child of darkness

"Yer ring, me darlin'," Pat Quinlan said to his granddaughter, pointing. "Mommy told me your bear friend gave it to you."

Troy nodded.

"It's a pretty thing. But also, Troy honey—it's a real ring. D'ye hear what I'm sayin' to you, child? Some things are make-believe and they are all for pleasure. But things like yer ring, they're genuine. Fact." He licked his lips that had gone dry and tried to make his point. "Listen now, girl. That bear playmate you mentioned, Troy sweet. Did he have a name?"

Quickly she replaced the ring beneath her blouse. "His name," she said finally, "is Sir Gat." She jumped from her chair, leaving him behind as she headed toward the stairway.

Pat Quinlan paled and stared at her retreating figure. Blood had drained from his face until the bushy brows stood out in relief. The *surgat*, his ancient aunt had told him, was a terrible demon to be avoided as man or woman loved the human soul. The *surgat*, sometimes willing to be controlled by children because their youthful capacity for belief freed it, motivated it, gave the awful demon liberty to prowl the countryside and kill at will. The *surgat* who, in grudging return, always gave to the unsuspecting child a bit of magic, an article of protection, in payment for having been again summoned to the sweet emerald isle.

Summoned, that is, from Hell.

Other Books by J.N. Williamson

**THE EVIL ONE
DEATH-ANGEL
GHOST MANSION
QUEEN OF HELL
THE BANISHED
PREMONITION
DEATH-COACH
HORROR HOUSE
THE TULPA
THE HOUNGAN
THE RITUAL**

We will send you a free catalog on request. Any titles not in your local bookstore can be purchased by mail. Send the price of the book plus 50¢ shipping charge to Leisure Books, P.O. Box 511, Murray Hill Station, New York, N.Y. 10156-0511.

Titles currently in print are available for industrial and sales promotion at reduced rates. Address inquiries to Nordon Publications, Inc., Two Park Avenue, New York, N.Y. 10016, Attention: Premium Sales Department.

playmates

J.N. Williamson

The odd forces seem to hang around dragon paths (or "faery tracks," as they are called in Ireland).
—Colin Wilson

LEISURE BOOKS ❦ NEW YORK CITY

An author is a strange bloke, at best. It's hard to know him truly, because he's so many people, including those in the book he's writing. A handful of people have made the ongoing effort where I'm concerned; they've helped in other ways as well. They include my colleen Mary Cavanaugh Williamson; my father Lynn; my son John; my sister Marylynn; Nancy Parsegian; Milburn Smith; Leslie Gelbman; Ron Duncan; and both my grandmothers. This novel's thanks must be divided among them, but the love I feel will easily go around.

I wrestled with reality 40 years ago and I'm glad to say I finally won over it.
—Elwood P. Dowd, in *Harvey*

A LEISURE BOOK

Published by

Nordon Publications, Inc.
Two Park Avenue
New York, N.Y. 10016

Copyright © 1982 by J.N. Williamson

All rights reserved
Printed in the United States

acknowledgements

Feeling more Irish than ever before in my life, I wish to express my gratitude—go raibh maith agaibh—to the following people and sources: *La brea* to *Fodor's Ireland 1978*, Edward F. MacSweeney and Richard Moore, editors, David McKay Company, New York, 1978; *Ireland* by Joe McCarthy, Time, Inc., New York, 1975; *Ireland in Color* by Harold Clarke, Viking Press, New York, 1970; *The Land and People of Ireland,* by Elinor O'Brien, Lippincott, Philadelphia, 1972; and *Mysteries* by Colin Wilson, G.P. Putnam's Sons, New York, 1978. My love to *daor* Ethel Gae Flanagan Mendenhall, me maternal grandmother, for givin' me the only genuine Irish flow in my otherwise turgid blood, and who, with my late father-in-law Charles W. Cavanaugh, showed me firsthand the endearing qualities of the Irish.

And to emerald Ireland herself, who was evergreen and glorious on every page I turned, with prayers for a final end to The Troubles and with the fervent hope that I may one day travel her storied shores and fall fully under the spell of her magical comeliness. With love and gratitude to every Eireannach, in truth or of the spirit.

pROLOGUE

> The blood-dimmed tide is loosed, and everywhere
> The ceremony of innocence is drowned...
> —W.B. Yeats

County Connaught, Ireland. A Sunday evening, early in the year.

It had seemed such a blessed day to Tom, those many hours ago when he picked up Lucy Kilkalien at her rooming house on Prospect Hill, that he never could have believed it would turn out so dishearteningly. In Ireland, love wasn't supposed to be unrequited.

Right from the beginning the day had a fresh nip to it—the temperature rarely descended below forty degrees, or rose above eighty—and an extra sweater was aplenty for the short trip through Galway's winding streets to Mass. Afterward, they'd gone to his favorite pub where they sang *The Men Behind the Wire* and told caustic, good-humored jokes with some friends who'd been fishing over in Clew Bay.

Later they'd played Bingo at Timmy's, on Flood Street. Timmy's used to be a small theatre and Tom loved being one of the boisterous crowd in the neatly lined seats, putting up a wee gamble of a bull or salmon for the chance to shout out the magical word. Then he'd capped it off by taking his Lucy to the newly opening Trust House Forte restaurant just over the O'Brien Bridge. There, he forked over two pounds plus a woodcock for their lovely meal from the snack bar. He'd consumed a juicy beef sandwich, barley soup, and a glass of wine with heartiness; she'd merely poked with a spoon at her cold plate and sipped some tap beer.

And then it was Tom realized, for the first shocking moment, how Lucy had changed since leaving Inishmaan. Hard as it was to confess to himself, she'd taken on big city airs.

Lucy spoke softly, confidently, of going to the United States when she'd saved her money, maybe even before she graduated from University. Tom hadn't known what to say. It was sad truth enough that people in Galway—in fact, all along the western coast—were forever catching an Aer Arann plane to America. There was even an airstrip on Inishmore (one of the other two Aran Islands), like some sort of damned air-lift of mercy (the arrogant fools). A saying had it that there were more Irishmen who'd flown off to American luxury than ever took a train halfway across their own country; maybe more than had ventured one minute away from their own dear Counties.

But Tom was born an Aran Islander, after all.

He'd considered it a mighty change simply to seek a job away from his dirt-poor islands. A year ago, at twenty, he'd faced a choice: Take a position with the quarry where they produced the famed soft green marble flecked with yellow and pink stripes, used for making jewelry; or begin tending to Connemara's fabled ponies, who were said to be of Celtic ancestry and traceable to the Ice Age itself, twenty thousand years ago. Because he'd always adored animals, and legends, and knew the clever versatility of the ponies who could work the land hard, race like lightning, or turn into fine show jumpers, the choice had been an easy one for Tom. But now, the way Lucy lowered her gaze from him, he wondered if he'd even cleansed himself of the smell his ponies left.

For Lucy's part, the sandy haired young woman with the thoughtful blue eyes was absolutely dejected by the way Tommy seemed so speechless about her wonderful idea. He, of all people, should understand why she never wanted to return to the islands of Aran, why she wanted instead to put thousands of miles between them and her. Others from the outside might find them quaint or colorful; she found them the roots of melancholy. Living among rocks in a dilapidated house constructed with geometric precision in a square or rectangle, peering out the one window on a side and trying to scratch out a life harder than the dismal stones lying like graveyard slabs everywhere, wasn't Lucy Kilkalien's style.

She wondered now if she could ever get the feeling of solitude, of stark isolation from her eyes, her memory, her bones. The dust of Inishmaan had penetrated her as no man ever could. Nothing had changed at home in one hundred years, from the obligation literally to make their soil, one bucket at a time, to fertilizing it with seaweed, to making their own garments. She remembered the old, brave boast—when all Ireland had given way to change forever, Aran would be just as she had always been—but seeing Galway, and studying at University there, had broadened Lucy's horizons.

She became downright moody when, leaving the restaurant, Tom didn't even seem aware of the Garda Siochana (Civic Guard) who was clearly waving his snow-white baton for them to stop. A traffic warden caught up with Tommy a block farther down, dispensing a stern lecture and a ticket, as the waning sunlight gleamed on the familiar golden band he wore round his hat. "Damned yellow-band busybody," was all the lad muttered as he drove on, barely swerving to miss one of the few pedestrians left on the street at the hour. She prayed that he'd mind the cyclists and, for that matter, not slam them helplessly against one of the roving neighborhood cows who were forever crossing Galway streets. Why was he so upset about her expanding herself, like the rest of the women in the world were doing, when she wouldn't remain in America more than a year or so?

It was irritating Tom that with misfortune tumbling round his generous ears, Lucy didn't even seem to recall the mutual pledges they'd made as children. He meandered silently across Dominick Street, which soon became Road L100, an N-class paved road which led to tiny Spiddal and beyond. Once there, Lucy asked quietly to stop for an inspection of the newest charmingly hand-knit cloth which was Spiddal's pride and joy. But right was right. Spurned, Tom only slowed when a donkey cart crossed the road; he stared with wounded brown eyes as two bent old ladies in black shawls hurried to catch up, then disappeared into their thatched cottage. If she wanted no more to do with him, he didn't even owe her the courtesy of an answer.

Each of them began to mellow somewhat, however, as they headed northwest toward Kylemore. The Connemara countryside was wild and beautiful to those who had the taste for it. *Timeless,* he thought; that was the customary word to be invoked. Now the dew was even heavier than usual and Tom had to switch on his windshield wipers. Driving on the lefthand side, he caught a glimpse across the road, to his right, of vivid purple heather and then the brilliant white bog cotton called *ceannabhan.* It looked to him then like the puffy flowers a leprechaun gentleman might take to his miniature lady. He reached his left hand to grasp Lucy's, wondering if he might yet romance her into staying. He felt a return squeeze, saw her give him a quick smile, then turn to see the way Connemara's mutable landscape switched in a breathless instant from greens, browns and blues to lavenders, greys and whites. The wind from the Atlantic, the only thing west of County Connaught, made the air indescribably clean and Tom rolled his window back down. An amiable farmer who was going "rambling" lifted a workworn palm in greeting before vanishing into a cottage that gave off the pungent smoke of peat. It was the peat, Tom knew, which provided fuel and peat moss that supplied the gardener. Above them, the jagged mountains of the Twelve Bens held them in their palm.

Cresting a hill, he looked in the rearview mirror

and saw the strip of white road twirling out behind them like a ribbon come undone from the head of a lovely lass. Somehow, he told himself, he would succeed in keeping Lucy home.

It was the last gentle, loving, and unterrified thought he would ever have in this world.

It was becoming quite misty when Tom turned down one of the many unmarked roads nearing Kylemore, where some of the grander homes remained. Lucy had told him, during supper, that a new University professor from America lived near here, a man named Quinlan. Aye, new friends were giving her the airs. Now Tom hoped to stop, to speak earnestly with her, to hold his girl close. Yet when they were within yards of the deep wooded area rising like the dark cliffs of Moher, another plan—less gentle, more dominating—began to breathe shallowly in his mind. He felt momentarily dizzy, and gripped the steering wheel hard. Inhaling the night air and finding it, off the main road and nearly a mile from it, oddly troubling in its scent, he headed directly into the woods. With Lucy's questioning, concerned gaze fixed on his dark profile, he swerved until the aging vehicle could no longer be seen by passersby. With as casual a sigh as he could muster, Tom turned the key in the ignition and heard the motor rattle to a tremulous stop.

Lucy allowed him to kiss her until the sturdy young man's hands began to rove. When they cupped her firm breasts she gently pushed him back and brushed a drooping lock of sandy hair away from her forehead. Her Tom had got so *rough!*

"D'ye have a *toitin?*" she asked, pronouncing it "thity-een."

Tom gave her a bit of a glare. "The old language, is it?" he said, fishing in the rough shirt pocket beneath his sweater for a cigarette and matches. Unlike most of the two thousand patient inhabitants of the Aran Islands, he had given up home woven, undyed wool, moccasins made of cured hides, the traditional *bainin* or homespun white jacket and heavy tweed trousers with a *crios,* or braided, girdle-like belt. His shoes were from Galway, not the *pampooties* made of heelless hide. Yet those were his major concessions and, beneath his outer sweater, he wore one from Inishmaan. "Is that your way of reminding me of my roots even when you seem to have forgotten them?"

Lucy shook her head in quick disclaimer. "I only know we cannot be living in two different universes at the same time, Tommy. It must be a total commitment, don't you understand? A dedication to the past or a dedication to the future." This was her new University way of speaking, he decided; but then she lapsed as her own internal uncertainty surfaced. "And I don't plan t'go on growin' potatoes in crevices between limestone, or watchin' you workin' with canvas to build a *currach,* only to go out in it and never return." She gave him an angry frown. "You men of Aran don't even think it's after bein' strange t'knit your names in your sweaters so your poor bodies can be identified! *Doar* Tommy, I haven't cared t'press ye—but it's come along with me to America one day or ye can live in *inne* till ye *do* drown."

Inne, he reflected, hearing the word as "anyay": *Yesterdays.* He saw the way she inhaled from her cigarette and let it ooze from her nostrils, making the peculiar stink of this spot even worse. He shook his head as he thought of her leaving for

America. No other lass in the ancient islands off Galway would dare such a thing. He drew himself erect in the front seat, feeling dizzy again but determined to be firm and dignified. "A man doesn't follow his woman, Lucy Kate Kilkalien. Nowhere in the world, leastways, that he's still a man!"

"Please take me home now," she said steadily then, crunching out her cigarette in his overfilled ashtray. Sparks rose dangerously. "At once."

"I suppose you'll be meanin' Galway, the big city," he said acidly. "Not—*home.*"

"*Now,* Tommy," she replied, risking a glance at him, tears in her blue eyes. "While we still have something to remember."

It might have been interesting, shocking, or appalling, what happened next. But no one ventured a foot through this tree-shrouded darkness— this solitary place—so late at night.

No one *human.*

"I'm thinkin' we need something *more* t'remember," Tom said, sliding over beside her and yanking her roughly against him. The ring on a cord round her neck—the one he'd given her, eons ago— swung free of her blouse. He felt hot; stifled. "Ye made a pledge when we was kids and now ye owe me something!"

Lucy was more angry and disappointed, at that moment, than frightened. His hand was beneath her skirt and she was conscious of a pebble still imbedded in one knee, a memento from a tomboy accident. It was Tommy who'd helped her up, carried her into the house—but not the Tommy *now,* the one with the rather glazed eyes and hot breath. Again she shoved him back and, for the moment, it was enough. Indeed, he fairly leaped away.

Now he glowered, panting, as he saw the way her short fingers toyed with the ring on the cord encircling her throat. He found words strange to him on his lips. "There's no reason why, if ye want t'be so modern—if ye want to be an *American*—we can't have a little fun. It isn't that sex is *outside* a relationship, not these days, girl. I—I've seen magazines from your sainted Yew-nited States with pictures the likes of which you'd never believe!"

She studied his face, curious about his change of manner. It wasn't like Tommy to perspire this way, to make taunting, sexual remarks that were off color, vulgar. But what really made her anxious was the way he had *altered,* twice, before her eyes. First to that absurd attack of his, when she'd swear he was as virginal as she; and then the way he almost bounced away from her, satisfied with talking . . . *that* way.

What got into me? he mused, panting. *I scarcely remembered my pledge to keep her here; I practically threw her away from me! Yet even now I want her so badly I can hardly stand it.* He put out his hand, tentatively, covering hers at her neck where she pressed the ring against her soft flesh. "Do it with me, Lucy," he urged her softly, intensely. "It'll be fine. I swear I'll be gentle."

She screamed. Not because she was terrified of Tommy but because, through the window on his right side of the car, *she had seen the creature.*

"Wh-what?" Tom demanded, startled and whirling to look, to peer at darkness. "What is it?"

She paused. "I d-don't know." Suddenly it was a little-girl tone, not the voice of a brazen nineteen with vast and glorious plans of a new life. There was a note of pleading. "It looked . . . like a bear."

15

Another pause. "I think. Anyway, it was absolutely enormous."

"A bear?" He chuckled lightly, feeling oddly relieved, more himself once more. "Shadows, darlin', I'm certain. Forget it." Whatever it was that had gripped him had suddenly fallen away.

Lucy realized she had been crushing his arms between her fingers and went into them, willingly, with a shudder. "Maybe I'll think it over, Tommy," she whispered. "Perhaps I'll stay here after all, at least in Galway." She kissed him on the underneath side of the jaw and, when he again tried to caress her breasts, she allowed him. "Nothing is definite, I suppose. Perhaps I. . . ."

The window on his side caved in, crushingly. It appeared almost to implode in a shower of fast-strewn glass, shards striking their faces like stinging needles, painfully pricking.

It had been the result of a single powerful blow.

Lucy issued low animal sounds and tossed her head from left to right, a sandy swirl like a dust shower. Her eyes caught those of her boyfriend and gripped them, pleadingly, asking him to chase away the terror.

Which was when Tom made his mistake. After a lifetime on Inishmaan he knew nothing could frighten him. If he hadn't been so sure of that, however, his mercurial reaction might yet have caused him to react as imprudently, because he was furious that anyone would terrify his own lass.

His fists cocked, a bold, fearless youth who'd had a confusing day and who had almost committed an act for which he'd have killed another man with his bare hands, Tom leapt from the car.

Lucy gasped in shock.

Tom was instantly lofted into the air—all five-eleven, nearly two hundred pounds of him—his feet now far above the ground with his arms pinned helplessly to his sides.

The embrace was, though, incredibly different than that he had received from Lucy. It was tight, tighter, *tightest*. A ghastly stench filled his nostrils, dizzying him once more. . . .

And then, at last, the fear came in, flooding his senses to overflowing, almost dominating the unforgettable pain as his bones began to break.

Lucy, mesmerized, moved halfway out the door and looked up. It was dark, hard to see. But there were hideous cracking sounds, so many now that it sounded like popcorn snapping in a sizzling pan. And it also sounded, she realized with fresh horror, like hundreds of bones breaking the entire length of a trapped human body.

Moonlight edged above the trees of the woods; lunar rays played along the tree spines, illuminating to some degree the form meeting her eyes from some nine feet above mother earth. Lucy saw enormous, hirsute arms gripping Tom close to an oaklike body. There was something sickeningly sensual about the embrace, something perverted; her eyes and soul wanted to turn away from the horrid intimacy. Now a noise mewled from the loathsome thing, a sound almost, but not quite, a growl.

Tom's feet began to kick spasmodically. At once they merely dangled, limply, over a yard up from her seated eye-level. Unceremoniously, without warning, his body was dropped—simply dropped. It plummeted like an emptied-out egg. His skull bounced frighteningly off the door, an ear striking the car fender, as she shrieked. Tom neither objected nor cried out. He lay there, immobile; paralyzed, Lucy thought.

She opened her mouth and, with her blue eyes clamped shut against hell, screamed piercingly into the wooded night. When she opened her eyes again the night was still, and she seemed to be disturbingly alone.

Tom!

Immediately she was out of the car, kneeling beside him in anxiety and terror, the ring on the cord around her neck bobbing free as she reached down.

A brilliant redness trickled from the corner of Tom's mouth, welled up from his lungs to make a pool in the dark grass near his head. When she touched his cheek in awful experimentation, his whole head turned languidly without resistance, limply fallen to the other side. Now his brown eyes stared back at her without comment, the dulled expression one of surprise, panic and terrible pain.

But it wasn't, in any sense, one of life.

Dimly aware of her unprotected aloneness, Lucy scrambled to her feet to peer wildly from one direction to another. "Help!" she screamed, then louder, with greater urgency: "Help! *Help me!*"

Uninvited, the silence rushed in at her from everywhere.

Farm houses, Lucy recalled; there must be farm houses or cottages or something nearby! Even on the other side of the woods, where that new professor lived.

Slipping, lurching, *gross* sound, breaking the silence. The noise of a huge heavy body beginning to move somewhere among the silhouetted trees only yards away.

Lucy turned, spun into the driver's seat. She had

never driven before but it was the only way out. The keys weren't there! Swiftly, catlike, she darted out of the car and fumbled beside Tom's body. The sounds behind her neared. With her left hand she pawed at Tom's sweater, then the pocket of his pants; with her right she clapped the ground a hundred places. The noises behind her had stopped; *nearby,* she thought, hands flying, it's very *close!*

Keys, half hidden beneath leaves. She got them in her hand with a flood of hysterical hope, leaping to her feet, pivoting toward the car . . . .

A massive, hairy arm descended with deliberate power. Like a felled tree, it caught Lucy Kilkalien in the center of the spine, the vertebrae making awful sounds identical to the ones that had issued from her Tommy. Her back broken like a twig, the force of the blow shot her sideways to the ground and deep into the valley of unforgettable pain.

For a moment, silence. Barely conscious, in more agony than she'd known existed, Lucy lay at Tom's side staring upward. She struggled to move, *ordered* herself to move, but all her limbs refused the command. Now she made out the creature, starlike in its distance overhead, saw it ignore her fully and half-squat beside Tom's mute form.

That was the moment she saw the face, a coarsehaired grotesque parody of a face with a dripping and snuffling square nose, with yellowish saliva drooling from the black rubbery edges of its wide mouth. Bearlike, perhaps, it considered Tom with an attitude that was almost calculating, almost humanly menacing.

Then, with a senseless swipe of its claw-studded paw, the creature struck Tom's head, disengaging it and spinning it away like a bowling ball. The head rolled quickly, lurching over its ears and veering slightly, maniacally, as if possessed by new life. Bodiless life. Lucy caught a glimpse of his grimacing teeth glittering in moonlight as the skull struck a rock and bounced high into the woods.

Lucy shrieked—she yowled into the uncaring night. Eyes pressed tightly together, warding off monsters, her sandy hair seeming to dig into the dirt beneath her own head, she screamed her anguish and inhuman terror over and over before passing out.

Time, always patient and never more so than at periods of pain, waited without boredom or the slightest inclination to hurry the unconscious girl. When she awakened with her memory instantly full, when she began mumbling hysterically, she made herself pray that when she opened her eyes she would truly be alone.

She wasn't. The creature was bent to her, now, unhurriedly. Not quite peering into her face, it centered myopically upon the ring on the cord around her neck. Head slightly averted, it snuffled. Wildly, like a lunatic, it occurred to Lucy that the thing had a cold. Then with one dexterous claw, it flicked the cord away and she could not see where the ring went. The idea too formed in her harried mind that if she remained utterly quiet, as one was supposed to do with a rapist, the monster might just go away.

But when at last she saw the eyes clearly, Lucy recognized that what was stooped above her was neither a bear nor a rapist. Its eyes were mad, demonically livid-red, yet shrewd and cunning. They were eyes that *knew,* knew things Lucy had never known and would never wish to know.

Gently, the immense paws touched the sides of her face. The pads on them were rough, leathery; the hard claws pricked faintly but did not break her soft skin.

Now Lucy smelled its breath.

It could not be possible, but that stench—that hideous, reeking *filth* of the creature's breath—was worse than anything she had seen or felt. It was, somehow, an all-consuming stink, deathly foul, both inhuman and inanimal. It was like the doors of hell had flown open and released the gathered putrescence of all the unclean souls who had been tormented for ten thousand millennia. It was, Lucy thought as her eyes blinked and she strove to turn her face from the creature, quite possibly a death-dealing odor.

"*Die,*" the creature said, quite distinctly. The voice came from deep in its hairy throat. "*Die, for Troy.*"

Then she tumbled into unconsciousness.

Tommy had had his way. Lucy was kept at home.

Forever.

PART ONE

My Derry, my little oak grove,
My dwelling and my little cell,
O living God that art in Heaven above,
Woe to him that violates it.
— *St. Columba*

one

It had taken coroner Bill Fogarty more than an hour to locate the dreadful death scene in the wooded dark because, in this "James Joyce country" that comprised Galway and Connemara, a man venturing into unknown terrain met endless bogs and dank moors criss-crossed by pocked roads which wavered and straggled all over the countryside. Bill had tried several of them to no avail, cursing poetically as he struggled to turn round his car, until he saw lights rising above the etched treetops—police lights.

The odd thing about the area, old Bill mused as he joined the others, was that this was yet another typical Irish paradox. Within miles of the isolation he was encountering there were excellent roads, fine hotels, and pocket-handkerchief farms quite as well maintained as any in the world.

And paradoxes proliferated in the old country, he thought, his slightly stooped, lanky body moving among the policemen without a word. While Eire was an island, after all, it had no sea tradition, no merchant marine, a navy small enough to have over for dinner, and only in recent decades, a fishing industry. That, of course, was because his countrymen considered fish "famine food." The Irish ate it only on Friday, and then as swiftly as possible.

Bill Fogarty had been sixty-eight when he won the election for coroner. Now, three years later, he felt one-hundred and eight. Tonight, especially, he was dog-tired and cases like this 'un—decent-looking kids out for a little petting—tended to age him by the minute.

Holding his broad-brimmed white hat in one hand, Bill scratched at his pinkish bald spot with the other. To the best of his ability, he avoided glaring at the deputy police chief who, after all once again, couldn't really help being an incompetent idiot. Besides, Chief Francis Muldowney was that rare incompetent fool who had the good grace to know what he was.

In this late summer night the woods, Bill felt, seemed unnaturally silent. It was almost as though nocturnal nature was pausing with curiosity to see what diurnal man would do about this little surprise it had dumped on him. Through the old coroner's age-weakened eyes the woods looked *furry,* somehow, a backdrop of stealth for the intruding puddles of pale light spilled by police beams. Everything in here, beneath the outrageous light, appeared unaffectionately soft.

Like the stomach of a hungry spider.

A ring of sleek cars circled the scene, as if by ringing-in the killed they might get exceptionally lucky and ring-in the killer. But this killer wasn't going to be apprehended all that easily, Bill Fogarty knew, not even if they had used almost every vehicle available to the Galway police department and one or two called over from Oughterard. Bill shook his head wearily. The terrible ones who did this much ugly damage to folks either did it insanely, from a perch on a building during rush hour, or skulked around in the woods in ebon darkness utilizing the native cunning of a hungry mountain lion. He'd always been dubious about killers like that, who used insanity as a defense. They were forever sane enough to take off and save their worthless hides.

Hungry moutain lion . . . The old man, glancing once more at the maimed boy, could have believed a lion did this dreadful thing to him—if there *was* a lion in County Connaught, of course. In these coarse and trembling shadows one might imagine that the poor lad had grown frightened and simply hidden his head beneath a blanket for protection.

Except there was no blanket.

"You find the boy's head?" He glanced some ten feet to where the incompetent fool, Francis Muldowney, was chatting light and easy with one of the new paramedics.

Voices carried, on a night like this. "*Ofche mhaith,* Doc," Muldowney replied, noticing Fogarty for the first time. "Don't tell me you're ready with somethin' already."

"I asked if you'd found the lad's head."

"Oh, yes. It's in the container, over by the ambulance." The husky career officer hesitated. "Are you going to want to see it?"

"Jesus, Mary and Joseph, *no!*" Bill snapped. "Who in Christ would *want* to?"

But the coroner crossed to the ambulance anyway, and he looked, and he examined the tissue around the terrible wound with his lower teeth biting his upper lip. No; the marks weren't right for a lion or any kind of cat. It had occurred to him that a circus might have escaped his notice and lost one of its animals. But it wasn't the hacksaw killing of some red-eyed psycho with the sweet touch of a surgeon either. No tidy Jack the Ripper behind this one.

Sighing, he stood, dusted at his tweed trousers, and returned to the deputy chief, mopping at new perspiration with a brightly-colored handkerchief. "Another query, Francis."

"Fire ahead, Billy," the policeman replied. But before the coroner could speak, he blurted: "Jaysus, this is a pretty rotten thing, I think." His piggy eyes almost twinkled in the high beam of the nearest police car. "What d'you figure slew the boy? A bear?"

Fogarty arched his shoulders and neck to relieve a recurrent tug of arthritis. Then he looked steadily at the younger man. "Tell me, Francis. Do you ever recall seein' a bear in County Connaught? Hm-m?"

"No, sir," Muldowney confessed, shaking his head with awe. "I surely never did see a bear in these parts." Then it dawned on him that he was becoming foolish again and his face crimsoned. "I understand your point, Billy. I guess nobody saw one tonight either."

Bill gave him a fleeting humorous smile. "Well, yes, it's possible they did. This night." He paused, thinking about paradoxes, thinking of the way he—a Prod from Ulster who happened to belong to the Fianna Fail party—had become a coroner obliged to deal with this Taigue member of Labour. "I wrote me a little monograph on bites, on clawmarks, ten years back. And I have t'say, yes, it *appears* that a bear has done this awful deed."

"A bear?" Muldowney murmured, sounding like the idea was all new to him. "Really?"

"But still and all, I am puzzled as all get-out by a pair of things." He eyed Francis with upraised brow. "Possibly you can be shedding a bit of light for me."

The deputy chief edged closer at once, confidential now, his own heavy brows lowered until he seemed simian. His voice was at the pitch of a lad in a classroom, whispering to someone across the aisle. "I'll surely try, Billy. What are your questions?"

"For three years I've begged you to call me Bill, not Billy. Or Fogarty. Or even Doctor Fogarty. Can you remember that?" He inhaled, and began counting on his long fingers. "Number one, where in hell would a bear come from? Second, in addition to the fact that the underbrush here is all trampled-down—crushed, as if an awful weight had prowled the site—in addition to that fact, Francis, have y'looked at the plant life? Chief Muldowney, it's *dead*." He gestured. "All the plant life is *dead*."

Francis Muldowney couldn't conceal his disappointment and surprise. "The *plant life* is dead?" he repeated, incredulous. He dug in one hairy ear with a yellow pencil, his look at Fogarty clearly implying that the old man had gone senile before his very eyes. "Well, pardon, Doc. But who gives a shit about *that?*"

Bill sighed. "I do, Chief; I do." His air was still benign, explanatory. He'd really hoped that Muldowney might have learned something at last and might, as well, have found an idea or two straying through his brain. He thought about a description he'd read once that called the Irish a "highly advanced pagan people collected from a variety of Central Europeans and sub-Asian

29

tribes" and figured, for the first time, that there was something to it. "At the scene of a crime, Francis, one makes the effort to gather and secure facts. Not selectively, either. *All* of them."

"All of them?"

"They are called *clues,* Chief. Now, most of them may be utterly useless, but we can't know that, at the outset. Some may appear peculiar, bee-zare even; they may not make a lick of commonsense. But when all of them are gathered, there is frequent-ly a wee tendency to reason backwards in quest of a solution." He patted Muldowney's shoulder with a fatherly touch. "D'you see, boy? *Do you see?*"

Deputy Chief Muldowney muttered something profane beneath his breath. "You needn't treat me as if I were a perfect fool!"

"No one, Francis, is perfect." Now Bill Fogarty tugged at the younger man's sleeve, bending slightly as he pointed. "Look, please. There. And look again, *there.* Here, too; and there."

The bony digit clearly indicated what he'd discovered: Wild flowers, grass, weeds, some vines— all dead. Drooping; withered.

"You see, Chief?" Fogarty asked anxiously. "You can see that it's all shriveled, almost like it was poisoned?"

Muldowney made a mighty intellectual effort as he knelt to peer at the dying flora. "Yes, sir, I see it now. And I see that you are suggesting some kind of—*human motive* for what's occurred." He scowled up at the old man, squinting. "So where is that leavin' your bear?"

"I don't create these little details to plague you, Francis. I only find them now and then."

"Are y'saying, then, that some lunatic was the

killer?"

Bill assisted him to his feet. Muldowney had put on weight since he got his assignment of Deputy Chief and began sitting with his feet up on the desk. "I honestly believe that will be up to you and your people to learn, Francis." He shook his head. "But I'll tell you true, I doubt seriously that any humans were responsible for all this. I only say what I can observe, understand? For example, even from this distance, I can look at that poor dead girl's throat and tell you she was wearin' a necklace or cord of some kind round it. Now, it's gone. Ripped clean away." He added, patiently, "You might want to look into that."

The two of them walked toward Lucy Kilkalien's body where it lay, face down, in the grass beside the decapitated boy. Leaning on their car, Muldowney explained what he'd found to identify them. "The lad, now," said the chief, looking in his notebook at his smudged writing. "You might not know it, since he doesn't tuck his pantslegs in his boots or hold his jacket together with a belt; but he's from Aran. Inishmaan, to be pre-cise. The girl has a Galway address, apparently a boarding house."

Bill had been examining Lucy with gentle, respectful fingers. "But she's originally from the islands too," he said softly.

"How d'you know that, Billy?" the chief asked in wonderment.

"It's *Bill*. I know because of the bra she's wearing." He looked sharply up at the younger man. "It's white wool."

"Well, at least we know *how* they died, don't we?" Muldowney chuckled at his challenge. "That's pare-fectly obvious, isn't it!"

"No, it is not." Fogarty shook his head, stood, and put his white hat back on his head. "True enough, her back is broken. Horribly broken. It didn't kill her."

"The boy?" demanded Muldowney, his face red. "His head—"

"Dead before he hit the ground, if I don't miss my guess." Bill glanced up. He looked some ten to twelve feet in the air. "Dropped when he died." He took a deep breath and joined the deputy chief in leaning on the car. Now he averted his eyes from these dead people fifty years his junior, who would never age, who would remain youthful throughout eternity. "Francis, it's sure the girl would eventually have died from the damage she sustained. But that's not what took the child's life." He paused again, hating to say it to this insensitive, unimaginative policeman. "Something *poisonous*—in the air, perhaps pumped into the car—killed them both."

"You are shitting me."

Bill made a face. "With my bowels, Francis, I wish I was." He produced a scrap of cloth he'd hidden in his hand. "Here. See how strong it is at the source."

The cloth had been torn from Lucy's blouse and Fogarty stuck it under Muldowney's nose. "Jaysus, Billy, it stinks like nothin' I ever smelt before!" He shoved the old man's arm away. "What *is* that awful stench?"

Bill shrugged. "No idea of the chemicals involved. Not yet. I'll be havin' some dandy tests run, though, you can wager a banknote or two on that!" He pursed his narrow lips, conscious that, at this hour, he needed a shave and wondering why he cared about the chief. "I've heard of stuff bad enough to peel wallpaper, but I never anticipated smelling it!"

Until now, the moon had been lurking behind a cloud far above the treetops. Lights from the police cars had been inadequate, failing to reveal detail. The paramedics approached at a tentative speed and looked expectantly at Bill Fogarty and then at Francis Muldowney. The latter glanced at the former for approval, though he was technically the man in charge. "Right," grunted Bill. "You can take these poor kids along now."

The men shuffled forward, shoes sopping in the heavy dew; a tall, redheaded paramedic paused. He lifted his long nose to the air in wrinkling disgust. "Goodness," he began, "what stinks around here?"

"The odor of untimely death, youngster," replied Bill Fogarty, not telling it all.

Until then, the old coroner's lanky form had shielded the victims' bodies, almost as if he were protecting them from further harm. When he stepped aside, the pair of young paramedics and the driver saw Lucy and Tom for the first time. Instantly, instinctively, each took a backward step and crossed themselves. "Mother of God," whispered the stout, burly driver. It was a prayer.

Now the redhaired paramedic—his name was Mike—reached Lucy, overcoming his repugnance, and stood staring down at her with his mouth working. He'd seen a lot but she and her poor boyfriend were difficult to stomach.

But Bill Fogarty had already been shocked, kept it to himself, and handled it like a competent coroner.

The girl's slender body had been left on its stomach in the reeking grass. Her thin palms were flat on the wilted, largely barren patch of earth as though proximity to the poisonous vapors had seared the ground itself.

But her face was looking blindly up at the redheaded paramedic, the sandy hair loosely spread as if she reclined on her pillow in Galway or back home, on Inishmaan.

Her pretty head had been turned completely around.

Taking a snatch of breath as he strove to recover his lost aplomb, the paramedic and his fellows stooped to place the girl's body in the stretcher. With the guidance of the overweight ambulance driver they moved with the utmost of care and respect, trying to behave as professionally as Doctor Bill Fogarty.

But the pert sandyhaired head suddenly became detached and tumbled cleanly off the twisted neck, rolling lurchingly for a yard or two, stopping against the deputy chief's foot. It jiggled a moment. Her vague blue eyes gazed up at him, appealingly; they pleaded with him. They were somehow full of a sight and a sound no Irish lass had ever seen before . . . except, perhaps, for one.

Chief Francis Muldowney rushed to the edge of the woods.

He barely made it in time.

two

Connor Quinlan had gone out to mail a check he could not easily afford to Kenning Car Hire, in Galway, but found himself walking instead of driving the expensive Mercedes he'd leased, upon arrival, from Kenning. Petrol—he made himself use the word in his mind, instead of the term "gas" with which he'd been more familiar through the years of his manhood—was costly. Even if one ignored the quality Caltex stations, where one tipped for good service, and visited Jet Petrol instead.

He told himself firmly, at the start of his walk, that he was afoot to save money. In midwalk through this pretty town of Kylemore, in Connemara, he switched his reason with a doggedness typical of the dark-haired writer, to a need for exercise. He'd been too long in his study behind the house. On his way home, he further compromised his interior integrity by deciding he only wanted to get away from Ethelyn and Dad for awhile.

Only when he was given a sincerely affable wave and a tip of the cap by a sweater-clad stranger on an ambling horse, the man's traditional mongrel dog trotting alongside with his tongue lolling happily from the corner of his mouth, did Connor admit that he really wanted to re-familiarize himself with the town. To give it a fair chance, especially if he were to be stuck here the rest of his days.

Because Connor had returned home, with Ethelyn and little Troy, for all the wrong reasons, and he knew it.

Fifteen years ago, at the precise manly age of twenty-one, Connor had fallen for the lure so many young Irishmen experienced and gone to America on his own. Pat Quinlan, his father, took the opportunity to opine patiently that Quinlans had lived and died in County Connaught for more generations than anyone could count, and further that the emotional tug of the old Kylemore house would eventually bring Connor home again. This had been Dad's proud method of denying that he wasn't having his own way, this time; and his means, too, of suggesting subtly that Connor was making a slightly treasonous error of judgment. Implicit in his words was the fact that Connor would always be welcomed back warmly, and that if they were reunited in Connemara, the final victory would belong to old Pat Quinlan.

Connor remembered a strange, touching scene from his boyhood when a man who was well into his forties wept as the coffin was taken from a funeral at his church. The man who'd died must have been in his eighties. But the middleaged man wept piteously, and cried: "Gran-da, me beloved Gran-da! And who'll jam me bread now?" The attitude was characteristic of Ireland. Here, if no place else on earth, a son still respected his father.

Despite himself, Connor found that he enjoyed the scenery. He grinned faintly. How could anybody who felt he had an iota of sensitivity fail to fall in love with these sights, these people? The cottages were gem-like, nestled at the foot of jagged, barren mountains which stretched-up like a warning hand to halt outsiders. Not that this was the view of the people, who were universally friendly. And besides, Connor was learning now that the many-fingered mountains only sought to keep people *in,* and threatened to clench their fists round the boy-o who returned so belatedly.

On his deepest plunge away from home, farther into the countryside, Connor had gasped, feeling himself abruptly cut adrift on another world. The hills were too steep to cultivate and took countless forms, like many-colored breasts rising to a multitude of lovers. Farmers separated themselves from their neighbors with neat stone walls which appeared to be extravagantly composed of jewels discarded by the sensual hillocks. Everything had a magical feeling. There was a planned look to the rectangular farmhouses as if they had been collectively persuaded to lift themselves, simultaneously, from the earth itself. Haymounds humped here and there like so many ancient menhirs. Everyone here was a trout fisherman who drew his tall tales from lakes of sparkling, purpling blue, especially Lough Inagh and, more distant, Lough Derryclare. Connor recalled from his childhood the soft, scarcely-moving mist over Derryclare and the subtle way it altered the land and greyed the sky. Still farther out, but yet within biking distance, the Connemara ponies were raised on a large promontory between Kilkieran

But here, returning home, Connor saw whitewashed homes which wore sloping thatched roofs like noncommittal toupees bleaching too long in the sun. The residences of the Quinlan neighbors looked not so much like dollhouses as like the homes of gloriously quaint, indescribable beings. Beings who were, the prodigal son mused, different from the rest of humanity. Beings who believed to their time-rooted souls in the wee folk who might still be summoned, and who must, on occasion, be honored and placated. He shivered despite himself, knowing that he was being silly. No more amiable, witty folk lived on earth. It was only the improbable pastel greens and blues and off-whites beneath the drooping roofs and the fact that, where the emerald of Connemara wasn't in evidence, obdurate stone—rock that might have been hunching there since before man walked the earth—was everywhere.

He drew within viewing distance of home—*Pat Quinlan's home,* he reminded himself; *it can never be mine*—and tried to shake off the underlying impression of guilt. He hadn't really failed in America nor had he failed to stay long enough to become an American at heart. Why, in a way, he was a self-made man like Dad, even if he hadn't earned the money old Pat acquired. His subsidy publishing company was well known in the industry and he'd even managed a few best sellers. Unlike others in his trade, he'd never taken the money for printing the book of a talentless unknown and run. While the chances of his finding great artists were always slim, he'd understood the ego, the needs of his authors. He'd felt for the way they desperately desired to see their writings in print and done his utmost to promote and encourage those with a flicker of ability. Where the others were concerned, the literary groupies who wanted to show their books boastfully to artsy friends in little amateur writing clubs, he'd made the facts clear to them from the outset: The chances of this work becoming a brisk seller ranged from slight to zero.

The subsidy publishing venture, back in Indianapolis, was only to enable Connor to promote his fonder aspirations anyway. In Bookquins he had created a publishing edifice that made it possible for Connor to search for another Fitzgerald, another Yeats, and also to publish himself, should he ever find the courage to write his book. Then with the founding several years ago of his Bookquins Newsletter, wherein he could express his thoughts on contemporary literature, evaluate trends, analyze the small successes of his subsidy writers and offer his advice, Connor had lost both his heart and his money. Like many men before him, he fell in love with an aspect of his business which scarcely paid for itself, except in coin of a realm that was rarefied, inspirational, fulfilling. For the first time he was putting his own thoughts on paper, and it was heady. Thrilling. He turned down several commissions for books to print. He let Ethelyn's job with Stern & Stern Advertising Agency provide their primary living.

And when they ran completely out of money because Connor had secured only a few hundred subscriptions to the Bookquins Newsletter, and his wife Ethelyn was discharged for failing to copulate with the younger Mr. Stern, there was the letter from Dad Quinlan, who'd been advised of his son's folly by a worried Ethelyn, waiting in the mailbox with an aura of triumph fairly reeking from the envelope.

Galway, Dad pointed out in no-nonsense terms, was now a lively university city. Everybody wanted their children to attend, to find a better, less hard existence than they'd known. It was only twenty-tree miles from the Kylemore home and writers were always welcomed with open arms as visiting professors, sure to be retained if they only remained sober. There'd been two television channels in Ireland since 1978. Most of them dealt with current affairs or were loosely formatted with discussion shows, and a man of the world like Connor could easily fetch his own program. Best of all, there was *absolute freedom from income tax* for resident writers or painters, composers and sculptors regardless of nationality, and had been since 1969. A creative type like Connor could easily live on little more than a hundred dollars a week, especially since he, his wife, and their little girl Troy—whom Gran-da was dying to meet, by the way—were entirely welcome to stay with him forever. Then Dad capped it off by remarking that the house was being willed to Connor, anyway, and, considering the old man's age, the younger Quinlans might as well get used to it. Thoughtfully, he added a simple postscript: "You aren't going to be happy till you write a book. You know that and I know that. It's quiet, beautiful, and practically free of tension here. Come home."

It had been hard to fathom whether the last two words were an invitation or a command; but Ethelyn made it perfectly clear that what *she* had to say happened to be an order at best, an ultimatum at worst. The decision was reached when she concluded: "There's no way you can't do the newsletter from Connemara anyway. And the Irish have provided as many top writers for you to support and encourage, *per capita,* at least, as any nation in the world."

Now Connor again approached his father's two acres, thinking, despite the ongoing impression of being trapped, and stifled, that there was charm about him everywhere. There was a grassy field of every color of green, gray and brown, growing at stubbornly independent angles and, like most of the estates in the west, rarely mowed. To the east was a woods, great in size for the county, to which young people from Spiddal, Galway, and Oughterard sometimes drove in order to make love in privacy. The house itself was very old, a two-story with a massive attic and a solid, contemporary roof old Dad had replaced since Connor's boyhood. There were two elongated windows on each side of the first floor and two small ones, little better than a foot in length, on each side of the second story. It was impossible to see into the attic from outside. The house, in good repair for its age, sat atop a rise several hundred yards from a waist high line of stone absurdly indicating the boundary line between Pat Quinlan's and his distant neighbors. Nothing about the estate, during the day, was musty, reeking of age, or eerie; but it was easy for Connor to imagine that any rare passerby at night might consider the house haunted.

Well, he thought as he opened the unlocked door and entered, at least Dad had greeted him with *"Cead Mile Failte"* ("one hundred thousand welcomes!") when he and his family arrived.

And perhaps the old devil was working his magic already, weeks into the so-called "visit," since he'd taken such a long walk. While Dad was too old to exercise outside so ambitiously, he chose all manner of odd hours for his noisy strolls around the house, scarcely pausing for at least an hour.

No one was around and Connor took one of the comfortable easy chairs in the front room, finding a newspaper waiting for him on its arm. Ethelyn, being thoughtful again, trying to make it up to him for her insistence that they move here. He sighed, opening the paper and spreading it in his lap. Undoubtedly this wasn't easy for her, either. She'd never seen Ireland before and taking up residence in a land foreign to her must be trying. Maybe now that she'd acquired a position at an ad agency in Galway she'd begin to relax and be more like her old self.

Perhaps everything would work out after all. Dad was fundamentally a delightful man of sixty-nine summers, eager that they feel at home, inclined to dote on eleven-year-old Troy. He approached the girl with an endearing mixture of Gaelic charm and ponderous solemnity which gave meaning to the child and warmed her young heart.

From Troy's standpoint, if Gran-da said it, it had to be right. And she had adored the woods from the first moment of their arrival, spending most of her free time there for the past three weeks. When she learned she had to go to school, her expression of disappointment almost broke Ethelyn's heart.

He leaned back in his chair, glad that Dad had it waiting. He'd acquired a bad back in Vietnam during his two-year tour and it needed all the coddling it could get. With the evening hours coming on, and the sun shining desperately in the window behind him, Connor began to relax. What did Dad's restless little journeys around the house mean, anyway? Why be upset about them? What difference did it make that the old boy was so mysterious about the locked and bolted attic?

That was another idiosyncrasy of Patrick Aloysius Quinlan that plagued Connor in his childhood, used to fill the boy with such curiosity that he'd felt he must burst. No one was allowed in the attic by him then and, Connor found the other day, no one was permitted there today, either. There was probably a chest full of old coins Dad kept there, the Irish harp glittering from everyone of them. Or maybe he had a cage of leprechauns— who could tell with Dad? Connor chuckled. The old boy had been a widower much too long. Mom's passing, shortly after giving birth to a second son, Michael, was followed by Michael's death in a fall when he was twelve. It was only natural that Dad would feel that all things, good and bad, were intrinsically linked to this house, and he was entitled to a special room. Or attic.

"Tired, Con?"

It was such a chirpy voice that he didn't jump, merely lowered the newspaper. "I guess I haven't entirely adjusted to the move. Besides, I took a long walk. Now I have to think up a lead piece for the

43

next Newsletter."

She took her chair across from him after turning on the lights. "Well"—it was her familiar, deliberate style that informed him she already knew what she intended to say, but preferred to make the idea sound fresh—"why not a paper about our move here? Our regained Irishness?"

Connor laughed. "'Our?'" he asked. "D'you really think that would interest our readers in the States?"

She made her Wise Face. "A lot of people who aren't even Irish *like* the Irish."

"Liking isn't wanting to read about them, or the people who return to Ireland." He squirmed. It had always depressed him, made him feel nervous, to be consciously motivated. "I dunno, honey, it could have merit. I'll have to think on it."

"Oh." The word dripped frost. Ethelyn's large, liquid brown eyes opened wide, not so much with surprise at his lack of enthusiasm as in an effort to appear surprised. And unjustly cast aside. "Well, it's *your* Newsletter, of course."

Connor smiled, pushed himself from the chair with an impression of *déjà vù*, and crossed the wood floor to her. By now, he knew how significant to Ethelyn were her fleeting, apparently inspired ideas. She was quite pretty, still youthful; yet in a society where she'd always been very short, female, and forced to seem "cute," she also felt obligated to battle an internal sense of inferiority. The weapon she used, quite proficiently within the realm of her advertising duties, was the Bold Idea. The flood of such never ceased and Connor admired her for it.

But what they did, in their writing, was completely different. Leaning forward with his meaty hands on either side of her to kiss her reassuringly, he wanted badly to explain the distinction. In ad writing, one shiny notion might be primped and padded into a convincing message on behalf of an advertiser. Copy writers earned a lot of money for as simple a thing as a logo, a catchphrase that appeared overnight on everyone's lips. But a Newsletter from a subsidy publisher must have comment of somewhat deeper, more probing merit; and it had better make the reader believe the piece applied to him alone.

Since it was an old skirmish, he didn't repeat himself but brushed his tanned forehead fondly in her dark-auburn mass of curls before kissing her head. "I really do appreciate your help."

"I'll bet." A beat. "I hope so."

Oddly, he didn't quite lie. While the specific nature of her ideas seldom propelled him to his typewriter, its freshness often resonated in his mind until hours or even days later, some useful hybrid of their two creative minds meshed.

Without being passionate about it much anymore, Connor Quinlan loved his wife.

Not taking his seat, he went out to the kitchen, glad that Dad had one of the few electrical hookups in the area. Life would be good with Ethelyn, even back in Connemara, if she could only have more children. Not that he was judgmental about it. Just as Ethelyn couldn't help having a life-endangering problem, he couldn't help being Catholic, by upbringing if not current practice. He was a robust man, favorably inclined to the notion of many offspring; and since they both eschewed birth control methods, Connor had a problem of his own which Ethelyn rarely cared to confront.

He took a swift swig of hearty Irish beer before returning to the front room. Ethelyn simply didn't have the pelvis for safe childbirth, just like his late mother Margaret. Dad's advice, unasked as ever, came in a letter one year ago: "Are you being a man and doing the right thing by your wife, boy? She can't have more tads, however much we might like that. Stand by her side with your head up!"

Connor slammed the door of the aging refrigerator; jars inside rattled their protest. He swore at himself under his breath. Thinking about their love-making was like discussing intergalactic travel, fairies, or winning with a longshot at the Kentucky Derby. Pointless. Etheyln could not help it that he awakened once or twice a week with an ache surpassing mere physical longing and verging into the state of sublime yearning. She probably felt guilty enough on her own. Worse, one of the reasons she'd prodded him to come home was because she felt certain he was seeing other women.

He went back to the front room, thinking both how wrong she was and that here, in a virgin's paradise, Ethelyn would certainly have nothing to worry about. People might marry at an older age, colleens might take older men for husbands, but adultery was all but unthinkable.

If it hadn't been for the Newsletter, and his precious little Troy, he would have small reason for living. Shoulders sagging, he took his seat.

Magically, it seemed, Connor discovered the child Troy herself entering rapidly through the front door and slamming it with the same force he'd used in closing the refrigerator. Not from frustration, of course, but sheer exuberance for life. Ah, they were so much alike—not physically, but where it counted!

"Hi, Mom." The greeting was perfunctory, accompanied by a cursory wave as she rushed past her mother and jumped boldly for Connor's outstretched arms. "Daddy, Dads! *Hi-i-i-i!*"

"My sweet kitten!" Delighted, he tossed her the expected foot in the air. His bad back groaned; he felt a pang of regret that this greeting of theirs would not be possible much longer. "How are you, you rare Gaelic sprite?"

She hugged his neck, kissed him squishingly on his large nose. "Oi am foine, me boy-o," Troy declared, doing the Irish schtick she'd done for years. But now she was learning it first hand. Troy landed on tiny feet, aware of her mother's oddly reserved eyes fixed on her.

"Well, what about a kiss for Mommy?" Ethelyn asked.

Troy's hesitation was barely discernible; miniscule. "Sure." Then there was a winning girl's smile there as she hurried to her mother, pucker in place.

Ethelyn discerned it and her glance above Troy's head at Connor contained a measure of jealousy. *Why,* it asked, *does Troy prefer you?*

Two things were wrong, however unfair they were, and Connor knew it. Mommy had been away each day most of the child's eleven years. She was seen now as competition for Dads' attention. Dads might also be gone, to the office he'd rented in Indianapolis; but everybody knew it was all right for Dads to be away. Troy sensed a problem between the two adults, believed Mommy's compe-

47

tition was fundamentally unjust. How could a little girl compete with the woman Daddy had chosen when she, herself, was merely an afterthought of their adult union?

Troy not only hugged and kissed Ethelyn but stayed beside her on the couch, her blonde head piquant and reflective on her mother's shoulder. At eleven, the impressions Troy claimed were a wildly incredible blending of mature accuracy tinged with the subjective evaluation of childhood. She was inordinately impressionable to everything around her, genuinely intuitive, and painfully imaginative. Born a Geminian barely out of the preceding Taurus, Troy might have been an earthy pragmatic instead except for the soaring insights of her imagination.

The strain between Ethelyn and Connor bothered her even though, at eleven, she was able to believe that her parents *might* love her. In their way. She felt that Daddy would love her more when Troy brought him a dozen grandchildren someday; she saw clearly that Mommy was happiest when she worked. Why, they'd been here in Connemara only long enough to make a few friendships in the woods, but Mommy was already employed again!

Without knowing a thing about sex, Troy also knew somewhat more. There was a sex-problem-thing between her folks. What's more, she perceived that Gran-da—who was entirely marvelous, in her experience—and her beloved Dads did not see eye to eye either.

She sighed and picked idly at Ethelyn's sleeve, yawning. Most of the time life was all so excruciatingly boring. That was why Troy had begun making certain changes, now that she was living with Gran-da. It had grown clear to her that the grown-ups went their own ways. To pursue some joy herself, Troy determined to do the same. *Her* way. Adjusting mercurially to the notion of independence, the girl found that it had its advantages, especially if she put her imagination to the task.

Thus it was that, deep inside little Troy Quinlan, there was harbored an unvoiced conviction of permanent aloneness, the impression that everything was somehow her fault, and an urge to remake humankind wherever she could along sensible lines.

"Oh, Troy, you've left your jumper on again!" Mommy was more hurt than angry. Once that was a useful weapon but her only child was emotionally in the process of disarming it these days. "I've told you a thousand times to wear your shorts or your jeans for—for messing around."

"I hate shorts," Troy retorted, shuddering at their very image. "I got rotten legs and it's just too damn hot for jeans."

"You *have* rotten legs. I mean, that's the way to say it." Ethelyn flustered easily. "But wear your jeans tomorrow anyway, and that's an order. And so, my girl, is this: Quit swearing." Mommy giggled. "It sounds like hell."

"Okay." Brightly, pertly; aware of her cuteness. Now Troy danced over to Connor, buried deep in his newspaper. "Guess what, Dads?"

He glanced up. Abstracted eyes, much like his daughter's colorless ones in terms of frequent, brooding reflectiveness, failed to focus at once. "What is it?"

"I got a new playmate."

49

He put the newspaper in his lap, crumpled, with a sigh. Still, Troy's imaginary friends always intrigued the amateur psychologist in the writer. "You *have,* not you *got,*" he corrected her.

"I know I have," Troy replied, playing dumb.

"Well, what happened to good ole Sir Gat?"

She shrugged lightly. "He's in the woods or whatever." Her former playmate, beloved a week ago, was dismissed. "But he *did* leave me a gift, right before he went."

"How nice," Connor said, curious. "What is it?"

"*This.*" Troy extended her open palm with an aura of profound mystery.

In the center of it, gleaming in the dying rays of the sun streaming through the window behind her father, lay a young man's ring.

A torn string, reknotted, swung from it.

The land of faery,
Where nobody gets old and crafty and wise,
Where nobody gets old and bitter of tongue.
　　　　　　　　　　　　　　—W. B. Yeats

three

Connor reached for the ring to examine it more closely, but Troy closed her small fist around it and slipped the ring calmly into the pocket of her plaid jumper. Her face wore a look of pride.

Curious, he wanted to question her about how she'd come upon the object; but it was nearly time for dinner, he was tired from his walk, and he really preferred talking about his daughter's imaginary playmates. They teased and aroused his own latent sense of Irish humor and awe. In a queer way they tended to make him feel young again.

"Will you miss Sir Gat, now that he's gone?" Connor asked, prying gently.

"Oh, no. Not really." Troy was always very solemn when she discussed these creatures of the youthful mind and the rays from the fading sun gave her colorless eyes a strange reddish hue. "Besides, he was pretty damn ugly, if you want to know the truth."

"Don't swear," he corrected her automatically, folding the newspaper and laying it carefully on the floor beside his chair. "Troy, I don't think I ever asked you about him. What *was* Sir Gat, anyway? A little green boy or a giant frog, or what?"

She seemed surprised. "Didn't I tell you?" She thought a moment. "Sir Gat was a bear, sort of. While *I* knew him, that is. I think he could be a lot of things, if he wanted to be." Musing, her slender fingers patted her jumper pocket, absently. "And he said that this ring will always protect me. From just about *anything,* good or evil. Ain't that neat?" She paused, then headed straight to her original refrain as children sometimes do. "I got—I mean, I *have*—a brand new playmate now." Her expression was judicious. "This is a *lot* neater one."

Dads gave her a gentle smile. "I'm relieved to hear it, darling. I'm so glad you won't be alone once again." Connor knew how badly Troy needed to have brothers and sisters to play with. Without looking her way, he hoped that Ethelyn was listening. "It's tough being alone at your age. Who's the new guy in your life, my colleen?"

She shook her head, bouncing on her heels in new excitement. "It's not a guy. It's—it's Ducie. A *she,* Dads, a gorgeous lady. A real, nice, superdooper lady with real long, red hair. And she's absolutely *beautiful.*" Troy's expression modified to sudden wistfulness. "Daddy, do you think I'll ever be beautiful too?"

"You already are," he replied with tenderness.

"There's no one prettier than Mommy's girl," Ethelyn put in across the way. She could identify with the need to feel lovely.

"You're the most beautiful thing in the whole, wide world to your mother and me," Connor swore, tears in his sentimental eyes. He cleared his throat, resuming the game. "Now, about this new lady friend of yours. Are you absolutely certain that her name isn't *Lucy?*"

"Nope, I'm positive. Her name is Ducie. Beautiful Ducie," she sang in a singsong, dreamy fashion. "But her breath smells *horrid!*"

She'd said it with wide-open eyes and perfect timing and Connor Quinlan burst into laughter, unable to stifle it. His more sentimental tears slid down his cheeks as he smiled. "Now, Troy, is that a nice thing to say about your brand new friend?"

Troy enjoyed Dads' sense of humor enormously, always responding to it. She smirked. "Well, I can't help it. It's true." Remembering something, Troy shuffled her feet. "Ducie is going t'help and protect me, she says. Just the way Sir Gat helped me."

"Help you do what, kitten?"

At that instant, for no reason in the world, conversing with adults became the dullest waste of time imaginable. Troy jammed her small hand in a pocket, fingering the souvenir ring, and turned away. Blankly, "Whatever," she answered with grand vagueness, smiling. "I better get ready for supper."

"Dinner," Ethelyn amended without looking up. "Even over here we aren't going to succumb. In our house, we have dinner."

Troy had reached the bottom step of the staircase. "Whatever," she agreed over her shoulder with a shrug.

Dinner had been good. Ethelyn was always a decent if uninventive cook and rather enjoyed shopping in Connemara stores. They threatened, Connor thought, to bring out his wife's inventive-

53

ness.

In Ireland, they discovered, the more weight-conscious no longer insisted on having potatoes at every meal. Still, baked in their skins—or "jackets," as people here called them—potatoes were still a staple, along with pork chops and bacon and cabbage.

Only Dad Quinlan had anything alcoholic to drink and that was the one careful glass of Scotch whisky he sipped throughout the meal. He explained that he knew the statistics on his country too well to ignore them. In a population of five million, experts estimated there were between fifty- and sixty-thousand alcoholics. "And I don't plan t'be one of them," Dad promised. "Not if there are close to twelve thousand pubs for the ones with a thirst."

Now Connor Quinlan perched on the edge of their bed on the second floor, large hands dangling between his heavy legs, idly glancing into the bathroom. His stare was aimless, actually; without intent. He felt tired—almost as if he still suffered jet lag, or the five-hour difference in time—and his active mind was drifting free, waiting for inspiration.

He found it in his wife.

Ethelyn came into view in front of the wash basin. He started to look politely away but his eyes remained fixed. There was about the moment a feeling of being discarnate, disembodied, as if others could not see him. She was naked to the waist, her small breasts with their high-placed nipples reflected in the mirror over the turquoise sink. Feeling vaguely like a voyeur—or rather, feeling like he *should* feel like a voyeur—Connor observed her ablutions and rested the palm of his hand in his lap. He saw the way her breasts changed shape when she moved, something he had always found gripping; saw the nipples harden as she passed a lukewarm cloth over her torso, sponging. His palm became fingers. Connor remembered other, happier nights, times when tension was needed only as a bridge to their mutual fulfillment, times when he had fondled and kissed her freely, when those half-moon hips lifted against him in reckless shared want, an earnest desire matching his own—when selfishness also crossed the bridge and blended in oneness.

She came into the bedroom a few minutes later, quite naked now, apparently oblivious to his existence. Her first Irish ad campaign on her mind, no doubt; ways to announce yet another furniture sale, yet another new gadget. Breasts dangling, Ethelyn ransacked through a dresser drawer for a clean nightgown, then turned in his direction. He saw the dark pubic thicket, felt it mesmerize him with hot longing even as he snatched his hand away from himself, nearly caught. Ethelyn's brown eyes saw where he was staring; they moved then to him, saw the violent swell between his thighs, caught his telltale desire.

She looked away. Connor stood, with awkwardness, took a slightly painful step as she swept the nightgown over her head in a silken shower of gold. Her body wriggled; it was hidden.

"It's the wrong time, sweetie," she chirped, patting his cheek maternally as she breezed past him to sit on the edge of the bed. She yawned. "Next week, maybe."

Wordless at the lips but filled with paragraphs,

he nodded mutely. His big hands moved to replace his shirt, the arms aching slightly; he left it unbuttoned and the dark hair on his broad chest caught the reflection of bathroom light, gleaming with heat. He needed to adjust himself; he turned away from her.

"Where are you going?" There was no concern, no panic, to the voice; it was barely an interested question.

"Out to the study, I think." He paused in the doorway, thinking his own voice sounded hoarse, tightly controlled. He guessed it was. "Can't seem t'get the old Newsletter off my mind."

"Well, don't stay up too late, Connie." In a little imitation she had done for years, Ethelyn pressed her lips with a small palm and blew her husband a Dinah Shore kiss. "Mmm-*wahhhh-h!*"

He smiled wanly, the *dèjù vu* overwhelming and easily identified, his fingers wriggling a farewell from his thigh, and left.

After a period in the bathroom he went downstairs. The old stone house appeared cavernous, replete with shadows carrying boyhood memories on tiptoe. He'd been much smaller then, he realized, faintly recalling how there were times when the house at night had frightened him. Often he'd stood before the stairs leading to Dad's attic, his pale, tiny frame immobilized by a combination of intense curiosity and incipient terror. *Great giants will come from that attic someday,* he'd thought, half nodding to himself. *Creatures one-hundred feet high with a dozen cruel eyes and 'lectricity for brains.* And once, at the age of fifteen, he'd administered to himself a test of manhood by sitting on the floor, his back against the wall, waiting for hours to see them descend. Dad had found him asleep on the lower step the next morning, laughed, and told his son with the aching back that that would teach him to butt into other people's affairs.

On the first floor Connor heard the subdued, tinnily-human buzz of voices from the television set in the den. He smiled in wonderment. Dad, of all people, hooked by the late evening programs. Perhaps it was part of the insomnia that made him walk the house so many times in the past. Connor paused, thinking about stepping in to the den to say a few words to his father. But it wasn't time, yet, to have the talk they were bound to have, man-to-man, someday. There would be a moment when they'd have to get it all out in the open, express their deepest thoughts like adults, in the hope of real peace. But this wasn't that moment.

It was warmer than usual tonight, the humidity high, and Connor hesitated just beyond the back door, searching for the sign of a breeze. But the breeze was somewhere else and he wished, more passionately than before, that he was with it.

He took a few steps toward the garage Dad had converted to a study for him and stopped. Peculiar, he thought, how damnably alone he felt so close to the old house. It was rather like stepping boldly out onto an uninhabited planet with a creepy sensation of alienness making the light sweat on his back clammy. He shuddered, stretched, to twist the disembodied hand away from his skin.

The woods were well off in the distance but didn't look all that far away. For a moment they looked within arm's reach, like a mirage that never grew nearer. Illusion, he told himself, starting toward his study. Now his feet felt heavy, clogged with dirt on the soles; it was like walking in quicksand and he tried to shake off a feeling of being oppressed, or watched. If he didn't know better, Connor thought, he might think he was having some kind of dark premonition.

The sounds from the woods increased in volume as he put out his hand to the doorknob of the study's only door. God, how wild, how *feral* were the night-noises of nature! Day and night were two separate and distinct worlds for the lesser creatures, cohabited in a fashion, yet with a massive isolation that no bridge of man's construction could hope to cross. Gone were the sweet, lifting birdcalls of the morning. They were replaced by a billion—*ten* billion—fierce predators' cries, and the sounds of their trapped and gutted victims. It occurred to him that the insects and small animals were no less awesomely violent for all their tininess than maligned man. Why, the carnage in the Quinlan woods each night, the savage loss of life, was beyond human ken, beyond computing.

Closing the door behind him quickly, Connor turned rapidly to the light switch. Locking the door securely, he grinned at his own foolishness. God was wise enough to keep his creatures separate; the bridge was rarely crossed. The tiny warring ones remained in their own vicious worlds, scarcely aware that a world of people even existed. And so he would be safe here.

Safe, in the civilization Man had erected like a shield about itself, a shield not really against lesser life, but to keep himself *in*, controlled. Connor had brought his own handsome walnut desk and comfortable leather chair. Dad supplied a decent radio/stereo combination. He'd spent much of his first week in Connemara cramming two homemade bookshelves with his favorite books, many of them from his own subsidy publishing house. Unlike the big stone two-story, the study was his, truly his, because he'd paid Dad for the simple construction work that was done and even managed to press a small amount of rent on his father. Pride satisfied, he was beginning to find the study a place where he could genuinely relax.

He'd lied to Ethelyn. He planned to do little or no work on the Newsletter. Other things had to be worked out, primarily the offer the University had made him. Slumping deep in his chair, Connor had to admit that Dad's estimate of his chances for employment was accurate. After giving only two lectures in Galway they'd asked him to teach regularly, twice a week, for an amount higher than Dad's modest guess. If the old man was right again, the TV station would also let him do one program a week and, together with what the University paid and his income from Bookquins Newsletter, he'd actually have more spendable income than he'd had in Indianapolis. But his workload would increase, too, especially if any talk shows he did stole another day from his personal working schedule. He could allow nothing to interfere with the Newsletter.

Just how stubborn a man *am* I? he wondered. Perhaps it was true what Sid Aronson had told him when it looked for awhile like he would have to cease publication. Sid had been trying to cheer his boss up when he said that nobody read the damn Newsletter except a bunch of faggot pretenders to literature, or kid journalists with more pimples than credits. But maybe, just maybe, Connor was right and the publication not only encouraged potential geniuses but informed fellow publishers that Connor Quinlan was doing everything in his limited power to make the subsidy business legitimate.

He switched on his radio and stretched out on the old sofa Dad so thoughtfully had placed in his study. Some old Irish ballads—not the ones Americans sang with beery tears in their Dutch and German and Italian eyes, but the genuine article— were playing. He arched his back, wincing, trying to get comfortable. He realized that while he'd never wanted to be a teacher, there was a need for an educated man that he'd never known before. After the British "intruded," by the mid-19th Century, the great famine had been a deadly exercise in "gentleman's genocide," as it was called, and the formerly rich land had been ruined —run red with the blood of innocents and the shouts of greedy cannon. Even today a recovery had never been complete and illiteracy remained high. A degree from University, some good pointers toward a better life, meant a great deal to these folk. Why, the great Gaelic writers were sometimes said to have taken up the pen because they were just too poor to buy a weapon!

And it was here, in the west of Ireland, that the brave exclamation "Hell or Connaught!" was coined. Once here in Galway the British had bragged in 1518 that "neither 'O' nor 'Mac' shall strut nor swagger through the streets of Galway." How sweet it was to the residents to know that Galway was the most Gaelic of Irish cities! That a Galwayman came to America with Columbus! It was here, too, that the dispossessed of Ireland's Catholics were sent into exile when Oliver Cromwell turned the lands in Kildare and Meath over to the English Protestants during the nearly-fatal 17th Century. What chance for progress, modern conveniences, or an education could they possibly have enjoyed? It was a miracle that the people survived at all!

Behind Connor's head the radio beeped twice, thrice, then caught its breath. A local announcer came on, trying to sound like Dan Rather: "This is a special news bulletin. Two young people, Lucy Kilkalien and Thomas O'Donovan, were killed last night in a woods near Kylemore, Connemara. The analysis from coroner Doctor William Fogarty indicates that they may have been slaughtered by a large and powerful animal, possibly a bear. Inquiries are being made round the clock," the baritone pondered on, "by the police departments of the region to ascertain if a circus or zoo has failed to report an escaped beast. In the meanwhile, residents of the area are . . . ."

Slamming his fist on the cement floor, Connor sat up to turn it off. A shiver trickled down his spine and he frowned. *Troy*. She'd have to be told to play in the house for a few days. While the youngsters had lost their lives on the other side of the large woods, that was no guarantee that the beast had departed. Always something, he groaned. He and Ethelyn would have to keep an eye on Troy until they located and destroyed the damned animal.

Connor rose and sat down at his desk, reaching for a book on the wildlife of Ireland.

Outside the garage-turned-to-a-study, from

somewhere in the nearby woods, came a sound that froze the publisher in immobility.

Distant and whimper-thin, it was a sad, tortured wailing. Like the noise of a child, or a woman, sobbing.

No, he changed his mind; it wasn't really like that. Wonderingly, he shook his head and then heard the sound again.

There was something underlying it, something beneath the surface grieving he had not identified at first. His eyes wide and staring, he listened intently.

Dammit, there *was* something else lurking in that sound and he couldn't quite pinpoint it.

With the noise dying out Connor continued to sit, frozen, trying hard to put a finger on the exact nature of the peculiar noise.

And finally he had it.

It was the sound of a creature luring its victim with cleverness, by an almost manlike ruse that was at once hypnotic and entrancing.

It was a sound with the basic quality of... *blood lust.*

> *All full of angels*
> *Is every leaf on the oaks of Derry.*
> —St. Columba

four

Ethelyn Quinlan was curled on her bed with a book, nerves twitching; restive. It seemed so *dark* in the house with no street lights outside like mute guards posted against unseen prowlers. She turned over on the bed again, trying to get somewhat better light on her pages. But it wouldn't really help, since her mind was unwilling to come to grips with the John Jakes historical novel. That irritated her, and further roused her from sleepiness, but not alone because she usually adored being swept away to more romantic and primitive times. The magic carpet seemed already to have left, her shoulders ached from holding the novel just so, and she was getting irritable with herself.

As far back as she could remember, she had been blessed with a swift flexibility of mind. It was the type that enabled her to adjust to fresh conditions while, at the same time, she succeeded in forcing a few major elements into line with her unspoken private wishes. The circuitous device was almost Communistic in the clever, involved process and quite effective. In stressful circumstances Ethelyn tended to provide a glittering smile, an easily understanding and agreeable manner, plus a cheery mask that kept others from knowing for a minute her secret displeasure. But when she was ready, when her chance developed, large or small, she displayed a remarkable eagerness to pounce upon that single means of establishing her point and was satisfied with having made a small but valuable gain.

Ethelyn was very much a modern woman.

In her marital relationship, she loved Connor Quinlan dearly and that long-lasting fact was the one blinding her to her customary perception of available loopholes in the marriage. He was always, she felt, so *unreasonable* with her on nights like this. After all, she often craved him sexually as much as he did her, or so she honestly believed, and only a deep seated survival instinct enabled her to refuse him. Tonight was but one of hundreds of other nights and depressingly typical. Dammit, she wanted badly to relieve that lonely ache she felt, to be transported romantically to some more familiar world, one in which she needn't learn the ad agency business all over again and feel that she was losing Troy to the winsome Irish charms. She wanted to feel like a woman, just as, she assumed, Con needed to feel like a man. A part of her yearned to find his weary, satisfied head relaxing gratefully, freshly unsexed—unfanged?—on the pillow next to her.

Her primary solace, as she placed the vivid novel on the paint-chipped table next to the bed, was that Connor might possibly feel as restless as she did. It was he who instigated these things; it was he who should be mostly miserable. Fair was fair.

Ethelyn loved her husband in a particularly

feminine fashion and as much as she was capable of loving something that was not a part of her own personality or body.

Stretching her short arms and legs as far as they would go, thereby flattening her small breasts until they looked like flesh-toned fried eggs—wishing her exertion would turn her tall, lithe, and tigress-like, a sleek fashion model every inch of her length—Ethelyn sought relaxation and finally decided it was beyond her reach.

For a moment she toyed with the possibilities, tight in a foetal ball, her tiny pointed chin resting on her knuckles beneath the yellow bedlight. Was it literally true that she must die if she got pregnant again? It sounded so unreasonable; Ethelyns did not perish. She'd suffered such agonized concern about the doctor's threat that she could no longer recall precisely any one thing the man said. She wished she might get Connor to sympathize with the fact that Death had become a viable, frightening, *personal* element for the first time in her thirty-two years. She considered its gaunt, sneaky shadow unappealing, mostly; just as bad, she must see herself as unchic, immature, oversexed and a trifle addlepated if she *did* get PG after what the doctor told her. Her chums back in Indianapolis would bring to life a charge Ethelyn heard many times when she was growing up, should she die: The charge that she was shallow and empty headed.

Now she made an effort to reflect in a level headed way and confessed that she must have been wrong in believing that Connor cheated on her. He left his home in Indianapolis with too little protest and without time to have smoothly dissolved any relationships. Perhaps it was only that *she* would have stepped out, if she'd been in his shoes. When there was no womb at the inn, Ethelyn giggled to herself, as a man she would have been *in* at the *womb!* But Dad Quinlan had instilled in Connor an outlet that wasn't so much Catholic as disposed to regard infidelity as gauche. It wasn't *proper,* in the Quinlan clan, to taste forbidden fruit—or, she added, her ad-trained mentality always working overtime, forbidden *fruits.*

And if Connor was not looking around, maybe she should begin cooling the way she continually flirted, herself. Not that she'd ever done anything *bad,* but it'd been close, a few times. That overset fellow from the TV station, for example—he was loaded, knew everybody, and had it *bad* for Ethelyn. The clot had whispered exciting suggestions every chance he got. And there was Will Jackson, who'd been Senior Account Exec for six months—*he* simply *drooled* after her, never making a change in the copy she wrote for his accounts, even with almost *no* encouragement at *all.*

Believing things of that sort used to get Ethelyn through the day. Now that she wasn't with her own kind any more, now that she was in an old country where fidelity was just the way the Quinlans liked it, her beliefs didn't seem to get her through the night.

Resigned to being awake, Ethelyn sat up, slid her small pink feet into gaily furry orange slippers, donned a frilly robe, and padded downstairs.

Patrick Aloyious Quinlan, her father-in-law, was no longer watching TV when she found him in his den. She glanced around once, looking for

Connor, realizing he'd gone out to the garage-study just as he intended. Good ole reliable Connie, Ethelyn thought; eat shit. She curled up on the immense overstuffed leather sofa across from Dad, softly little-girl-like in her scurrying, and said Hi.

The old man looked up sharply; then he relaxed, smiled, and waggled his fingers comically at her. "Ah," he murmured, "another restless Quinlan!"

"Too much on my mind," she admitted, watching him and thinking that Connor got his dark good looks from old Pat.

He had watched television until it went off, well before midnight, and then began to browse through his personal library. At sixty-nine, Pat was an erect six-one in height, perhaps an inch taller than his son, with a face that appeared to have been made of the same leather used in his sofa. Naturally dark-complexioned, his eyebrows and smile were his most notable features, the first bushy with the latter a sunny sparkling of dry humor in a fleshy face. He was, Ethelyn felt, jowly without being overweight and looked splendid in the smoking jacket she and Connor had brought him from the States. By day, of course, Pat always wore a tweed jacket over a sweater and, beneath the sweater, a white shirt buttoned to the neck. When she had seen the old man outside he'd worn a plaid cap, the tilt of which bespoke both humorous wariness and self-assured arrogance.

"I was listenin' to the TV, hearin' about the troubles to the north," he began in a voice that would rumble, then suddenly lilt to an emphasis-making tenor, "and remembered a quote from Daniel O'Connell." He held up an old book in his meaty hands and stooped to get light on it. "Ye

67

might like it: 'Bigotry has no head and cannot think; no heart and cannot feel. When she moves it is in wrath; when she pauses it is amid ruin. Her prayers are curses, her god is a demon, her communion is death, her vengeance is eternity, her decalogue written in the blood of her victims...'" He peered over at Ethelyn, the shadows making his eyes deep and wise, and smiled gently. "Approve?"

"Very much," she whispered. Of all the things she'd seen in Connemara, indeed, in all County Connaught, she liked her father-in-law best. He'd been the one to stand in her corner when they needed help; he'd opened his doors to them. "What else do you have in your library?"

He turned with a grin and a gesture. "It's mostly my people, I fear. *The History of Irish Literature* by that weird, wondrous 'A. E.' The *Yellow Book of Lecan,* and the Fenian cycle." Pat snapped shut the book from which he'd drawn the quotation and reinserted it, with careful respect, in the proper place. "The complete works of Boucicault, William Butler Yeats, and St. Columba." He pointed with finger like a cigar. "There's Sean O'Faolain and Frank Connor. O'Casey's *At-Swim-Two-Birds* and *The Cattle Raid of Cooley."* He paused, smacking his lips. "Once, a long while ago, I wanted to be like these fellows. But I didn't suffer enough; I got three squares a day."

His wistful tone disturbed her; it indicated, she felt, some deeper grief, something he could not discuss with anyone. Ethelyn was always at her best in conditions of this kind. Her intuition was often correct; even when it wasn't, it brought out her husbanded compassion. "Troy is so happy to

68

here with you."

The old man took a chair opposite her and his [s]kin crinkled like cracks in fine leather. "And I'm [s]o happy she's here. The lass has a rich imagina[ti]on, I'm thinkin'—richer'n mine ever was." He [r]aised a judgmental index. "It could be that the [fl]ow of Irish talent has merely skipped a couple of [ge]nerations."

Ethelyn made a face. "She doesn't like school all [th]at much. She hates it that she has to go. Even [he]re in Kylemore. But I made the arrangements [to]day and Troy will find out tomorrow." She [si]ghed. "I do hope she'll buckle down and do some [w]ork for a change."

Dad looked somewhat anxious. "But ye will [h]ave some time, will ye not, t'see some of Ireland? [In]cludin' Troy? I started making plans even before [I] come." He anticipated her thinking and [sh]rugged, his grin elfin and disarming. "Not that [I] plan t'become a typically oldfashioned Gran[d]a who *forces* his attentions on the young 'uns. [H]owever, I *did* have some little ideas of places the [fo]ur of us might go, seein' as how Connor has that [fa]ncy little machine at his disposal anyway."

"Why, you rascal!" cried Ethelyn with a laugh. [Y]ou're going to make us Irish to the core just as [fa]st as you possibly can."

Pat made a sly face. "It's only smart to be [kn]owin' what yer new countryside has t'offer. [B]esides, betwixt the two of us, I'm delighted to [h]ave another clean shot at your husband. Troy can [cl]aim she's half-American and you're all-Ameri[ca]n but Connor, well, he *belongs* in these parts."

[Th]e grin had gone, leaving a sober-faced and [se]rious expression that only hinted at the depths of his sincerity. "It ain't natural t'be born in Connamara, in County Connaught, spend twenty-on[e] years here, and not know more about his peopl[e] than Con knows."

Ethelyn didn't know why, but something in h[is] tone vaguely disturbed her. "I think I'd like to hav[e] something to drink. May I bring you somethin[g,] Dad?"

He stared up at her as she arose. "Hot tea woul[d] go down nicely about now," the old man acknow[l]edged. "There's always a cup on the pot, as th[e] sayin' goes."

Pat Quinlan was as good as his word. She foun[d] the tea brewing, red-hot, and brought them eac[h] back a steaming cup. He sipped it gratefully and [a] trifle noisily while she mused. "Tell me, Dad. If w[e] have some free time, what are the magical place[s] you'd be, ah, 'after takin'' us?"

He waved his wide palm negatively at her. "N[o,] no, girl, don't y'be tryin' to catch the ring [o'] *Eireannach's* talk." He chuckled but meant i[t.] "The lilt don't be comin' that easy to ye." H[e] leaned forward in hunching eagerness. "We[ll,] t'answer yer query, Ethelyn, we could go salmo[n] fishin' where the Ballynahinch empties into th[e] Bertraghboy and stay in the very hotel we[re] 'Humanity Dick' Martin lived."

Ethelyn blinked. "'Humanity Dick'...?"

"Martin," Dad finished, with much the tone a[n] American might use at the failure to recogni[ze] Benjamin Franklin's name. "Ole Dick founded th[e] Royal Society fer the Prevention of Cruelty [to] Animals, he did, and he lived here in Galway fro[m] 1754 to 1834!"

She hid a smirk. The old fellow made it soun[d]

like ten years ago. "Where else might we go?" she inquired.

He tilted his big head back, the light from his floor lamp giving him a certain golden enthusiasm. "Well, now, any weekend we could skip over to the Aran Islands for a *ceilidhi*—a party after the pub closes." He winked broadly at her.

"An after-hours joint?" Ethelyn gasped.

"Indeed!" He nodded grandly, definitely. "There's a band ever'time. Generally an accordion player but sometimes he brings a drummer along. We'd take the one taxi on Inishmore and go 'jaunting.' That means riding round the island in a sidecar which is none too securely fastened to a horse-drawn buggy. The folks who get to the *ceilidhi* and back have a rare old time." Finally he quit teasing her and managed a laugh. "No doubt it's all a wee bit primitive for yer tastes, lass. Father Dunnehy acts as an unofficial chaperone each week, the boys and girls begin on either side of the pub and then sort of *whirl* together, cloud-like, in a lead-footed kind of dance. But it's nice for the Aran folk, who don't have much." He hesitated again, as if a switch had been thrown, the glee replaced by an ambience of sadness. "They're an unfortunate lot, them islanders—and an intuitive people. Very psychic, in most things. Acourse, nobody kin figure out *everything* that's goin' to happen."

He stopped talking abruptly, turning away slightly, and the shadows in the library reached across the room like probing, cold fingers.

"Dad, what is it?" Ethelyn asked anxiously. "Something's on your mind, isn't it?"

He ignored her and took a breath. "Now, down in

71

Salthill—that's what ye'd call a suburb of Galway, seems to me—there is a long promenade of ex-*traor*dinary beauty, and it possesses an amusement park. Little Troy would be enjoyin' the place, I reckon."

"Dad, *tell* me," she begged, frightened now. "What is it? How may I help?"

He felt her gaze beseeching him and lifted his head to meet her eyes, considering this daughter-in-law of long standing whom he'd known for such a brief period. How much was she capable of understanding? What did she believe in; what feelings of the heart did she hold dear? Just what *should* she know about the awful things he suspected?

"Did you hear the news?" His question was casual, nearly offhanded. He waited until she shook her head. "The authorities in Galway reported that two kids from the islands were murdered last night." He tapped his fingers on the chair nervously. "On the other side of the woods. *This* woods, the one out back."

Ethelyn shuddered. "Did they catch the murderer?"

Pat Quinlan shook his head, then averted it. "They say it might have been a bear. And y'see, Ethelyn, there are bears and then, well, *there are bears.*"

She studied him again before commenting, seeing that Connor's eyes were generally wide open while his father's tended to be crinkled in good humor and wit or, as they were this minute, fixed at a half-mast that gave nothing away. He had oversized ears and full lips; like Con, he was a fluent speaker, willing to consume twenty minutes just to get to the punchline of a joke. But Connor preferred to talk of facts while this old man dwelt in a soft fancy bred in his blood. "I'm not sure what you mean, Dad," she said at last. "But I warn you: I'm a very modern kind of woman."

"I know," he retorted with sadness, "I know. You miss a lot."

"Really?" she teased. "I thought we got so much more than ladies of earlier times."

"Certainly not!" He was firm, almost convincing. "Not only did ye give up on bein' Cinderella, and looking for yer handsome prince. Y'gave up on a lot of very pee-cool-yer things which happen to be true." He inclined his large head. "Practicality is limiting, you know. 'Specially when it conflicts with unfamiliar facts."

She laughed, edgy despite herself. "Is this going to be a catechism class? Or *cataclysm* class?"

"Nope, not religious in the customary sense." Dad leaned toward her from his chair. "When I was just a tad here in County Connaught, me own aunt told me often of certain . . . bee-zarre things. Things that live all *around* us." He looked around, to the back of the house, as a rill of thunder sounded with the quality of an oboe in practice. "Especially . . . in the woods."

"You mean, leprechauns?"

"Oooh, my, I'm *so* weary of them little people!" He pointed his finger. "Leprechauns is only a small part of a *bigger* picture, Ethelyn Quinlan. They must have had a good ad man, like you. But there's far more to it than leprechauns. *Far* more."

Ethelyn relaxed, thinking, What a dear foolish man he is. She snuggled deeper into the sofa, her fuzzy-slippered feet behind her. "Tell me more."

"Tell me: Ever see the Internal Revenue Service?"

"No," she giggled. "Thank God!"

"But y'*believe* they're out there. Don't you? Because ye sends 'em a check now and then. Some kind of proof *that* is!"

"And because," she argued goodhumoredly, eyes wide, *"everybody"* believes in the IRS. We *know* you have to send them what they want, or else."

Dad's expression grew dreamy. He ignored the loudening rumbles beyond the old house and folded his hands over his abdomen, delighted she'd walked into his trap. "Everyone here, when I was a boy, *knew* you had to do what the *ryanees* wanted. Or else."

"The who?" she demanded.

"The *ryanees.*" He spelled it for her. "Tiny folk. We didn't see much of them, either, and we also didn't want to. But ye had to put good food out for 'em, right on schedule, or—"

"Or what?" she asked, frightened again.

"Or they come and they *got* ya, that's what! Just like your IRS." He opened an eye to see her plain. "Do you know what happened after you put the food out for the ryanees?" She shook her head. "It got *eaten.* Yep," he nodded, "when ye went after your saucer and cup, they'd be empty. Cleaned. Just like the IRS takes your check and returns it to ye, cancelled."

She giggled, a female mixture of apprehension and amusement, even joy.

"There's a whole lot more, daughter," he promised. "Never overemphasize the significance of what a bunch of folks *believe.* That could be the worst and the last mistake y'ever make." He lit a cigarette, the flame and the lamp making yellow hollows in his cheeks. "There's sound foundation for every belief from cats bein' the familiars of witches, to vampires, to much worse creatures. Demons come in many guises other than wolves, bats, and serpents and goats."

She paused, honing in on his emotions. Something in his tone of voice had been modified again. "You aren't *serious,* are you, Dad?"

"Serious as yer taxes, me girl. I was thinkin' about those two kids in the woods. Often, Ethelyn, creatures from—from *Below*—come as wild animals." He leaned toward her and she realized the nature of his emotion. He, too, was afraid. "And there's little or less to combat them. And if they also happened to be *summoned*—"

Ethelyn leaped. Both of them spun their heads to the stairs.

There was the sound of crying, from upstairs.

"I think that's Troy," Ethelyn mumbled, rising swiftly with a certain gratitude for the interruption. "She must have been crying in her sleep."

Pat A. Quinlan stood too. He hesitated, watching his daughter-in-law hurry from the room on her foolish, flashing orange slippers.

Then he hurried after her at a slightly stiff-legged trot.

It was pitch dark inside Troy's room except for moonlight splashing in a golden pool around the sleeping child. Her pale yellow hair was sprinkled damply on the pillow, her eyes squeezed tight. Troy's lips were working as if she struggled to fight off a nightmare. Dad was there now and watched Ethelyn reach out to soothe the child, to stroke her soft hair and murmur hushing sounds.

They saw it at the same instant.

That ring Troy found, she'd put it on a fresh string and tied it round her slender neck.

And the ring, inexplicably, *was glowing dimly but decidedly in the dark.*

Curious, Ethelyn wondered what rare oddity of lighting caused such a luminous shimmer. "*Don't touch it!*" cried Pat Quinlan, warning her, putting out his own arm to deter Ethelyn.

But she already held it up from the girl's throat, working it between her fingers as she stared down at it in puzzlement. "Troy said her friend Sir Something told her this ring would protect her." Was it her imagination or did it give off a faint, pleasing tingle? "Isn't that cute?"

"*Maith dhom e,*" he apologized, "but I don't rightly know if t'is." His soft voice was lower because of the sleeping child, but there were other reasons as well, and they had more to do with fantastic age than innocent youth. "My experience has taught me that whatever protects one person almost always seems to . . . to *harm* the other person."

His gentle, superstitious gaze met Ethelyn's eyes and her smile, without malice, was yet disbelieving. Pitying.

Pat looked out Troy's bedroom window, the only one there was. It was fringed by lacy curtains, a souvenir of America Troy's mother had brought to Ireland. As a guarding object, he doubted it would be nearly enough. A parade of ancient images of stolid evil taunted him, moved like servants of Satan through his mind. In the distance, in the drifting quiet of a gentle rainfall, he saw the trees of Connemara lift their plaintive heads to the night sky and he listened to the woods grumbling to itself. And he thought, without wanting to be sure, that he heard another sound, of crying. But it was hard to tell.

Involuntarily, the old man crossed himself.

Evil comes to us men of the imagination wearing as its mask all the virtues.

—Yeats

five

After Ethelyn had finally fallen asleep last night, dreams of Troy in mortal danger from an entire cave filled with marauding bears prevented her from sleeping well. Thus she had awakened feeling terrible and, while three glasses of fresh milk assisted in quelling a queasy upset in the base of her stomach, she continued feeling ragged and out of sorts.

Nevertheless, Ethelyn threw herself into preparing a solid Irish breakfast. Eventually she hoped to have a chance to bake bread their way, in iron pots with red coals of smouldering turf piled atop the closed lid. It was supposed to be delicious. As well, many women in County Connaught still boiled their bacon and cabbage in fireplaces instead of on stoves and she looked forward to trying that, too.

Puttering in the old fashioned kitchen, Ethelyn was happy to see that Dad Quinlan happened to have the money to keep things in condition, even if there were few modern appliances to help her cook. She doubted if the Irish had heard of a microwave oven, but there was a toaster. The water supply was plentiful, piped in; and while Dad's house still used peat at times for the sake of tradition, gentle blue smoke lifting from the chimneys of the area, he also had central heating.

She cooked a typical breakfast of the community for Connor, Troy, and Dad: Hot cereal, one egg and one strip of bacon each, toast and rolls, both hot coffee and tea strong enough to open their sinuses. She'd remembered to buy marmalade in Galway and that soon earned her an appreciative cock of the jaw from the old man. There was so much to do, to measure up, Ethelyn thought as she toyed with a roll. Her arrival had retired an old neighbor lady named Annie Flanigan and Ethelyn knew perfectly well Dad was sitting there comparing her cooking to Annie's.

Well, whatever magic this quaint place worked on an old city girl from the States, Ethelyn told herself determinedly, she wouldn't begin spinning and weaving the way many of the neighbor women occupied their time. Nor could she imagine Connor emulating the menfolk, crafting straw-thatching with the odd grass they called simply "bent." Unless Dad concealed, beneath his oft-enigmatic crinkle of a smile, more secretive "hidden persuaders" than either she or Connor conceived.

"Troy," she called across the table, "under *no* circumstances are you to leave this house today." Her voice, even to her own ears, sounded more cross than she had intended. When would this annoying tummy upset pass? "Please, darling. Mind Mommy?"

Troy knew perfectly well it was a question and so did Gran-da, who regarded the child with tolerant amusement. She gave the impression that she had completely tuned the others out as she gulped a second glass of milk without replying.

"Troy! Did you hear what Mommy said?" It was Connor, his own tone a notch sharper than usual. Deeply concerned for his daughter's danger in the woods, he put down his coffee cup and tried to catch Troy's eyes. "*Neither* of us wants you to go outside today. All right?"

She peered at Connor with eyes of indeterminate color but also with a glint of disappointment for him. "Mommy told me I'll be starting back to school soon. So it's like the last of vacation." She paused, looking hurt. "What did I do wrong?"

He hesitated, wondering whether to tell her. "Nothing. There are some—some bad things happening in the general neighborhood."

"Things a little girl shouldn't have to know about," Ethelyn interjected.

"Oh, them." Bored, Troy played with the ring on the cord around her neck and pushed back her cereal, untried. "More of those rapists and pervs and things, huh?"

"Troy!" Mommy exclaimed.

Connor grinned at his daughter's cool. For a long moment he thought of explaining that this crime was on an entirely different level of brutality than those crimes of which they customarily warned her. But he knew he'd face a battery of countering questions, if he expounded, and doubted that he had any accurate answers. All he knew was that the woods might contain something deadly and he needed to guard Troy from it. He glanced at his wristwatch.

"We must be going, darling," he said, looking at

Ethelyn. She was staring absently at the chalky bottom of her milk glass. "You don't want to be late for your new job and I plan to stop at University this morning." He stopped talking, drumming his fingers, unsure at the last moment that he wanted to make this definite. "Well, I decided to tell the administrators that I'll lecture twice a week."

"I'm so glad," she replied, soberly, her enthusiasm spoiled by the nagging misery in her abdomen. "I think you should get involved away from the house, Con, instead of developing the habit of spending all your time on the Newsletter." Pushing away from the table to stand, Ethelyn staggered lightly, weak-kneed. As best she could, she camouflaged it. When Troy lifted a patient cheek for her goodbye kiss, Ethelyn turned her own cheek. "Mommy thinks she's getting an attack of 'germans,' darling," she said cutely, apologetically. "I don't want the invasion to spread to my girl."

"If only you'd been at Cadigan's longer you could take the day off," Connor said with concern.

"Takin' anything for it?" Dad inquired, looking solicitous.

Ethelyn merely shook her head. She was afraid the old man would force some weird home remedy down her throat, and went bustling in pursuit of her handbag. Troy watched her and Connor, making ready to leave, silent as a mouse. There they went again, off to do their own things, and here she sat at a table in a strange country, condemned to a day of boredom.

Patrick Aloyious Quinlan saw Troy's watchful stare and misinterpreted it. "I'm sorry you're to be stuck with an old codger."

Troy patted his hand, almost maternally, and wiped back a strand of blonde hair with the back of her other hand. "I didn't mean to hurt your feelings, Gran-da. We'll have lots of fun together."

Dad looked up as his son and daughter-in-law opened the front door. "Be sure to wear your overshoes!" he called.

"We don't have any," Connor responded with a curt smile.

"Ye'll learn," the old man said to the closing door. "Ye'll learn."

He heard Troy giggle appreciatively and settled back in his breakfast chair, watching her, to light his first cigarette of the day. There'd be no more than five others, unless the day grew long and his strong will weak. "Tell me, me darlin'," he began, fixing his gaze on the girl. "When was it y'got your first playmate in the woods?"

Because Gran-da treated her seriously, she answered all his questions in the same manner. She nibbled on a bite, reflecting. "The same day we moved in with you. He was Prant."

Gran-da allowed a polite, carefully incurious smile. "And who was Mr. Prant?"

"A pixy, he said."

Pat blinked, mildly surprised. "Where'd you pick up that word, Troy?"

"From Prant. I told you," she answered, gesturing with her fork.

"Fair enough," the old man averred. "Tell me now. What did your pixy companion look like?"

She adjusted to her remembering-face. "Well-l-l, Prant had kind of long ears and almost no nose at all. His skin was green, sort of. Greenish."

83

The grandfather's eyes narrowed and his heart began to beat more quickly. "Think now, darlin'. Was Prant a boy or a girl pixy?"

"I couldn't really *tell*, Gran-da," she said truthfully, then giggled again, clapping small hands over her mouth in embarrassment. "He didn't wear any clothes but there was just *nothin'* down there! Not even an ole belly button." She laughed and it sounded like Ethelyn.

Pat Quinlan made himself look away from the ring on the cord she wore, the ring that had glowed in the dark. He could see the back lot from where he sat, through the window, and sensed the woods beyond it. "Where was it you saw your Mr. Prant Troy sweet?" He kept his voice under control with difficulty. "Here, in the house?"

"Oh, no." Troy shook her head. "In the woods. My friends are almost always in the woods, Gran-da. Because they don't like grown-ups much. Prant told me I'd meet a whole lot of his nice friends there and they'd all play with me. And Gran-da—" her face lit up with joy—"Prant was ab-so-lute-ly right! Do you remember when Dads was tryin' to get me to read last week and I had trouble with the big words? Well, *that* was when Nabby showed up."

"Go on," he urged her. He knew, now, he would have to discuss these matters tonight with Connor, whether it alienated them further, whether it shook his son's concept of reality, or not.

"Well, Nabby had this deep, *deep* voice—deepern' yours and Dads', and almost like thunder. Y'know? He even told me he drew his voice right *out* of the thunder in the skies. And he touched my forehead and helped me learn to begin ex-press-ing myself better." She enunciated the word precisely

84

as she'd been instructed to do, her colorless eyes enormous. "Nabby knew just about *ev'rything*, Gran-da, and he talked and *talked* to me all day!"

There were shadows out back, the old man saw, drifting ones. He cleared his throat, trembling slightly, and then slipped the offending hand in his lap. "Troy, lass, tell me now: What was Nabby? He wouldn't be a sort of, *ah*, a sort of . . . *crow*, would he?"

"Oh, Gran-da," Troy cried happily, jumping down from her chair, "You're almost as smart as *he* is!" She ran to give him a bear hug.

Unresponsive because he was somewhat fearful of moving, Pat Quinlan looked across her small shoulder at the distant window and tried not to blink.

"I want you to tell your Gran-da the truth, always, Troy," he said when he could. "You haven't been gettin' into me things, have you? Like my books, for example?" He paused. "Or my room? Or—or Gran-da's private attic?"

She didn't reply for an eternity. "No, I really haven't," she answered him at last, pushing back from him to look the old man directly in the eye. The way Mommy taught her, whenever her word was questioned. "I wouldn't get into your things like that, Gran-da. Why, I *love* you."

The aging man sighed and ran his large hand through a mane of dark hair with infrequent gray streaking, then kissed his granddaughter's nose. It was a relief not to have to punish her. "Okay. D'ye recall any of your other chums from the woods?"

"Sure," she said brightly, resuming her place at the table and brushing at crumbs from a roll.

"There was a dog awhile. Named Kuan. He said that he was really a boy, or used to be. Kuan's been helping me learn what trees and plants are there for."

He chuckled softly. "I'd always thought they was there to provide oxygen," he remarked, relaxing a little but painfully curious about the source of Troy's unusual knowledge. "And of course, for bein' beautiful."

"You're so silly!" Troy exclaimed. From her jeans pocket she produced a small pouch made of soft material and fumbled inside. Out came a few sprigs from a tree. "These are from one of them nice ash trees over by the pond," she explained with adult patience. "They keep lotsa evil things away. Or things you *think* might be bad for you. Kuan showed me."

But Gran-da didn't seem to hear. He was staring out the window at the back, toward the woods, considering how nature appeared to reveal its beauty generously and yet hid, beneath the surface serenity, a virtual alternate world of peculiar life— a life that never overstepped, so long as man remembered his place. Because, under ordinary conditions, only man transgressed.

Troy had spoken utterly without guile, but she filled his heart with terror. Unless she was experiencing some kind of racial memory brought on by contact with Pat himself, the child was learning things that were told *him* when he was a boy. Things he was quite certain the modern Connor and Ethelyn would never have told her.

Because the elders used to say that sprigs from ash trees kept away many kinds of restless evil and Pat would swear on his late wife Margaret's grave that he'd never even passed the information to Connor during his childhood. So where else could Troy have acquired such an idea?

"Did anyone t-tell you about these ash springs?" he pressed, voice low.

"Sure," she said. "I told you. Kuan did." Her expression reflected disappointment in him. Couldn't he remember anything anymore? "I just explained, Gran-da."

"I had in mind," he explained, "*human beings.*"

"Oh. No, just the dog." Suddenly she brightened. "He also helped me to see the leprechaun with my own eyes. The only one I ever got t'see."

"How very nice." His smile was warm, engaging, and totally unfelt. How could he get to the bottom of this mystery? At least leprechauns had enjoyed good public relations, to use Ethelyn's term—P.R. In the well-populated world of Irish mythology in which Pat had lived his life, the leprechaun was always considered a respectable spirit. "But how come y'saw only the one wee one?"

"Well, he just wouldn't stay." A cloud swept over her intelligent young face. "He claimed he didn't like my other friends. Kuan was all right, he said, because he'd be either good *or* bad to become a boy again. Then Kuan sort of chased him away, barking all over the woods."

The grandfather held her hand in his two big ones, noticing a new light creep into the little girl's eyes. She was either wary now, as if there was more she could tell, or perhaps she was merely bored with being cross-examined. He shrugged to himself. Possibly *he* was the one being childish, being superstitious. Here, after all, was a lovely child having the kind of pleasant fantasies he would have liked Connor to experience and he was on the verge of terrifying her with his grown-up questions. Spoiling it all for her.

He took a deep breath, deciding to end their talk, perhaps play some games with Troy. But then he was reminded of last night by her small fingers twirling the ring tied round her neck. In the sunlight from the window he couldn't tell if it was glowing now, or not.

"Yer ring, me darlin'," he began again, pointing. "Mommy told me your bear friend gave it to you."

"Uh-huh." Clearly her flow of communication was beginning to dry up.

"It's a pretty thing. But also, Troy honey—it's a real ring. D'ye hear what I'm sayin' to you, child? Some things are make-believe and they are all for pleasure. But things like that, like yer ring. They're genuine. *Fact*." He licked his lips that had gone dry and tried to make his point. "Listen now, girl. That bear playmate you mentioned, Troy sweet. Did *he* have a name?"

Quickly she replaced the ring beneath her blouse and the pouch in a pocket of her jeans. Lips pressed, she was done with talking now, ready to move on to other concerns. Watching, Gran-da told himself that her new impatience was typical of any child, that it wasn't—pray mother Mary—that she was *hiding* anything.

"His name," she said finally, "is Sir Gat." Now she jumped up from her chair, leaving him behind as she headed toward the stairway. Over her shoulder she made it clear for him. "The bear's name was Sir Gat."

Pat Quinlan paled and stared at her retreating

88

figure. Blood had drained from his face until the bushy brows stood out in relief and he sat in the stillness of a posed mannequin. Oddly, he felt unwilling to lift his gaze from the spot where she had been. After all, it would lead directly to the window and thence to the carnivorous woods at the back of his property.

And as he stared in silence, Pat marveled. It was the first time since boyhood that he'd thought of a dreaded creature whom Aunt Peg described to him. She'd been the one who kept the old stories alive in the Quinlan family, a rare colleen once who turned, under the press of a hard life, to a crone with lines and cavities in her face like the craters of the moon. He could see Aunt Peg now, with eyes the color of crows, the parchment skull, the fury of secret knowledge that must be passed on.

And it was the *surgat,* she'd told him in her hushed, beguiling tones of sanctified superstition, who was a terrible demon to be avoided as man or woman loved the human soul. The *surgat,* sometimes willing to be controlled by children, to do their bidding, because their youthful capacity for belief freed it, motivated it, gave the awful demon liberty to prowl the countryside and kill at will for the sheer bloody joy of taking human life. The *surgat* who, in grudging return, always gave to the unsuspecting child a bit of magic, an article of protection, in payment for having been again summoned to the sweet emerald isle.

Summoned, that is, from Hell.

And one of the *surgat*'s favorite guises had been, since the dawn of Time itself, that of an enormous, incredibly powerful, absolutely vicious, man-killing bear.

It is not abnormal men like artists, but normal men like peasants, who have borne witness a thousand times to such things; it is the farmers who see the fairies ... It is the woodcutter ... who will say he saw a man hang on the gallows and afterwards hang around it as a ghost.

—G.K. Chesterton
(in a discussion of W.B. Yeats)

SIX

Connor and Ethelyn drove companionably in his leased Mercedes, the temperature a brisk but sunlit fifty, coming in on Mill Street. With virtually no traffic to impede their progress from Connemara, it had taken them less time to reach Galway than either of them anticipated. Ethelyn, still warmly beneath Pat Quinlan's subtle charm and abruptly finding herself intrigued by her new home, asked Connor to drive slowly through the narrow streets.

He looked at her, rather surprised. He was also more pleased than he would have confessed. Sleeping all night in the garage-den, close to the humming woods, had merged with his decision to lecture and awakened some of his old affection for the ancient isle.

They took Dominick Street to the Claddagh Quay and Connor pointed in the direction of the Dominican Friary, reaching back to the 15th Century. "Six months from now," he said, "in mid-August, it will be the start of the herring-fishing season and a priest from that friary will bless the sea. Then the fishing fleet, resplendent with gay flags, will move slowly down Galway Bay. The fleet stops in more or less stately array," he chuckled. "And they lower their sails. The priest, toting his own flag, offers his blessing."

Nearby, they passed outside the renowned Spanish Arch, a beautiful cathedral where Christopher Columbus was believed to have prayed before going to the New World the first time. Galway, to Connor, seemed ideal for such an adventure. After all, he pointed out to Ethelyn, Columbus sought to establish a fantastic dream of his own and, in the process, discovered a magical new land. But traffic was beginning to pick up and, with a sigh, Connor merged with it. While the make of cars might be different, Galway looked little different in mechanical flow than the noisy swirl of vehicles common to any good sized city.

What Connor really wanted to show Ethelyn was the statue in Central Square. There, they were fortunate to find a space at the curb where it was possible to hesitate for a few moments. Leaving the Mercedes' motor idling and trotting like children across the grass, they stood hand-in-hand in quiet admiration of the famed, roving story teller, Padraic O'Connaire.

Old Padraic, looking impish, self-satisfied, and bemused, was perched like an amiable leprechaun atop a high pile of rocks. It was easy, in this land of encouraged imagination, for Ethelyn to believe that a troop of wee folk might soon pop up around the writer to hear him weave his spellbinding tales.

"Dad named me for him," Connor told her quietly, "Spelling my name somewhat differently. I think he may have jinxed me, made me something of a writer from the beginning—or perhaps the old man sensed what I would become. The Irish seem to be the most intuitive people on the face of the earth. Everything is an omen or warning to them, I guess."

She laughed but it was with appreciation. "I don't remember seeing a statue raised to a story teller, an author, anywhere else in the world, except Stratford, and Central Park. No wonder you didn't fight when I wanted to come here."

He squeezed her hand, feeling closer to her than he had in a long while. "Old Paddy was beloved in Galway, still is. I imagine Dad hoped I would be, too." He thought about agreeing to lecture at University. "Who knows? Maybe there's still time."

Galway, they saw, was thriving. New industry, new shops, burgeoned. And perhaps it was time, Connor thought, aware of how the city had changed since he left County Connaught. In the 1840s, innumerable families had grouped together on the dock in hope and fear, then sailed away from Galway Bay for the golden opportunities they felt awaited them in America. But now emigration was down to a trickle. Modern civilization, in the form of business and bustling factories, was starting to edge into the country's most Irish city.

Once, Galway had been walled in and more aggressive. It had enjoyed its largest burst of growth, until now, during the 13th Century. The Spanish Arch he had pointed out to her was a relic of those bygone trading connections Galway enjoyed with Spain and France. He let the Mercedes idle briefly before a time-touched little church on Lombard Street, explaining that it dated to the year 1320. Here, exceptionally, the aisles were peculiarly wider than the nave. She looked at the church with something like awe, impressed by its great age, the durability that implied. There was a mist floating near the top of the old building that gave the entire structure a light-blue, shifting tint, like a pledge of Forever.

"May we bring Troy here some Sunday?" Ethelyn inquired huskily, sounding like a child herself.

"Of course," Connor replied gently, glad they were having this time together. "I believe you are beginning to understand why the Irish persist in considering America the 'next parish to the west.' Any of us can learn to be at home here."

But when Ethelyn was dropped off in front of Cadigan's by him, she soon found herself deeply involved in an advertising campaign. Quickly she was reminded that the world of commerce changes very little, that it is primarily the same everywhere in the world: bristling, busy in hectic spurts, crammed with pointless meetings, wary of its competition, a little paranoid, and inclined to devour its young.

Her own reception at Cadigan's, Ethelyn found extraordinary and a trifle confusing. She was given a private office, something she'd only been able to claim briefly in Indianapolis; and while it was a cubicle that made her recall Irish-American Fred Allen's line about how the mice were hunchbacked, the courtesy was appreciated. On the surface, everybody was like the people she and Connor met elsewhere in Galway and Connemara—warmhearted, charming, and casually friendly. But beneath the surface, she suspected antagonism from the other employees and, on the part of her employer Mr. Cadigan, something tightlipped and vain. It was as if he dearly wanted her Mad-Ave-style know-how but unconsciously preferred verification that he was doing it the Right Way.

Cadigan's was more informal than agencies in the States, she'd found. There were few business suits in sight. Most of the employees wore tweed, sweaters were everywhere in evidence, and a few people proudly displayed jeans and jeansuits. But while they were quick to cater to her imagined expertise in advertising—even old Rollie Cadigan, the agency president and founder, deferred to her long enough to collect her opinions—they also appeared slow to accept anything she told them.

"Now isn't that a tiny bit flashy?" Rollie would inquire with brow cocked, a smirking man of sixty with outrageously dyed red hair. Or, from the pursed lips of Eddie Fagan, "Don't y'think that could be considered a spot boastful?"

The other women at the two meetings Ethelyn attended that morning—a pale natural blonde named Kathleen O'Skelly, to whom every male eye swiveled as if magnetized and who said "fuck" in all the wrong places—went to great lengths to agree with Cadigan, Fagan, the artist Petey Rafferty and Cadigan's son Terrence. There was an embarrassing smattering of "right on," "Let's run that up the flagpole," "That's my bag, chief," and "Whaddya want to be when you grow up" which sounded every bit as out of place as pygmies discussing the score of the Steelers' game or American admen commenting on the future coronation of Prince Charles.

It's going to take time, Ethelyn told herself with lip-biting patience, to be really accepted on my own merits. And it may take the rest of my life to teach them one simple, modern principle of advertising.

None of which made it a bit easier, since Ethelyn felt no better than she had at breakfast. Sometimes the sharp abdominal pains passed, but they were replaced by feelings of nausea, and worse—deep in her rather neurotic mind—feelings of some impending, dreadful loss. She worked hard on some improvements in copy for an upcoming newspaper ad; but always, troublingly, she sensed the impression that something horrid lay over the horizon, something from which she might never recover.

As the morning sluggishly gave way to the lunch hour, she found herself thinking more about Troy, about her dubious safety at Dad's house. Perhaps that was where her feelings were intuitively pointing, she mused; perhaps she should have remained home with Troy. Whether the little girl would follow her orders and Connor's and stay indoors away from that awful woods was hard to say. Normally, she knew, Troy was an obedient child who liked pleasing her parents. Especially her beloved Dads, Ethelyn noted mentally with a twinge of jealousy. She'd never been any trouble, not in eleven years.

But ever since they came to the house in Connemara, Ethelyn saw, Troy was subtly changing, right before her eyes. She was stretching those lanky legs toward independence. And while she figured that was inevitable, Ethelyn was in no rush for it to happen and had no intention of encouraging Troy's adventurousness. Especially since there were times, really, when it was so much *more* than a growth stage. It was almost like Troy was trying to show that she didn't really need them anymore, at all.

Which had to be silly, she told herself, munching on a ham sandwich she'd called out to have delivered. Plain silly. Every young girl had to have *somebody* to turn to, for companionship and counsel. Could any of this, to any degree, be Dad Quinlan's doing? Was it possible the old rascal was more an influence on Troy than she'd cared to admit? The old boy was certainly friendly, certainly conversational enough—he'd talk for hours on end, if she'd let him, and about the strangest things—but he also had a secretive side.

Last week, Ethelyn remembered, she'd taken two curious steps toward the attic when Dad Quinlan came out of his own room and explained, pleasantly enough, that the damned place was a No-No. What in the world could he *have* in there that was so confidential, so private? Could the attic's contents have something to do with Troy's newfound interest in liberty or even in this procession of quaint imaginary playmates Troy kept describing to her and Connor? For an instant Ethelyn wondered if the playmates substituted, in a childish way, for her and for Troy's precious Dads. But that sounded silly, too; after all, they loved Troy, didn't they?

Early in the afternoon, when her feelings were hurt by Mr. Cadigan's smiling refusal to update a display ad scheduled for the weekend paper, Ethelyn ransacked in the drawer of her desk in search of Kleenex. It wasn't just the corporate turndown that bothered her. She was feeling worse by the moment, even faint whenever she stayed too long on her feet. There was nothing but desk drawer beneath the Kleenex box, unlike her old desk at Stern & Stern in Indianapolis. There, she'd kept a collection of potential scalps: Eleven or twelve snapshots plus two dozen business cards of the clients who'd made it perfectly clear to Ethelyn how gorgeous she was in their eyes. How *supported,* how *wanted,* they'd made her feel—patting Randy, leering Sol, hugging Larry, dirty-talking Ted, who'd whispered in her ear that "broads with little tits are the best lays in the world." Not that she'd ever been unfaithful to Connor, but she really missed those cute guys now, in a universe where fidelity and propriety remained words in common use. Why couldn't Connor appreciate the sacrifices she'd made, in being true to him and in coming to this darling/lovely/backwards/guilt-creating land? The bastard, she'd given him *everything!*

The phone jangled on her desk, the black instrument jiggling like something alive. She snatched up the receiver as an image of Carl French, six-one with sleek black hair and a moustache and bedroom eyes, rose hopefully, impossibly, in her mind. "Ethelyn Quinlan," she said pertly, hoping it sounded beguiling.

"Hi, sweet girl. S'me. Just called t'see how my girl is feeling. Any better?"

He was always so damn' considerate, Ethelyn scowled, loving him and sensing wells of guilt at the same time. Kleenex crumpled in her palm, her nimble little fingers grabbed a red pencil and tapped it between an ashtray and a container of paperclips. "I'm—better, I think." She paused, envisioning Connor at the university, how dark and strong and good he was. Suddenly she simply adored the fact that he'd telephoned and broke into tears. "Oh Connie honey," she wailed. "I'm *so* glad you called!"

"What's wrong?" his baritone came in her ear, sharp, ready to defend her. "Want me t'come get you?"

She sighed, wiped one eye on the tissue in her palm. "A combination of things, I guess." Memory. "They didn't like the rewrite I did on a display ad."

"That's happened before. It isn't all, is it?" he pressed, concerned.

She raised her eyes and gazed out at the Galway streets, a story down. They were narrow and unfamiliar, foreign and suddenly alarming. It was like finding oneself in Morocco, in Casablanca, or something. Behind the tiny stores and low-lying buildings *things* seemed to crawl, muttering about her. "I feel . . . a little frightened."

"Of what?" he demanded.

She laughed. Just then she couldn't remember why she was afraid but knew that it couldn't be put into words, whatever it was. Could change of life begin in your middle thirties? "I'm being absurd, Connie. I really d-don't know. *Why* I'm f-frightened. It'll pass in a minute."

He paused in silence, confounded by women's words. "Well, then, I guess I'll see you at the house for dinner."

Ethelyn remembered. Connor had no other appointments and would be going home soon, ahead of her. It had been her idea. Old Mr. Cadigan had to visit his Da in Spiddal and had told her he didn't mind going a bit out of his way. Suddenly the idea

99

of the remaining hours of this day, of Connor twenty miles away, of riding home at night with an old man she scarcely knew, compounded her fright and she was entirely unable to speak. "'Bye love," he was saying in her ear; and then there was the buzzing sound.

She replaced the receiver, her gaze falling on the circle of data printed on the base of the phone: LOCAL, 5p. *What the hell am I doing in a place where a phone call costs "5p," and what does that mean anyway?* Ethelyn moaned to herself. God, it wasn't quite three p.m. here—and it was only quarter to ten in Indianapolis! She made a noise out loud, terribly disoriented and newly frightened, then spun slightly and sat down in her chair at the desk, hard.

Ear-splittingly—so screamingly loud it brought Ethelyn's shocked hands to her ears—the incredible howling sound rushed into the office and enveloped her. It was consuming; it seemed to come from everywhere at once, somehow feminine even when it subsided, and then lingered in the air like musk, drifting down over her skin, draping her like a veil.

Or a shroud.

Kathleen O'Skelly, more pale than ever, threw the office door open. It smashed against the wall, knocking over a hatrack. She stared in at Ethelyn with alarm. "What the hell was *that?*" she demanded, violet eyes wide.

Then Petey Rafferty was there, the artist with the shock of black hair. At once wiry and frail, he looked for all the world like some Irish poet who'd misunderstood the muse's message. "Jay-sus," he breathed, clearly trembling, "are ye all right, lass? What *was* that terrible shriek?"

Ethelyn began breathing again. Her eyes were enormous as she looked around at them. She felt naked, as if her drawer of masculine mementos had fallen to the floor. "D-don't ask me, folks," she replied with a nervous giggle. "It wasn't me."

"But it seemed t'come from your office," Petey persisted, stepping warily inside and glancing around. "If I believed in the old ways I'd think I'd heard a banshee's wail."

Her dazed brown eyes registered the time on a clock posted on the opposite wall: 2:53. "It's your city, people," she managed a fragment of her old working-woman-of-the-world manner. "I just work here."

Eventually the others backed out the door, shaking their heads in wonderment, as if the American possessed some secret compulsion or perhaps some secret disease, that made her lose control of herself.

In a way, their assumptions weren't entirely off the mark.

"Great Lord, Mr. Quinlan, what *was* that?"

Connor Quinlan looked up at his secretary, Lurene Shanahan. She'd been his secretary for approximately two hours now, since he officially committed himself to two lectures a week at University, and he noticed two things about her at that moment: First, she was a perfectly beautiful woman of twenty-nine or thirty. Second, her expression probably matched his own—stunned, half-deafened, scared, and needful of some rational explanation.

But as he shrugged, helplessly, Connor realized

101

that none was coming. "Honestly, Lurene, I have no idea." He rose, crossed over quickly to the window of his new office on the third floor, and stared out at the university grounds. Peculiarly, everything seemed normal. Students weren't even looking around, or up. Which meant that the noise was somehow localized, limited perhaps to this building.

Still seeking an explanation, he switched on the overhead bank of lights and then switched them off, paused a second to listen for reverberating echoes that would suggest failure in the various power services supplied the building. Nothing, no indication of trouble. Connor shook his head.

Somewhat recovered, he glanced at his watch. "Two fifty-three," he said aloud, as if memorizing and remembering the sound would somehow clarify it. "Sure was one hell of a racket."

He realized he was mumbling, almost talking to himself; then he realized *why* he was.

Insane as it sounded to him, Connor felt that the noise was *intended* for him. Like the bombs that fell in World War II, one of them, a crazy buzz-bomb of hellish noise, had had his name on it. And it was a *personal* message.

Perhaps a warning.

Lurene remained in the doorway, her heavy breasts still rising and falling with some rapidity. She tried a discreet laugh for size. "Quite a welcome you're getting, sir," she said. The voice was all lilting music. "Pair-haps the hospitals are experimentin' with a new mode of siren." The word came out "si-reen."

He located his natural voice and smiled. "Well, whatever it was, it hasn't been repeated. Thank

God." He found his gaze entangled with hers and the part of him that was eternally masculine observed how Lurene Shanahan was drawn to him. Or, at any rate, how she liked him. "I guess it's All Clear now."

She lowered her eyes. How could this handsome American simply dismiss such a terrible racket? Maybe it was true, what they said about folk in the U.S., and they were used to gangsters squabbling in the streets. She made a small, aimless gesture, muttered, "Well-l-l, good fortune," and slowly retreated, closing the door behind her.

When she was gone Connor trailed his eyes across the handsome paneling of the walls, saw against the expensive reproductions of Jack Yeats' paintings—W. B.'s brother—and finally looked appreciatively at his new desk. It, too, was handsome. Despite his earlier doubts of the wisdom of agreeing to lecture here, he had to admit that he richly approved of his new environment. Except, naturally, for the way something *screamed* at him! He returned to the window, parting the drapes.

University College, Galway, was a constituent college of the National University of Ireland and they were eager for instructors and lecturers with a knack for reaching out to inspire the students. It was one thing for the elders in County Connaught to urge their young to attend college, to improve themselves; it was something else entirely to get them to perceive that they could secure a better life for themselves. Possibly, in the process, that might also improve things for everyone in Ireland. It would be hard.

He tried not to think of the shriek and of the bizarre impression he'd had that it was a warning, as he peered out. This building was one of the newer structures, created to accommodate the rising yen for education. Around it stood other buildings built in the Tudor style some one hundred years ago. From where he stood Connor could discern the new cathedral, made of fine Galway limestone, built on the site of an ancient jail. It was constructed in the form of a towering cross surmounted by a marvelous dome, and accommodated three thousand parishioners. Connor thought, with affection, of the fabled Notre Dame in his old state of Indiana. But these fighting Irish of Galway were trying to win more than football games. Their victory would be an end to ignorance and to poverty.

He turned away, thinking of the dreadful murders in the woods near Dad's place. His hand on the phone, he considered phoning Ethelyn again to see if she also had heard the ghastly sound.

But that was ridiculous. She was safely ensconced in an office building on the other side of town. Home, even this temporary one, was miles away, meaning that little Troy hadn't been endangered by the noise. Clearly, Connor felt, his loved ones were out of range of the inexplicable shriek.

What a fool I am, he mused. *A lot that Dad implies with those long stares of his is probably right. There's some natural explanation for the sound and I'll read it in the papers.*

I ... discovered that for a considerable minority—whom I could select by certain unanalysable characteristics—the visible world would completely vanish, and that world summoned by the symbol would take its place.

—*Yeats*

seven

It isn't so much that the person who prefers the imaginary to the real has no use at all for reality. It's simply that the imagined has the decency to be shy, and stay out of the way, while that which is real continually and obdurately intrudes.

So little Troy Quinlan gave a friendly pat of distinct camaraderie to the huge, gnarled tree trunks as she ventured among them again in that special place she had come to think of as *her* woods.

Once she could not be seen by passersby in Kylemore, she paused to brush away a curving strand of yellow hair with easy feminine grace but without hard feminine vanity. The gesture, instead, was one that allowed her to look blissfully up and observe that she was already shielded from the somber light of Heaven by the distant green canopy folding itself like multiple arms across a dreaming breast. A glance at her feet reassured her that nothing Dark could penetrate the solid, packed surface of earth.

Here, the woods gave Troy the impression that they were guardlike, thickly muscled and coated with a layer of sweaty myrrh. It was as if they'd worked out in thoughtful preparation for her expected coming and planned to delve gladly within their vital parts to produce, for her alone, something unique. Something lying close to the secret heart of Irish mystery.

Here, too, Troy felt that she could truly be herself without fear of the erasure and scribbled rewrite of adult intervention. In her woods there was no need for artifice or an agile tongue, no need to please anyone.

Perhaps there was not even the need to please any*thing*, but Troy was less sure about that.

The point was that when she was at this unguessable distance from others but no longer cut off from her own urgent, private dreams, she sensed her importance. Because it was true that, long before she reached her objective in the woods, Troy's special nerve fibres and the invisible quarks tumbling nimbly in those parts of her mind accessible only to Troy Quinlan had reached out and made contact. Aloneness was merely a lie; she knew that she was surrounded by friends.

Fragrance from the unsullied grass, stirred now by her child's feet, rose like a heady cloud of spray cologne. At times, she giggled aloud, it was almost dizzying—even drugging. But the experience was nature's high and she bobbed her blonde head affably as miniature creatures darted past, some, knowing who, and *what* she was, pausing to regard her humanness with bead-like bright eyes.

And other times, less frequently, unfamiliar things of intermediate size and unaccountable life-force stared from chocolate shadows, gripped in waiting by her unique friendship and by their mutual need. They, too, had bead-like eyes; but behind them lay an extraordinary intelligence that was not precisely animal and surely not precisely human.

Utterly without fear, Troy moved ahead. She knew where the clearing was, knew somehow that she belonged there today. It was true that Dads and Mommy wanted her to stay in the house. But Mommy really had Dads on her mind and Dads was only saying what he was supposed to say. Now when he left the house, he was trying to learn where *he* belonged. Troy had no guilt because she *knew* where she belonged, and what she was supposed to do. The knowledge was small, at this point; it was only partly formed, yet perfect, and Troy knew that the knowledge would grow.

Suddenly the bright orange sun of twilight burst through with coloring-book flares of dripping light, the sky clearly revealed as a victim of blood poisoning. She had emerged in a foot-fringing tangle of wild flowers. The kaleidoscope of hues warmed Troy's eyes, tickled her bare feet. She scanned the clearing proprietorially, appearing a golden haired exclamation mark etched against the quietude. Beneath her, the flowers were grown at the direction of some idiot geometrician; or possibly it was that the geometry was of a kind man could not perceive.

Clusters of the vivid flowers dotted, circled, and swept across the clearing to the pool Troy loved— placid, cool and still, a sheet of gentle azure and turquoise in which, Troy knew with confidence, *things* dwelled that only a child could see . . . and live.

Yet today the pool was being gently agitated by

the crying woman who was her new friend and who knelt beside it in work. "Hi, Ducie," Troy called lightly.

For an instant there was no answer. It was as if some incredible barrier of time and place—a curvature of inverse realities, realities that sometimes might be unlocked if one but discovered their secret aperture—existed between Troy and Ducie. The opening, Troy understood, could not be discovered by stealth or by science. One simply waited for the door to open.

And at last the beautiful redhaired woman lifted her head, asking Troy in, and brushed back a lock of her scarlet hair. "Hello, Troy. I am glad ye came."

If that was true, why was there that familiar catch in her voice, the audible whisper of a sob? "That's okay," Troy replied, moving forward to the woman. "I wasn't doin' anything."

She crossed the clearing to sit, cross-legged and watchful, some twelve feet from Ducie. She saw that the woman, tears staining her cheek, was washing something in the pool. Something of cloth, her motions careful, industrious, thorough. "I'm happy we're friends, Ducie."

"And so am I, me darlin', though every friendship has its price." She glanced up from her work, her cheeks glistening even as she smiled tremulously. While her upper lip protruded slightly—was prominent enough to suggest an almost harelike quality of mercurial vividness—it did not prevent her from being lovely. "Why do ye not perch close to your friend, child?"

Troy hesitated. Ducie's breath was horrid. But it was rude to refuse and Dads would not approve.

"Okay," she said finally. She jumped up and edged round to the side of the tiny, pretty woman, finally sinking into a comfortable position on the ground. "You got such nice red hair."

"Thank you. You also have pretty hair."

"Naw, mine's washed out." She had a sudden thought. "Yours is *really* red, too, not orange or— or *kind* of red like most ladies'."

Ducie stopped a moment to look at Troy. "D'ye realize your hair is blonde but your father and your mother have dark hair? Does that seem unusual, Troy?"

Troy couldn't answer for a moment. Poor Ducie went on sobbing as if the emotions tugging at her heart were of such penetrating misery or longing that nothing would ever halt their pathetic expression. She considered Ducie's query. "I s'pose it's kind of odd, Ducie."

"No, my sweet. It is only *meant* t'be." Now the small woman's breath touched Troy's cheek, overpoweringly. The sun had gone behind a cloud and her face was partly in shadow, giving her thin features a skull-like appearance. "You, Troy, are a child of the woods. A child of the true nature, my dear. You belong here—not there."

Troy scarcely heard her words. She was staring at Ducie, amazed by what she saw. In the tiny beauty's upturned nose, there was a *single* nostril. Until now, Troy had believed Ducie to be another human being, not the kind of creature Sir Gat had been, or Kuan, the boy cursed with being a dog. For a moment she held her breath as she looked at Ducie, blinking.

"No matter that you have not heard me—yet." The redhaired woman smiled gently. "Ye shall hear me—ye shall hear *all of us*—in time."

Then she brought the garment she was washing slowly into view. It was drenched with water from the pool, and smelled the way Ducie smelled.

"That's my mother's dress you're washin'!" Troy cried, pointing at the wet and shiny object dangling limply from Ducie's small hands. *"What are y'doing with my mother's clothes?"*

For an instant Ducie did not answer. When she sighed, it was shuddering and caused her slender form to tremble. "It is something I must do, child."

"Why?" Troy asked desperately.

"Because," Ducie shrugged, "it is what I am here for." She lifted the dress a few inches from the water. Its wet gloss lent it a sort of sealskin life. Ducie pointed at a dark stain, her expression sad. "That is your mother's own blood, Troy." Again, Ducie sighed and lowered the dress into the pool, scrubbing hard at the spot with a bar of yellow-green soap. "Ay, child. I *must*."

"Why, Ducie?" She shifted on the ground in intense curiosity. "Why d'ya wash other folks' clothes?" She ignored a miniature black beetle scoot-slithering down her bare arm. *"Why?"*

Now Ducie turned her dazzling beauty full on Troy Quinlan. Her eyes were large, emerald-green, deeply-set in a face with an alabaster complexion. Someone older than Troy might have found hers a classical beauty, of the kind that has always existed. The tears left twin furrows on her cheeks as though Ducie had been crying all her life. The smile on her full lips was infinitely sad; seeing it whole, Troy felt tears well up in sympathy in her own odd eyes.

Ducie made an effort to stop shaking with

sorrow. "I do it, child, because it is believed by enough of your people that I *do*. Because, y'see, all the tides of belief are beginnin' to shift now. Many of them are good, but they're dyin' all the same. But now and then, Troy, beliefs may be restored by those who return—those who have a child with the gift of belief." One tear dropped from her cheek and landed, hot and sweet, on Troy's small hand. "And lass, what is *believed*—truly believed, by enough— is still the strongest thing in all the universe. Nothing whatever can stop it."

Troy glanced at her wristwatch.

It was 2:53 P.M.

Connor had come home again to find no one around and scratched the crown of his black head, a trifle put out by the absence of companionship. People were always underfoot in droves when a man wanted peace and quiet, but they were borne away to God knew where if he wanted a little friendly chatter. Feeling a bit sorry for himself, he passed into the living room, where the lights were out and, for a moment, everything seemed musty, draped with cobwebs, vaguely threatening. He knew that was silly, because Dad's friend Annie still came round to sweep and tidy up; but the feeling remained until he'd turned on all the lights.

He finally remembered that Ethelyn would be home later, delivered here by her new employer, and settled into his chair. Dad was probably upstairs, bumbling around either in his own room or that damned secret attic of his. What had been a good mood faded the rest of the way out of his mind and heart, quickly supplanted by a series of shadowed images flickering in his memory like scenes from an old silent film.

As nearly as he could judge, the whole attic was taken over by Patrick Quinlan's precious, lifelong secret. What in the name of all that was holy could he keep up there? The old man even had two heavy locks on the single oak door and constantly kept the keys on his person. Once, before Connor left for America, he'd come out with it and asked Dad about the attic.

"Allow a lonely old codger his foibles, lad," Dad had replied. "Maybe it is that I'm buildin' a time machine, ay? Or discoverin' a cure for all manner of disease." He'd winked in a comical conspiratorial manner. "Pair-haps it's a space ship to travel to another galaxy. Or maybe I ain't the man y'think I am an' I have a harem of aging colleens kept prisoner till the white slaver comes!"

Grumbling to himself, Connor arose to pour himself two fingers of stiff Irish whisky and, returning, sank down on the couch, stretching out with a smile. Whatever the old boy was doing up there, he felt sure, it wouldn't be anything evil, like drugs. It might be—

He sat up again, assaulted by memory. Until now he'd completely forgotten the one moment when, as a lad of no more than six or seven, he'd had a sort of brief glimpse into the attic. Yes; he remembered now. He'd been waiting for his father, standing on the little landing outside the attic, as Dad came out.

And in his memory Connor now drew out an old impression of . . . *age*. Yes, of great, dry, musty oldness—as if he had stood at the entrance of the world's oldest museum, and sought admission. A museum wherein no amount of care or room deodorizer could conceivably chase away the nose-twisting stink of age. Now he recalled that night, when he'd lain on his bed in the dark, thinking of it with his little boy's mentality, envisioning the lost secrets of Alexandria, precious secrets of such antiquity that man must wait until he is ready again for them.

So what would that attic room be like now, he wondered with mild disgust, after another quarter of a century of mustiness piled on the dust of the old room! Why, it would even be dangerous, piled perhaps with stacks of tattered and yellowed newspapers, even now on the verge of. . . .

"A bit early for heavy drinkin', isn't it?"

Patrick Aloyious Quinlan had come into the room in total silence, wearing his soft leather bedroom slippers, and Connor gave an involuntary jump. "Dad!"

"Didn't mean to startle you, son," he replied with a sheepish grin.

Sitting up, Connor studied the man whom he so closely resembled and a sudden spontaneous upsurge of affection suffused him. "Guess I was noddin', Dad. It wasn't your fault." He hesitated. "Besides, I'm worried about Ethelyn."

"Yes, she was feelin' a mite poorly in the ayem." Dad lowered himself carefully into his own favorite chair, considering whether to broach the subject of his granddaughter's strangely familiar playmates. "Is she due home soon?"

"Any time, I guess. Where's Troy?"

"I fear she's out in the woods, Connor. Playin'." His expression was guilty.

"Dad! We told Troy to stay inside today because of those two kids who were killed." He turned the whisky glass in his hands, worried and displeased. "It's not like Troy to disobey us this way. Why did you let her go out?"

"Well, lad, I didn't exactly allow her." He shrugged his smoking-jacketed broad shoulders. "I went up t'grab a few winks. When I came back down, she was gone. Listen now, I must talk with ye about that child. Some odd things have been happenin' around here."

But Connor wasn't listening. He'd finished his drink in a single swallow and slapped the glass down on a nearby end table. And he'd found a scrap of grade school theme paper there, printed legibly if childishly: "Gone out to play. I'm fine so don't worry. Love, Troy Q."

"It's after five," he said aloud, glancing at his father. "I'd better go out to the woods and...."

The awful howl came again, that anguished cry. It was so mournful and piercing it froze both men in place. There was a hint of a tormented, broken bird in the cry, something peculiarly human—female—too. It was brief this time, yet it permeated the old stone house and lingered with the staying power of a creature agonized or demented: baleful, intent, somehow ... warning.

Pat Quinlan's stricken face peered into his son's. *"Bansidhe,"* he whispered.

"You know what it is?" Connor demanded, gaping at his father.

"Oh God, not so soon, so *soon*," Dad prayed, turning away with his shoulders slumped, almost frail as he groped for a chair. "Not yet!"

"Dad! *What is it?*"

Dad turned his head back. Amazingly, his expression had grown quickly icy. He was already under control. He looked Connor in the eye. "I have no idea at all what it is."

"But you *said* something," Connor protested.

"A swear word, perhaps, in Gaelic," Dad snapped. "Nothing more."

Troy! Connor whirled, ran through the house with his heart thumping. He knocked over a table, then a chair, rushing to the back door, planning to find his daughter in the woods, praying she'd be all right.

It was dusk already. Shadows crept like sad ghosts across the gray ground between the stone house and the edge of the woods, just beyond his own study. Again Connor ran, not thinking now, almost panicstricken , . .

. . . As Troy came from the woods, idly twirling that ring of hers on its cord, *smiling* at him.

Her appearance seemed magical in the queer way that dusk plays sly tricks. She seemed, just for an instant, something. . . portentous; knowing. . . with the woods foreshortened by her abrupt emergence. Her face was pale and wise in the dying sunlight, her eyes fixed on him.

"Troy!" Connor shouted.

Then she was running toward him—his little girl, his princess pumpkin—her jumper stained from play, the hem damp, jumping toward him with the old confidence in her father, tumbling happily into his outstretched father's arms. "Dads! Dads!"

"Kitten! Are you all right?"

Her eyes were guileless. "Sure, Dads. Why?"

"That—that terrible crying sound, like a scream. What *was* it?"

Clinging to his neck, her ankles round his

thighs, she looked at him solemnly and truthfully. "It was my friend, Dads. The redhaired lady."

"Lucy?" he asked, astonished.

"*Ducie,* Dads, Ducie." She dropped to the ground and began skipping toward the back of the house. Then she paused, turning back to him, pretty and pure in the dying sunlight. "But you don't have to worry, Dads," she said. "It's not for you."

> . . . *Open-eyed and laughing to the tomb.*
> —*Yeats*

eight

It was an hour later that old Rollie Cadigan, Ethelyn's employer, showed up at the front door of the house in Kylemore. By his side was his other feminine employee, Kathleen O'Skelly, and between them, hanging with most of her slight weight upon their necks, was Ethelyn herself.

"Sorry, gang," she managed, looking weakly at Connor, Troy, and Dad Quinlan. "I guess I'm a party pooper after all."

"Honey, what's wrong?" Connor took her in his arms and saw the look of relief on Mr. Cadigan's face. "What happened?"

"She began getting sick right around three or so, Mr. Quinlan," explained the sleek Ms. O'Skelly, her tone brisk and businesslike. "Just about the time that siren, or whatever, went off."

Connor blinked in surprise. Then she had heard the scream, too.

"Then I went in to fetch her at closing time," continued the impossibly-redheaded Cadigan, obviously still breathless and concerned, "to take her home. She was unconscious, lyin' across her desk. Somehow she stayed the whole day."

"Get me—to bed," Ethelyn gasped in Connor's ear. "Just want—some rest, some sleep."

Without another word he scooped her up in his strong arms and headed for the stairway. When he had made her comfortable in bed, carefully tucking the covers up to her chin, he stood helplessly beside the bed trying to decide what to do. The nursing standards in Ireland were very high, he knew, but he didn't know a doctor in Connemara. Finally he made her wake up just enough to slip a thermometer between her lips, and sat on the edge of the bed, his expression agonized.

After a minute, he withdrew the thermometer and held it to the light from their bedlamp. Nearly 102°, he saw with further anxiety. Determined now to get help, he moved quickly, quietly toward the door.

"Connor?" she whispered. He whirled to her. "Connor, I really wanted you to be happy here. To *find* yourself here."

He blew her a kiss. "Everything's going to be fine. I'll be back after a while and check up on you."

He ran downstairs and met Dad at the foot, starting to climb the steps. "A doctor," he said, half out of breath. "Ethelyn needs a doctor."

Pat Quinlan's eyes seemed out of focus as they met his son's. For a moment it appeared that he had something to say, something he found it hard to utter. Then he held up the address book in his hand, anticipating Connor's need for it, and spoke tersely: "In the M's," he said. Then he touched Connor's arm with fingers that shook a little, and headed on up the stairs, slowly.

Connor sat down at the telephone, his fingers fumbling with the address book until he located

Dr. J. Arthur Malone's number. He sensed someone standing beside him and glanced irritably around.

It was Troy, her face very serious. "Is Mommy going to die?"

He made himself smile reassuringly. "Of course not, punkin." He patted her pale cheek and smiled. "She's just running a little fever."

Troy seemed about ready to turn away, balancing on one foot. Her lower lip trembled. "I didn't think it'd be so *soon*," she said plaintively. "And I didn't really think it would be Mommy."

"Later, princess," he said, barely hearing her as he began to dial. "Later."

After making the phone call Connor went back into the front room where old Mr. Cadigan and the fashion-model type, Ms. O'Skelly, were politely waiting.

Both Dad and Troy were not in evidence.

Pat sat on the edge of his bed, the Bible in his hands, his shoulders bent to his reading. He looked very old, just then, but there was no one around to see and he didn't try to stop his hands from shaking.

Finally he stopped reading, tucked the Bible in his smoking jacket pocket, and left his room. He crossed the hall to the stairs leading up, paused only for an instant, and then began climbing the stairs. He moved slowly and, as he went, looked in his pocket for the right key. Then he was on the landing outside the attic, looking briefly down to make sure he was still alone. He found it difficult to unlock the two locks because his hand continued to tremble, but he got the job done.

It was very hot in the attic, and very dry. Pat locked the door after him. He stepped past the space heater going full-blast—there was another, similarly activated, at the other, distant end of the attic—and began to perspire. The temperature was kept in the middle eighties here, year round. It always was, always had been. Pat unbuttoned the smoking jacket, tugged the much-thumbed Bible from his pocket, and sat down at the one chair in the entire attic.

He looked wearily out at the compartments and sighed. It was there, in the center of the huge room, that it was hottest. Shoulders bowed, he let his arms dangle between his legs, the Bible nearly touching the floor. It was more a comfort, now, than something he planned to read in this place. In a way, he supposed, it would be sacrilege to read the Bible here, in his attic, unless it was done the way Van Helsing did it in front of the fictitious character Dracula, with a cross raised to ward off evil.

For many years he had come here to discuss things, even though he never received an audible reply. Under the circumstances, that was natural for him. At last he lifted his head and there were tears in his eyes. "Can it really be right to prey so heavily on the young ones," he asked, aloud, "to deprive them of their rightful future?"

He looked at the places that were filled for an answer, not the ones that were waiting. He hadn't really expected an answer, not in so many words, and he didn't get one.

"Yes, yes," he answered himself quickly, a trifle irascibly. "I know it's true that I did not personally lift a finger against the young woman. It isn't my fault, not directly." The fingers of his right hand pressed the Bible more firmly, seeking moral strength from it. "But soon, I shall be asked again, won't I? Soon, I'll have t'do it again. Isn't that right?"

While no words were formed by the customary means, answers nonetheless began seeping back to him from the compartments, carried on the steaming air that hung swamplike above them. Pat Quinlan listened intently, possibly to whispers from other beings and possibly, instead, to the creaking cogs of his own conscience.

Finally, his head still raised high, he closed his eyes and nodded. "Of course, there is only the one way for us all. I accept that; I always have. And it is *our* way."

He rose, perhaps more determined now but surely no less tired of it all, and then hesitated for a last dry scrap of conversation. "My little granddaughter," he said carefully, testing the words. He stared at the center of the attic floor, to where it all began. "Troy. I fear it is possible that her own sweet beliefs must soon get in our way. She is . . . strong. A very strong child indeed."

Now there was certainly no answer. The breath-stealing air seemed held in haughty waiting; it refused to answer things that were so obvious. When Pat saw that this was so, he went trudgingly to the door and unlocked it. There, he paused, his hand shaking on the knob before he turned slightly.

"Of course," he said again, and left.

Dr. Malone hadn't come yet but Connor promised, the last time he visited her, that he was on his way. She hoped she could hold out. Alone in the room again, Ethelyn moaned and kicked off her covers. Lord, it was suddenly so *hot* there and she found that her bra and panties were adhering to her skin. "I feel so bad, so *damn* bad," she said aloud with tears in her eyes.

After awhile she turned over on her back once more but kept her eyes closed. It was getting darker by the minute, now that night was here, and she hoped—no, *prayed*—for sleep. Much of the immediate pain in her abdomen was gone but it had only spread, with the fever raging inside of her, throughout her small body. While it wasn't intense in any one place, there was residue of pain everywhere.

She wasn't alone.

The thought came to her, crystal-clear, not as a guess, an impression or suspicion, or even as a threat.

It was simply a fact that she wasn't alone anymore. With her eyes still shut, she called out softly, "Connor? Connor, that you?"

Words were not given in reply. Instead, from somewhere deep in the gathering shadows beyond the foot of the bed near the window from which they could see the woods, came a gentle, wistful singing. Someone was singing a song!

It was so excruciatingly distant, in a way, that it might only have been the aimless rustle of the wind in a small clump of weeds. Ethelyn frowned, faintly, but kept her eyes shut as she listened, fascinated. It was really quite pretty, she thought. It was also like nothing else she'd heard in the past, foreign—no, *alien* in a fashion, and she relaxed, because the music was, as well, sweetly, unstoppably hypnotic. As she heard the simple, mellifluous refrain repeated over and over, she found that she was beginning to hum along with the tune. She liked it, really; liked it a lot. It spoke to her of vanished yesterdays and the absence of frightening tomorrows. It soothed her, told her all was fine because all was eternal. It lifted her, gently, out of herself; it coaxed Ethelyn with a plaintive air that might have been sung somewhere in the shifting, steaming sands of Saturn or that might well have been the first lullabye a prehistoric mother sang to the babe in her arms. A *dead* babe.

When she opened her eyes she saw the shadows floating near her bed, beginning to take on coherence, personality, while the melody continued; and Ethelyn joined with it again, humming sweetly, softly, the line she'd heard now so often and began to focus upon even as the shaping shadows revealed, at her side, a tiny feminine form with long, red hair. Scarlet hair.

Because the little woman smiled at her, a radiant yet torturously sad smile that had seen the miscarriages of saints and the sickness of God, and went on singing her droning rondeau, her dirge fantasia, and Ethelyn returned the smile without speaking a word and continued humming the air. Yet, in the American's puzzled brown eyes, the question surely must have been mutely asked: "Who *are* you?"

There were two answers, one the progress of the mesmeric, binding lament, the other a motion lovely Ducie made to approach Ethelyn—to lean forward, above the ill human woman, and look down at Ethelyn with tears flooding her cheeks.

For a microsecond Ethelyn reeled away, pushing the back of her skull into her pillow as she smelled the overpowering, reeking, filthy breath on her face....

And then, with a relieved smile, resumed humming Ducie's song. Her eyes, locked with the other female's, trusted; believed at last. *And again Ducie leaned forward, her perfect tiny hands touching Ethelyn's cheeks, the melody stopping only when her luscious red lips pressed passionately upon Ethelyn's. She stayed there some time, red hair and brown hair mingling, as the hopelessness in Ducie was caught in Ethelyn's breast, mirrored there with something like female gratification, so that when Ducie parted from her and began to sob, Ethelyn sobbed with her in absolute empathy; and when Ducie began to cry, Ethelyn joined the tiny creature in a dirge-duet of absolute agony and absolute loss. Soon, their wailing became two screams as they reached for a crescendo of misery; and then suddenly, only one wailing shriek remained ... and again, Ethelyn was gently lifted from her pain.*

When it stopped, Ethelyn Quinlan's room was emptied of all living souls.

'The Banshee,' says McNally, 'is really a disembodied soul, that of one who in life was strongly attached to the family' ... To a doomed member of the family of the O'Reardons, the Banshee generally appears in the form of a beautiful woman, 'and sings a song so sweetly solemn as to reconcile him to his approaching fate.' But if, during his lifetime,

the Banshee was an enemy of the family, the cry is the scream of a fiend...
—*Thistleton Dyer*

nine

They buried Ethelyn Quinlan many twisting miles from her Indianapolis home in an old cemetery of softly rolling hills overlooking a peaceful lake, near Headford, east of Galway. Her stone would become one of unnamed thousands dotting the landscape, freckles on an immense emerald death's head.

Beneath the canvass canopy prepared for the family, as a priest with cheeks like a chipmunk's intoned his solemn perpetual message, the three principal mourners presented—to any objectively critical onlookers, of which there was precisely one—a collective image of individual loss, isolated sorrow. Instead of the groping way some families linked arms and hands, sharing their tragic grief, the remaining Quinlans of Connemara appeared to be burdened by personal feelings which they dare not express. Until Ethelyn's remains were at last deposited in the ground forever, they did not touch.

Behind them, a few friends of Patrick Quinlan, all of them bent, craggy-faced, correctly reverent—and the office force from Cadigan's, none of whom had known Ethelyn well at all, waited with mixed emotions for everything to be over. Lurene Shanahan, Connor's new University secretary, was closer: white-faced, discreetly apart from the others, watchful of her new boss. Unnoticed by all of them, on a rise near a hulking marble tombstone, coroner Bill Fogarty stood like an icon with his perceptive eyes taking everything in. Soon, Bill felt, it would become necessary to speak with these people. It only remained for him to find the decent way, one that didn't sound insultingly absurd even to his own ears.

Old Pat Quinlan was a study in silent guilt. He knew it was true that he had nothing to do with the death of his daughter-in-law. But he also knew that, in time, he might very well have been instrumental. Sometimes things happen that bring old deeds, old remonstrances, to the mind's surface simply because of their basic similarity. Dressed in his only suit, his shoulders hunched, he couldn't manage to ignore the way that others had gone to their deaths while still in the full flush of youth. Finally, haunted more by the mysteries of his private attic than the charming spirit of the woman they were burying, he accepted the heavy burden of knowledge that he wasn't entirely free of responsibility for the similar destinies of other people. Badly, just then, he wanted to talk to Connor about it. But it wasn't yet the time and he knew it.

His granddaughter Troy was outwardly no more than unreachable. At the mortician's she had refused to approach the open coffin, even under her Dads' gentlest pleading. Looking beautiful and feminine in her best American dress, her pale blonde hair streaming between her narrow shoulders, Troy had yet to formulate a single emotion or thought. Hypnosis would merely have detected a numbing realization that her life had just changed forever and that, in some furtive way Troy could not quite decipher, she might herself be partly the cause of the change.

For Connor's part, the primary theme of his emotions was not unlike that of any man who had lost his wife. He hurt, deep inside; he suffered. But fraying feelings of all kinds were radiating out from the nucleus of personal, painful loss and foremost among these was a realization that he was probably bound, for good, to the place of his birth, even to the house where he'd been born. Part of it was that Ethelyn would remain in County Connaught always and he was a man who believed in visiting the graves of his loved ones. But a more important element of his feeling of permanence in Ireland was the personal knowledge of Connor Quinlan that told him he wasn't a man who could uproot again. Not without his wife, his partner and other half, to motivate him. And from this strand of emotion Connor was already, without knowing it, reaching out to his father, to the house and interests of his father and his fatherland; he was beginning to settle in.

Later, when he was no longer bereft, he would seek the manly steel to fight back with his old determination, to be sure it would be on his own terms. He would try, he hoped, to make life content again.

The following day, scheduled to present his first lecture at University College in Galway, Connor gruffly brushed aside the telephoned insistence of

Professor Donnelly that "you abide with your grief awhile longer." "If I abide with it much longer," he told Donnelly, "I'll turn into a vegetable forever." Then he drove into the city. Work, Connor had always believed, was the best and certainly the most decent answer to unhappiness—or for that matter, to most things. When he was informing Lurene Shanahan of what he wanted typed for his first class, Connor was already making plans for the evening. Until he could learn how to sleep alone again, he would spend hours in the study, toiling over the Bookquins Newsletter and catching up on correspondence, until he finally collasped on the sofa.

At home that afternoon in Kylemore, Pat Quinlan had finished reading some political tracts from the Fine Gael party and came upon Troy sitting on the stoop beyond the back door of his house, tears coursing down her cheeks. So, he thought wisely to himself, the belated bawl. She didn't hear him approach and he stood a moment with his hands on his hips, watching, his heart going out to the child. Hers was silent crying, the worst kind, an awful thing indeed to see in a little girl, her shoulders shaking spasmodically and her small fists screwed into her eye sockets.

He stepped forward quietly into the sunshine and rested a large, gentle hand on her thin shoulder. "Troy, darlin', *Conas ta tu?*"

He'd pronounced it "Koo-nas thaw shiv" and she didn't know what he meant. "Huh?" she asked, blinking up at him.

"I asked," he said with a half-smile, "'how are you?'"

"Not so awful good, Gran-da," she replied with a

sigh and rested her chin on her balled fists, elbows on bare knees. Wearing the shorts was a sort of afterthought tribute to Mommy. "It's all such a dreadful mistake."

"Now, me girl, don't speak of the Lord's will that way," he chided her gently, squeezing in beside her on the stoop. "It's after hard to understand His ways, sometimes; but I'm sure He had a sound enough reason for calling your mother t'Heaven."

Her head, arms, and torso swung sharply from side to side in a negative motion. "You don't get it, Gran-da. You really don't." Her gaze was somewhere in the distance, deep in the woods. Perhaps, accusingly, centered on a lovely pool in a flowered-bedecked clearing.

"*An dtuigeann tu?*" he repeated her charge with a forgiving grin. "I thought I *did* understand ye, darlin'. Pardon me for intrudin'!"

Troy finally looked up at him again, almost with resentment in her colorless eyes. "The lady didn't *tell* me it was to be *Mommy*. Sure, I saw what she was washin', but I thought that was just a way t'get into the house. Like a password." She hesitated, dropping her head to stare disconsolately at several ants making designs between her feet. "I thought it was s'posed to be you."

He leaned slowly back against the cement stoop to consider what he'd heard, largely bemused but aware of a disturbing feeling that an understanding of Troy's meaning might come close to demolishing him.

"That lady whom you mentioned," Gran-da bravely honed in. He also kept his stare on the busy ants as they labored, so detached from human concerns they might have been on Neptune. "What lady might that be?"

She didn't seem to hear him. Tears rushed to her eyes anew, squinting them. "And today, it's not just Mommy who isn't here. I'm all alone." The idea frightened her, he saw, more than even he was. "I've looked absolutely *ev'rywhere* in the woods for Ducie, but she's g-gone." Troy paused. "And the woods is so awful quiet, so *still,* with no one around."

He stayed perfectly motionless, looking more at his interior thoughts than at any ordinary thing in his backyard. There were icy fingertips touching his heart. In some terrible way they recalled his reaction when, only hours before Ethelyn died, he'd heard a dreadful howl . . . "Tell me, child. This Miss Ducie. Is she, by any chance . . . redheaded?"

The aroused glint in Troy's colorless eyes held a little of her old appreciation for this aging man's extraordinary knowledge—wisdom she'd thought was entirely her own property and province. Hers, that is, and the creatures who lived in the woods. "Uh-huh. And she has just one nose-hole." Her head swiveled; her gaze demanded to Know. "Is Ducie what you thought she was, Gran-da? How do *you* know her? You're too old t'be acquainted with my friends."

He pressed his wrinkled fingertips as he mused, thinking that, in a manner he could not understand, they might be coming for him at last. The coldness at his heart was worse; it was also, somehow, closer. "It's all such a dreadful mistake," young Troy had said about her mother's passing. Worse, "*I thought it was s'posed to be you.*" Maybe it *was,* originally, meant to be him—

before his son and daughter-in-law brought Troy. Certainly it would have been more just for them to have chosen him; he didn't doubt that for a moment.

"Troy, me girl," he began again, a shiver of fear whispering along his spine, "your friend Ducie. Honey, Ducie was a banshee. In the Gaelic, a *bansidhe*. D'you realize that?"

"Oh, yes," she said quickly. "Ducie told me."

A pain throbbed through his temple. "But she didn't say what that *meant*, did she?" He felt it was urgent to know that but he wanted her, badly, to reply No. "Did she, Troy?"

Troy reflected. "She only said that she had t'do what she did because some people still believed she would." Her face screwed up in deeper concentration. "And she said that beliefs are changing but they can have new life from those who return—" Troy smiled happily at Pat, getting it all—"and have a child like me!"

"'Those who return.'" The old man mulled it round. "I guess that means your Daddy, lass."

"But what does 'banshee' mean, Gran-da? Is it like bein' a Knight of Columbus or a Shriner? Or is it more like Kuan being a boy who looks like a dog?"

He didn't answer for a moment because he was staring across his property into the woods. Lord, he'd looked there a thousand times before, without fear. In his earlier years he had walked them, on pleasant mornings, enjoying the scenery. Who and what was it who had stared out at him? Suddenly it was freezing cold on the stoop, so much so he wondered if he could ever be content out there again. "A banshee, Troy, is one who comes t'warn the Irish family that death is comin'. *Soon.* And there are those people, child, who claim that she is literally the one who steals away the precious breath of life with her lovely song and her foul breath and her sweet, sweet kiss."

Troy said, "Oh," noncommittally, and moved closer to him. For a second or two she was quiet. The wind was picking up when she spoke again. "I didn't want Mommy to die and I didn't want Ducie to move away either. Now there's just you, Dads and me left, Gran-da."

Feeling stiff, he gave her a hug and rose, stretching. "Darlin', don't ye worry about losin' your companions. Hear me?" He looked down at her, deeply pained by what he had to tell her, even though he knew it would please the girl. The late afternoon sun in his face merely accentuated the lines. "I'm sure, Troy, you'll be gettin' . . . *other* friends. Soon. Real, *real* soon." He lifted his tired face to peer helplessly at the heavens. "Ah, dear God, I'm dreadful sure of that!"

To the Gay Laugh of my Mother at the Gate of the Grave!

—*Sean O'Casey*

part two

> *Spirits, whom Yeats called "Gate-keepers," have "but one purpose, to bring their chosen man to the greatest obstacle he can confront without despair."*
> —William Butler Yeats

ten

The days of adjustment to Ethelyn's untimely, sudden death crept by slowly for the Quinlan family, each experiencing the change in his or her own way. To handle the chores, aged Annie, who'd cooked and cleaned for old Pat before his family came to Connemara, resumed her duties. While the crone registered her polite social grief for Ethelyn's passing, Connor thought he detected a gleam of victory in the old woman's eyes. It didn't make him angry and he supposed that was natural. Extra funds weren't all that easy to come by in County Connaught; what Dad paid Annie could well be the margin between her life and death.

Young Troy began school in Connemara and, so far as her father could tell, seemed to be faring well enough, perhaps better than she had in Indianapolis. Occasionally the girl asked for assistance with homework; but mostly she continued going her own way, whenever she could, just as she'd begun doing before her mother's sudden demise. On days when he was toiling on book submissions or his adored Newsletter, Connor would sometimes look up to see Troy quietly wending her way past the garage-study, headed for her beloved woods. Since nothing more had been said publicly about the killing of the two youngsters on the far side of the woods, he let the child go without comment. The poor kid deserved solace from life after losing her mother. For him, the Newsletter; for Troy, the woods.

It did not occur to Connor that, for father as well as daughter, their choice of solace might have been a better one . . .

On Easter, they discussed driving in Connor's leased Mercedes to the two-day Irish Grand National at Fairyhouse, over in County Meath. But they knew, when Dad brought it up, that they would not go. It seemed somehow far away from home; perhaps, too, it was still too soon for something pleasurable after Ethelyn's funeral. It didn't do any good for Dad to point out that Ethelyn would have wanted them to go and stop grieving. Connor was adamant; and besides, Dad thought wryly, he wasn't all that sure the self-involved Ethelyn *would* have wished them to stop grieving.

Later, they passed on attending Cork's International and Folk Dance Choral Festival, even the Maytime Festival at Dundalk which Troy's own Gran-da swore she would love. Connor came close to giving in; but Troy's own lack of enthusiasm curtailed their plans. It sounded silly to Connor but the girl was reluctant to leave her "playmates" in the woods. Now and then he felt that her imagination was getting out of hand—in the evening, one day, he considered taking her all the way to Dublin for a psychiatric evaluation—but it was a harmless pastime, clearly enough, and Connor didn't want to deprive her.

Each Quinlan fell into an unrelated routine, the days swept by, and suddenly it was sunny June. Pat Quinlan began talking of taking his family to climb Croagh Patrick's stony slopes, late in July. It was an annual event that honored St. Patrick himself and Dad assured them they'd "never feel your Irish blood run hotter or redder in your lives." It appealed to Connor—the out-of-doors; the exercise; the excited yet reverent crowds—and he told Dad he'd think seriously about going.

But by now he was feeling drawn more each day to Lurene Shanahan, the lovely blonde woman who acted as his secretary at University. While he continued working on Bookquins and seeking worthwhile authors during the rest of the week, Connor found himself avidly looking forward to Tuesdays and to Fridays. It was on those days that he lectured, and spent considerable time with Lurene in his office at the college.

Not that he'd so much as spoken an overt word, touched or kissed her. He was working hard on making himself believe that it was too soon, after Ethelyn, for such things. Even too soon to sit down and think over the possibilities which he sensed were present in a relationship with Lurene.

But he knew that he enjoyed her company enormously, never tired of the little typically Irish traces she revealed whenever her secretary-to-employer attitude broke down. Right from the moment he met her he knew, with a certainty rare in a man who'd never been a philanderer, that Lurene instinctively liked him, too. Eventually . . .

One day in June when the temperature was in the high sixties and the sun was in fine form, Connor had spent most of a Tuesday morning working with Lurene in his office and the stream of fresh air through an open window both beckoned him and gave him an enormous appetite. On the spur of the moment, he looked up from his desk-full of notes at the blonde secretary across the room.

"You must be starving," he said lightly. "I know I am. What would you say to a hearty lunch?"

She gave him a grin that rivaled the sun for brightness. "I'd say, 'Ye are the living end!' Isn't that the American term?"

He jumped up from his desk and went around to her. "I suppose it is, but it's probably ten years or more out of date." He fetched her lightweight jacket from the coatrack beside the door and held it up for her. "My treat."

"Is it a *ceapaire* and an *ol deoch*, Mr. Quinlan?" she asked, teasing him. She slipped her arms gracefully into the sleeves and turned to face him.

Connor pinched his nose thoughtfully and repeated what he'd heard: "A 'kapareh' and an *'Ole, dy-uk?'* No, Lurene, I'd really rather have food."

"Oh," she said with a nod, "ye want *bia*," pronouncing it "be-ah."

"I'm too damn old to learn a new language," he groaned as they went out the door to the elevator. "*Bia* obviously means food. What in St. Paddy's name do those other words mean?"

"A sandwich and a drink," she replied easily, laughing.

He loved the way she brushed her long, blonde hair to keep it from being held down by the jacket, the remarkably friendly way she laughed. He was also finding it nearly impossible these days to keep from staring with longing at the way her full breasts pushed against her sweaters and blouses and the way her skirts crept high above her knees. There was, he saw, an interest in work which made her careless of her costume and he liked that, too; because it told him that Lurene Shanahan was a woman who knew how to make the most of her life, whether she was deep in her duties or out for a good time.

"Shall I get my car?" he asked, on the sidewalk.

"Let's stroll, Mr. Quinlan, if y'don't mind." She paused, then allowed him to take her arm. "I'm thinkin' that ye still haven't really seen Galway in a proper style.

"You have a deal," he told her, walking easily beside her. "But only if you stop calling me Mister and remember what my first name is."

First they stopped for a few moments at Kennedy Square, so that he could explain his connection, by name, to the great storyteller Padraic O'Connaire. She listened with more amusement than Ethelyn had to his little anecdote because of the heavy, self-impressed voice he was using. "I rather doubt your Da marked you, or anything like that, 'Connaire Quinlan,'" she said with a teasing look on her face. "But it's always pleasant t'be havin' somebody else to blame when things don't work out just as we'd hoped."

He turned to her, annoyed. "Just what is that supposed to mean?" he demanded.

"I'm not a stick, Connor." She put a hand on his upper arm. "Just because I'm a gen-yew-ine Irish girl doesn't make me an ignoramus and I know a wee bit about psychology from me own days at University. You aren't going to feel entirely content, sir, until you write a book all your own. Until ye get your own thoughts and experiences in permanent form."

For a long moment he stared at Lurene, his lips parted in amazement. "I was married for years and Ethelyn never understood that," he confessed. "In fact, I rarely ever admit it to myself."

"It's time y'did. Come." She linked her arm in his again and led him left of the square at a steady pace. "There are some interesting things you may not have observed."

The sun was high above Galway's narrow streets and it had brought out more than a few strollers, smiling people who paused to peer into picturesque shop windows or who crossed the streets in affable defiance of the traffic wardens. Here, stores tended to open at nine A.M. sharp and close, rather desultorily—when enjoyable customers stopped dropping by—at five-thirty or six in the evening. On Wednesdays, of course, Galway recognized "halfday closing" and workers in the oft-charming shops were given the afternoon off from one o'clock on to catch up on their private needs. As for people who, like Connor and Lurene, liked taking their shortcuts across the streets, there was little risk from the city's taxis which did not cruise but operated from fixed stations.

She stopped in front of an aged edifice and said, "Now, then."

He looked at it, surprised. "It's just a bank," he offered. "We *do* have them in the United States."

"It's a bit more than that, Connor. It's Lynch Castle." Lurene assumed a storytelling pose of her own, one long leg crossed over the other as she leaned against the building, arms folded and an index finger at the side of her nose. "Here it was, in the 16th Century, that the place was a tower house owned by a man named Lynch. Mr. Lynch hanged his only son because the executioner refused to do it.".

"Good God, Lurene," Connor gasped, "that's horrible! Did they punish Mr. Lynch properly?"

She laughed, a string of tinkling Irish bells. "Not exactly. It seems the Lynches had had a houseguest, a Spaniard, and young Lynch murdered him in a quarrel. The old man dragged the boy off to jail, insisting he be put to death; but the executioner respected the Lynch family so much he refused. That's when old Mr. Lynch took the law into his own hands." She pointed her index at Connor. "Most of the oldtimers around here say that Lynch killed his son *primarily* because it was a breech of common courtesy to have taken the houseguest's life!"

"You must be kidding!" he exclaimed.

"No, I'm not. Here; look!" Lurene took him by the sleeve. Near the Colegiate Church of St. Nicholas she stopped again, pointing to a marble stone beside a walled-up door. "You wondered if old Mr. Lynch was punished. Well, Connor, this stone commemorates the good taste of the man. And later, in 1493, Lynch was elected Mayor of Galway!" She laughed at his astonished expression. "And *that*, sir, is a foine lesson in good manners and their just reward!"

Arm-in-arm, after lunch, they began strolling back to University. Midway there, it seemed suddenly natural to hold hands. "In a way, Connor," Lurene said dreamily, "this part of Ireland is rather like the old west in America."

He nodded. "I can name two or three famous American badmen who wound up sheriffs and marshals."

She waved her free hand in a broad, encompassing gesture. "There are five thousand square miles of rich land around us, Con. When we say 'the West' we refer t'everything west of the Shannon River. Especially Galway, Mayo, Roscommon, Leitrim and Sligo counties. And like your old west, it's there waitin' to be improved, ordered, changed for progress." She squeezed his hand. "But we certainly hope that more than the Aran Islands will still look Irish when it's all over."

Back in his office, Connor told her how much he admired the landscape by Jack B. Yeats on his wall. "There's a wild purity to it," he suggested. "Clarity."

"Jack was the brother of William Butler Yeats, a talented family." She stood beside him as they looked at the print, conscious of his proximity. "There've been several excellent Irish painters, y'know. Sean Keating and Maurice McGonigal are two others ye might look up."

Playboy of the Western World, the play by Synge," Connor remarked. "I just found out that Synge meant western *Ireland,* that he based many of his experiences here." He turned to her, taking her fingertips in his big hands. "But d'you know, Lurene, the real beauty of Ireland is in its people." He tipped her chin up with his index finger, peering deeply in her eyes. "And the most beautiful creature I've seen here is you."

She came gladly into his arms. Her lips were parted, but not to speak. His tongue explored between them. *The strength of the man,* Lurene thought, *he's what I've prayed for.* And Connor, kissing a woman other than Ethelyn for the first time in more than a decade, felt startling tears form in his eyes. Perhaps his life would not remain a lonely one after all.

During lunch, at school, Troy found that a boy named Bobby McCuffy insisted on taking up her time. They were in the schoolyard on this lovely spring day, the pale blonde girl perched on a swing and Bobby—darkhaired, roundfaced, bespectacled, an inch shorter than Troy and transiently bothered by an outbreak of acne—sat at her feet. It occurred to Troy, when her irritation began to mount, that a good backwards push with her feet up, and the resultant swing forward would send the presumptuous boy flying. What did she need with him when she had all the friends she required in the woods at home?

He had been plying her with questions about what it was like in America and couldn't seem to accept the fact that Troy had never seen an Indian in her life. "You just don't want t'tell me about 'em," he persisted. "Y'wanna keep even the *memory* of 'em t'yerself!"

Okay, if he wanted to play *that* way. Intentionally, she sighed grandly. It occurred to her that it was possible to play an entertaining game with this upstart boy, if she played it smart. "Well, when you've seen one Indian," she said, testing the lie for size, "You've seen them all."

He was fierce with delight. "That's what I thought," he cried, glowering at her. He filled quickly with almost insatiable curiosity. "D'yever see 'em scalp anybody?"

Bobby would have been a charming lad but for three primary faults. He was disinclined to believe anything said to him, unbearably suspicious. He had the habit of standing quite close, asking the same things over and over. And he had that damned curiosity. Troy's look at him was withering.

"Lots of times," she said loftily. "But the law doesn't let them do it much anymore." Conspiratorially, she leaned forward in the swing and spoke for Bobby's ears only. "T'tell you the truth, Bobby, I've seen more neat things here in County Connaught than I ever saw in In'di'nap'lis." Her pointed fingers measured off a small amount of height.

"Really?" Inches from her face, he was all ears. His breath smelled of something pungent he'd had for lunch. It was steamy. "A leprechaun, maybe?"

Troy moved away from him, laughing. She gave a toss of her light blonde hair. "Sure, but a lot neater things than just leprechauns." Her look scorned him, scorched him. "For Heaven's sake, Bobby, didn't *you* ever see a leprechaun?"

He looked away. "Maybe once." Sheepish, he wadded his empty lunch sack into a crumpled ball. "I wasn't sure, exactly, because it was rainin' cats." He hooked the sack toward a waste container a few feet away but it fell short. He left it. "I guess."

"Leprechauns is common," she told him, sneering. "They're like trees and flowers. They're ev'rywhere." She hesitated, plotting. "Bobby." He looked up. "Bobby, d'you like me?"

He crimsoned promptly. "Sure. Yes, I do." He glanced at his overshoes a size too large because they'd been handed down by a cousin over in Headford. "I like ye a lot, Troy lass."

"Okay, then. I'll let you meet the O'Sheas." She nodded and it was done.

"Who're they?" he asked, disappointed by the common name. "Neighbors?"

"Golly, don't your mom and pop tell you *anything*?"

"My da says fairies and stuff are superstitious," he replied stoutly. "He says they are dark throwbacks to the very worst of the way Ireland used t'be, and we should all come into the 20th Century with the rest of the world."

"The O'Sheas," Troy whispered intently, "*are* fairies—and I'll show 'em to you. You'll see 'em with your own eyes, clear as day."

"Well, then, what makes them more special than leprechauns?" he inquired. But even as he spoke she could see his modern da fading into the background of Bobby's thoughts.

"You'll see for y'self. Why not find out?" Troy touched his hand, let the fingers linger. "Want t'meet 'em, Bobby? Or are you scared?"

He stood up with a scowl. "McCuffys aren't feared of nothin'!" he boasted, adjusting his glasses and ready for combat. "Nothin!'"

"Then be at my house right after school," Troy urged him, arising from the swing, then brushing at her dress. Quickly, she left him there.

"But you'll have to be *very,* very quiet and nice and you can't tell *nobody* you've seen them. Because the O'Sheas are my friends."

For a moment he stared at her vanishing figure, slender, mercurial in thought and motion, the long blonde hair almost reaching her waist. *In the woods with Troy,* he thought with happy anticipation, a twelve-year-old boy suddenly filled with fantasy. *Wow!* Bobby McCuffy licked his lips. Then he went over to the crumpled sack he'd thrown, stooped, and dutifully dropped it in the container.

One's only real life is the life one never leads.
—*Oscar Wilde*

eleven

Patrick Quinlan spent half an hour more or less alone in his attic. He'd been drawn there by forces which he could never have described, uncertain whether he actually heard the summons or sensed that they beckoned him or, the other possibility, that he merely imagined them. A very long while ago, Pat Quinlan had confronted the terrifying question of whether he was insane or not, and it had made for a long winter. For weeks that became months he agonized over the decision—mad or sane—and finally concluded that he wasn't crazy.

After all, insanity implied delusion. A lack of reality, a total lack of it. It meant that nothing ever really happened, at all, except in one's abstracted thoughts. Everything was a dim, frenetic fantasy when you were mad, with absolutely no basis in fact.

That meant he couldn't have gone crazy, then, because many things had happened in the house in Kylemore, Connemara. Some of them were terrible, hellish things. So that suggested that he was sane and was obliged to bear it all on his Christian conscience.

And now, as he sat quietly in his chair, Pat knew

that the awful things must happen again. In a way, he didn't need any of the others to point it out. Already his hair was getting grayer by the day; his back hurt the way Connor's did; he felt wearier, more needful of sleep and rest, even though neither seemed to help him this time any more than they had in the past. Faith, it was never *permanent;* it never "took." There was always a need for another, then another, still more; and now he heard the insistence that time was almost up again.

He heard them telling him that, if nothing better developed, it would simply have to be Troy. His own granddaughter.

That made old Pat grieve but there were no tears in his eyes. After all, the constant repetition of the identical unfortunate procedure has a way of dulling the senses, even those painful ones of grief over personal loss. Age, he accepted once more, straightening, still had its privileges.

Bobby McCuffy was at Troy's front door five minutes after she herself arrived. He was trying very hard not to appear anxious, not to show how very much he wanted to meet the O'Sheas; but he was devoured by curiosity and, when Troy offered him a chair in the living room, he shook his head nervously. "I haven't a lot of time," he said, taking off his hornrimmed glasses long enough to mop at a lens with the tail of his shirt. "Maybe we could go meet the O'Sheas right away?"

Despite the things that had happened, Troy Quinlan wasn't an unkind child. She sighed to register her feminine protest at being manipulated—which she had fully expected—and went in search of her sweater.

She led Bobby across the deep backyard, past her Dads' garage-study ("What's that place Troy, huh? Who stays there?" and, after she'd answered, "Does your da write about fairies? He doesn't sleep out here, does he? Does he write horror stories?"), and to the edge of the thick woods. There, she stopped the boy.

The sun had begun to go down and there was a bumbling breeze, whispering. Troy was chilly. She pulled her cardigan sweater close around her thin chest till it left a spine of cloth, which she gripped. "There are things you must know, Bobby. Things you got to obey." Her voice was firm but she was annoyed and distracted by the hot, almost sticky way his myopic gaze fixed intently on her face. With the bottlebottom lenses and dreamy mind, Bobby's eyes sort of *surrounded* a person; they seemed to see her from every conceivable direction, with nothing much registering. "First, the fairy kingdom isn't like other Irish people."

"I know," he put in, fairly dancing with eagerness. "It's all tiny-like."

"No, Bobby, not all of it." She was recalling the hulky Sir Gat. "What I mean is . . . they aren't exactly friendly. They don't want to be pals every time someone comes around." She reflected on that a minute, searching for the right words. "They're more exclusive. More particular."

"Why?" he pressed. "Does that mean they're snooty like the rich in Ulster? D'they have their noses in the air and lots of dumb rules and regs, like British?"

She folded her slender arms across her boyish chest. "It's just," she explained, "that most of the time ordinary people can't *see* 'em. Grown-ups never do, 'less they've done something terrible t'make some fairy *mad*. But if they *do* make friends of a human kid—because she'll believe in them absolutely—they'll also let themselves be seen by the kid's friend." She groped for a concept she'd recently learned. "Adults, y'see, only pretend to believe in anything at all but they only believe in themselves. So it's the adults who are snooty, Bobby, not the fairies."

All she got for her careful explanation was a nod meant to rush her along.

"Y'see, children often have just the right mixture of belief and something called empathy," Troy continued, "to recognize one. Grown-ups have learned to hide their wild side even from themselves. But even kids only get that one look, that one chance to believe. And if they pass that magic test, they're accepted right up until they grow up too."

His head bobbed in assent. "Okay," he concurred, prodding. "Right-o."

"One last thing," she said urgently, ignoring the way Bobby was bouncing around, "is that you must never tell a soul you met the O'Sheas. Nobody, hardly, would b'lieve you anyway except maybe my Gran-da, but they'd make you tell everything you know. And that's not allowed by the O'Sheas. Promise to keep it to yourself?"

"Sure," he said, grabbing her arm and starting to drag her with him into the woods. "It's a deal."

She held her ground. "Bobby, I mean it. It'd be very dangerous if you told. And just as bad would be if you tried to visit the O'Sheas *without* me. Until you're completely accepted and all, I mean. Not all the fairies are nice people, see? Some get *real mean* if they feel you crossed 'em. You got to promise me that you'll remember all this. Do you?"

"Do I what?" He'd scarcely heard her.

"Do you promise those things I told you—cross your heart and hope to die?"

"I told you so," he replied with irritation, making the sign of the cross on his chest instead. "Now are ye satisfied? Can we go see 'em now?"

She paused, uncertain. Finally she nodded.

Hand in hand they plunged into the woods. It took Bobby time for his eyes to adjust to the way that the trees crisscrossed above them, taking away adequate lighting. It wasn't pitch dark, of course; but the boy was so nearsighted to begin with that he needed five minutes to see clearly enough to identify anything.

They heard the music before anything else.

It lay ahead of them still, a tinkling, musical sound that was like nothing Bobby McCuffy had ever heard. When he paused to listen, Troy grabbed his hand and pulled. "C'mon," she urged him. "We don't want to miss the parade."

After another five minutes Bobby wasn't sure he knew the way back. Troy's movements by now were swift and automatic. Like an Indian scout, he saw, she seemed to recognize signs that weren't evident to him—flattened blades of grass, an isolated patch of flowers, the coloring or markings of a tree. The small boy began to pant from his exertions. As a rule, Bobby didn't get much exercise. He spent most of his time away from school reading or drawing. One of the reasons he wanted to be with Troy this afternoon was to see how closely his imagined sketches of the wee folk hit the target. Not that he absolutely, positively *be-*

lieved he would see anything at all. But that was all right, if he could just have Troy alone long enough to steal a kiss and maybe put his hand on her knee.

Ahead of them, as they hurried forward, Bobby saw a rising knoll of grass. It wasn't much of a climb, even for him, but he followed Troy's tugging hand and joined her, sprawled at the top of the knoll where they could look down on the emerald grass beneath them.

For what seemed a lengthy period to Bobby McCuffy they lay quietly, watching, and he was aware primarily of two things. One was how heavy and noisy their breathing sounded when there wasn't any other sound. The other was how close to him Troy Quinlan lay; why, he could even feel her left thigh touching his right one, just faintly. With the discovery, Bobby's breathing came faster and became somewhat irregular.

The remainder of sunlight was on the verge of vanishing and Bobby was going to ask her to take them back when Troy said, in a hoarse whisper, "*Look!*" She pointed her finger enthusiastically.

On the plain of grass below the grassy knoll was a sight Bobby had tried to draw but had never anticipated seeing in life.

A seemingly-endless procession of miniature creatures had appeared round the bend of the knoll, costumed regally in clothing and armor that might have come from the time of King Arthur. Bobby gasped. The forms were tiny, almost jewellike. Some of them were afoot, preceded by staffs gripped stiffly in their hands, while others were atop horses and unicorns no more than an inch or two high. At the forefront of the parade were several miniature musicians playing cornets and trumpets, the sounds of which were the tinkling, feathery sound Bobby'd heard before. Midway in the procession was a carriage supported on the shoulders of small but powerful slaves. Tumbling at the side of the parade were several acrobats; and each instant that one of them landed agilely on his feet, he would cry, "Zounds!" in a triumphant voice no louder than the scratch of a mouse.

"You are watching," said Troy in Bobby's ear, "the regal court of the Dana O'Shea, moving to another part of the forest."

He couldn't find the words. Spellbound, fascinated, young Bobby McCuffy merely stared down at them in awe, his heart thumping loudly in his chest. Overall, he thought, it was like a glittering, golden string trailing across the floor of the woods, pulled by the powerful hand of an invisible giant. But there was no golden string. The little people moved of their own volition in an absence of sound so total, just then, that it was like putting down on an airless planet. When Bobby rubbed his incredulous eyes with his knuckles and then looked again, however, they were still there, silently going about their business. And the only giants intruding on their miniature universe just then were Troy Quinlan and Bobby McCuffy.

"They're kind of stuck-up and really not too nice," Troy whispered to him. Somehow the slight whisper was deafening. "They know me—that's why we're permitted to see 'em at *all*—but they hate strangers, I'm told. They probably won't stop the procession even t'speak t'me. Because they have dreadful dark secrets all their own and have no need at all for human people. Unless they need a sacrifice or something."

He barely heard her speak, he was so enthralled. The Dana O'Shea were tiny and it seemed to take them forever just to cross the width of the grassy knoll on which the children reclined. Bobby wondered if, when God saw man upon His oceans, he looked like that to Him. Why, moving all the way across the woods was a first class adventure for the O'Sheas—a titanic expedition, like Columbus discovering America!

But by now most of the first half of the procession had passed and Troy, accustomed to these marvels, was sitting up and looking away. She felt pleased with herself for giving Bobby McCuffy something to think about, because she was merely a girl and the Irish boys had shown her what they thought about that. Ignoring him completely, grandly, she jumped up on their side of the knoll, and stretched.

That was when the crimson curtains of the tiny carriage borne by the measureless slaves parted and, to Bobby's total amazement, a microscopic maiden leaned out, looked up at him—

—And winked!

Instantly he was smitten, gone, hopelessly in love with her; for the inch-high queen of the Dana O'Shea was ineffably, perfectly beautiful from the diamond tiara on her rich, golden head to the haunting smile on her full lips, from the exquisitely created little body to the gorgeously glittering gown encasing it. He hadn't known such beauty existed in the universe.

Meet me here, Bobby, urged the feminine voice in his mind, the sound a husky whisper of seductive promise, a mental caress, *at midnight! I'll wait for you!*

Even as the parade disappeared round the other side of the knoll, a drifting waft of heady perfume left teasingly in the air behind them, Bobby went on staring where they had been—where *she* had been. In the oft-lonely world of a young boy he had only imagined such a female form or such a bell-like female voice. Somehow, perhaps, he could be rendered *their* size and live the way *they* lived, finding excitement and adventure beneath every twig, every fallen leaf. Perhaps, then, he could slay a dragon or a lizard or fox and win the hand of the O'Shea's seductive queen and reign as her king forever!

When Troy finally got him in tow and they began retracing their steps through the darkened woods, sure-footed and casual, he felt confident about finding this place. It was as though a new world of knowledge filled his youthful mind and gave him, as well, a courage he'd never known before. She called over her shoulder to him: "Remember the things I told you, now. You must remember these are *my* woods, Bobby. These are *my* friends. I want you to promise that you'll never try to come here without me."

He fell back a step or two behind her. She was almost out of sight. "I promise," he told her with a ringing note of sincerity.

But he had his fingers crossed behind his back.

*Our hearts were drunk with a beauty
Our eyes could never see.
—"A.E." (George Russell)*

twelve

Last Friday, after class, a number of Connor's students had cornered him in the corridor outside his lecture hall and convinced him that a majority of his pupils who were serious about writing wanted him to discuss a certain topic.

This Tuesday, then, in his afternoon lecture, the Irish-American broached the subject with the disconcerting impression that it had been virtually forced upon him. Gripping the lectern hard with his strong hands, Connor began speaking about books that were made into motion pictures.

Merely mentioning the topic brought half the class forward in their chairs, rapt with attention. He looked out at the eager, generally lean faces and at the plain, even homemade garments beneath them, at once full of understanding and a realization that he had to set them straight. "Mixing books with movies," he began, "is worse than mixing apples with oranges. I cannot adequately impress on you two salient facts: A motion picture is *never,* really, the *book* in any meaningful sense of the word; and most books optioned for films are never actually transformed into films. I could name ten well-known writers who've sold their screen rights several times and never expect their books to become movies.

"And that," he continued, lifting a bushy black brow, "may be all to the good. In all too many cases, a book and a motion picture with the same title have nothing but the title in common. I would, in fact, go this far: The number of writers who are genuinely satisfied with the translation of their novel to the filmic form could perch on the head of a pin next to an entire chorus of angels and never force a single one to spread his wings in flight."

There was a little burst of laughter which was mingled, clearly enough, with a suggestion of disappointment and surprise.

"I'm absolutely serious," Connor said firmly. "The ultimate aim of the author of any book should be to see it published, properly promoted and circulated, and selling briskly. Outstanding reviews might be a consideration but seeing the novel sold to the movies isn't even on the list. Most well-read men and women who go to see the 'movie version' of a best seller come away richly expressing their dissatisfaction. Which is undoubtedly because it *was* just a 'version.' If the author had preferred a different version, I'm sure he would have written it."

A young man with hair as black as Connor's raised his hand. The hair was spread not only in waves on top his head but in a snarling torrent of a beard. He stood, scowling. "Are ye sayin', then, that books and films are mutually exclusive?"

"Not at all," Connor replied instantly, "although there are times when they should have been. Tell me one outstanding 'version' of a novel by Fitzgerald, Hemingway, or Wolfe—just *one* which is among the finest films ever made. Don't you think at least one of them *should* be that great? After all, those authors' books are generally considered among the finest works of the entire century.

"I shan't bother," Connor continued, "to indicate reasons why the translation from book to cinema fails with such frequency. Some of you, I'm certain"—he looked directly at the bearded youth—"are more interested in writing for the screen than for books. That's fine, but never confuse the two. They aren't the same thing at all, never will be, and require entirely different writing skills. But I do wish to impress upon you that the only truly valid reason for an author to yearn for his novel to be filmed is monetary. Yes; you are all quite correct in assuming that the writer probably earns a considerable amount of money for selling his screen rights. After taxes, some of it may be left for the poor chap to use in paying his psychiatrist." Now he pointed his index finger at the twenty-eight people in the room, one by one, with fine deliberateness. "To those of you who plan to write a book to the best of your ability, let me tell you plainly that simply getting the tale between covers is accomplishment enough—a very good trick, indeed, considering how few publishers will even *look* at a first novel anymore. And to your family and friends, people," he completed, lowering his head to fix them with a watchful frown, "make it clear as a bell that simply completing work on a book is a fine achievement indeed. If you *sell* it, it's even more remarkable. And if you become one of the people working full-time at the literary trade, you'll be in an exclusive circle comprising no more than *eight percent* of the writers in the whole world! Seen in this light, movies are nothing more than an afterthought!"

Pleased with his own brash handling of a tricky topic, Connor asked Lurene Shanahan to dinner. They ate in the restaurant of a Ryans' hotel in Galway, surrounded by pleasant people in tweeds and Irish-patterned, handknit sweaters. Connor saw two ladies wearing cocktail dresses and, when he pointed them out discreetly to Lurene, she whispered across the table: "Very few ladies in County Connaught own more than one good dress. This must be the birthday or anniversary of the ones across the way."

After dining, he drove her to a two-story apartment building off Eyre Square and, to his pleasure, she asked him in.

"I can offer you a little wine," she called, hurrying to the kitchen, "or tea, of course."

"Of course," he echoed her sardonically, smiling and taking a seat on an aging couch. "Tell me: Do you have ice?"

"Wait, I'll see." She opened the refrigerator; he heard it clunk against a wall or door. "Yes, I think it's ready." He smiled. It had been ten hours since she left the apartment. Without being in the kitchen to see the thing, he imagined an old-fashioned icebox fastened together with scraps of wire.

"Well, then," he called to her, aware of his American boldness, "pour the hot tea in a tall glass, fill it about three-quarters full, and add that ice you discovered. Three or four cubes, please."

Lurene appeared in the doorway from the kitchen, hands on her hips as she made a face. "Ah Lord," she said, shuddering. "I'm toilin' for a savage!"

"A bona fide Druid," he agreed lightly, listening to the cheery sound of liquid being poured, tinkling musically.

Waiting for her to come out, he looked round the apartment and sighed. There was so much progress in the United States that people took for granted. This was probably one of the average middle class apartments in Galway and it reminded Connor of certain coldwater flats he'd seen in British art films of the fifties. Not that it wasn't clean and just as tidy as Lurene could make it; but the linoleum just inside the door and the wallpaper—flowery, overly ornate—were faded beyond the tolerance of the most indigent American. He half-expected Sir Laurence Olivier or Laurence Harvey to materialize at the front door, juggling oranges or murmuring slyly of how they'd somehow make room at the top despite all the odds. Where a television might have squatted in Indianapolis, there was a table with a vase; the flowers in the vase were probably quite genuine.

Happily, Lurene wasn't a middleaged Simone Signoret depending upon her fading charms and desperate heart when, later, she slipped down beside him on the couch and came easily into his arms. Her heart was beating so fiercely that he could count its beats through his shirt. She was, Connor felt, more beautiful in a natural way than any screen actress he'd ever seen, so chalk up another one for literature. Half leaning on his torso with her face scant inches away, she smelled of some good Irish soap and of one lovely Lurene.

Tenderly, he reached behind her ears to lift the mane of golden hair and, at the same moment, draw her lips to his.

At first, shyly, astonishingly, her mouth was pressed nearly shut. Breath escaped with a hissing sound of leashed desire; the kiss was hesitant, actually chaste. But before he could even probe with his aching tongue, her lips parted with a hunger that caught him off guard. Now she lay against the full length of him on the couch, her hands tangled in his own black hair and her breath panting against his mouth. His tongue met hers, tasting; impossibly she tasted of cherry and strawberry, though he knew it was only the honey of a wanting woman.

When he released her head to reach low and cup her buttocks, pulling her still closer in toward him, and she felt his erection prodding at her lower body, she nearly succumbed. For an instant her hand was on him, slipped between their bodies. Then Lurene sat up quite suddenly, swinging her long legs over the edge of the sofa, gripping it with her fingers. A hand leapt; she brushed the hair nervously back from her temples and took several deep breaths. "I am not customarily," she said with obvious difficulty in speaking, "quite so forward."

"I'm sure you aren't, and never were," Connor said softly. Cautiously he extended his arm, touching her thigh where the tweed skirt had climbed, leaving it full and pale and bare. It was as if electricity jumped between them, but she didn't halt the light caress. Gently, with great care, he rested his whole palm on the thigh. "You're quite the most beautiful woman I've seen in my lifetime."

"It's too soon, Connor Quinlan," Lurene said, turning her head as if it hurt, looking down at him. Clearly she was acutely conscious of his hand, unmoving where it lay high on her leg. Her breasts, beneath the thin blouse, lifted fast, three times, and he sensed that her nipples were taut and long. She kept her legs pressed together, tightly, as if to open them was to advance her position beyond all defense. The way she sat on the couch was militarily erect, her sweetly-curved back so straight now and so stiff that he feared it might snap. "It's too soon after your poor wife's passin'."

He couldn't answer, he only listened to the way, under stress, her accent became sharply, lyrically Gaelic. In other circumstances, with another woman perhaps, Connor might not have felt the way he did. But he wanted Lurene's good impression of him; he liked the fact that they respected one another; he did not want to spoil that. And so he simply sat up beside her, kissing her panting mouth a last fleeting time, and retrieved his iced tea without a word. There was nothing in the world he could say that would not put them, together, in her bed; and there was nothing he could say or do, just then, that would not end their relationship forever the moment he dressed himself and left— unless it was that he loved her, and the complexities of that were more than either of them were ready to handle.

"I want you hugely, Con," she said, patting his knee with a grateful smile. "When it's proper, we'll do it your way. Why, we'll do *everything* your way." She blinked and, without moving from his side, sought a different topic. "Tell me about your family. About your father and your little girl."

"I will," he agreed, taking a breath and staring, "if you'll put the skirt down over those wondrous knees of yours." He saw Lurene's profound blush, her quick movement, and laughed, squeezing her hand. "Dad is another wonder of Ireland, Lurene. He's past seventy but he might pass for the mid-fifties on a good day."

"I met him once at a funeral and he was the most charmin' man in all the Isle," she said, noting his pride. "Leastwise, till I met his son. But there's something *else* in your voice, lad. What is it? D'ye hold somethin' back about your old man?"

He looked helplessly in her eyes. "Dad keeps secrets. Not that there's anything *wrong* with that—and it certainly isn't because he's senile, since he's had one particular secret as long as I can recall." He hesitated. "Sometimes I think I'm being foolish and sometimes I believe there's something *awful* going on in that private attic of his." He stopped, sipping his iced tea, changing the subject back to where it was. "All the men of our family live forever. I can remember his father, my gran-da, a little, and Dad says he was going strong right into his eighties. And his father before that."

"But?" she prompted, concerned for his attitude. "What's wrong with that?"

He studied his fingertips, more disturbed than he'd have cared to confess. Whether it was the frustration he felt over wanting Lurene so badly or only that, in expressing his anxiety for the first time, it was gathering force, he felt that what he was saying might be important. "The same pattern isn't true of the women in the Quinlan clan.

They never seem to live to be particularly old. My own mother died in childbirth, and my grandmother before her. Then there's poor Ethelyn, my wife."

"Whatever are y'saying, Connor?" she demanded with a frown. "My goodness, you're after bein' just as superstitious as we're all supposed to be!"

"I have two good reasons for wondering if there is some—some stupid *curse* hanging over Quinlan women, or something in the blood... an anomaly, like a virus passed down from generation to generation." His gaze held hers again. "My girl, Troy, is all I have left right now. Lurene, she's a delightful child, pretty and even fairer than you, extremely bright." His enthusiasm grew as he spoke of Troy. "And her imagination is incredibly inventive. Most of the time she plays in the woods with playmates she's just made up from whole cloth. She has a positive gift for making certain she's never lonely. But she *does* need what I cannot give her: mothering."

"And Pop Connor Quinlan thinks, secretly, that little Troy might become the writer he hasn't yet made of himself?"

His mouth fell open. "How'd you know that?" he demanded. "I never admitted such a thing to a soul."

Lurene laughed, musically. "It's clear as crystal to one who bothers t'understand ye, Connor." She remembered then. "You said you had two reasons for wonderin' about a curse on your womenfolk. What's the other one?"

He looked straight into her lovely eyes. "You, Miss Shanahan, you. I'm not about to bring a woman so full of life and love into my family if

169

there's even the slightest chance of endangering her very existence."

Now it was in the open. What both of them was thinking; what each of them hoped might be, someday. He was amazed by what he'd said aloud, but didn't for a moment wish he'd remained silent. Finally, because there was nothing else to say just then, he stood before her; and she arose, coming into his arms with a passion that, while limited in time and scope of expression, was nonetheless all-out, at once yielding and wildly demanding. They stood toe to toe, skin to skin the length of their bodies, pressing till it hurt, mouths linked and working with such a practiced harmony that it was amazing after such short experience. When she stepped away at last, panting, they knew it was not the last time but only the dearest of beginnings.

He hadn't been asleep long, he thought as he shoved himself on his elbows, scarcely aware of long, lusty dreams about the beauties of Lurene Shanahan. But when he clumsily raised his alarm clock with the luminous dial—a gift of Westinghouse to the older house of Quinlan—Connor was surprised to see that it was nearly three o'clock in the morning.

Who could be knocking at the front door at such an hour? A neighboring farmer clad in leprechaun-green, claiming he'd misplaced a cow?

Slipping on a bathrobe and one slipper—the other had apparently vanished into thin air while he slept—Connor hurried down the hallway. Behind him, he failed to observe, the light in the attic above him went off. Connor took the stairs two at a time and trotted awkwardly across the front room to the door.

Two people in his own general age grouping stood apologetically on the threshold, draped with mist and wearing polite expressions that did little to conceal their obvious concern. The man wore a peajacket and patched trousers; the woman had merely thrown a coat over her robe.

"I'm Sean McCuffy and this is my wife Sheilah," said the man, a thin, tall fellow with hornrimmed glasses. His nod indicated a plain, brownhaired woman with a wide, generous mouth and a frightened expression. "We sorely hate to bother ye at such an ungodly hour, sir, but our boy Bobby is a classmate of yer daughter."

Connor paused, struck by the absurd premature notion that Troy had somehow seduced the boy and even now hid him in her bed. "Come in, please," he asked, thinking how the imagination got wound up during the night. "How can I help you?"

The parents followed him into the front room and simply stood before the chairs they were offered. "Bobby is missing," said Mrs. McCuffy, accent-free and strangely dignified despite her worried face. "Other than us, the last person who saw him was your Troy."

Connor frowned. "I'm afraid I don't understand. Do you mean Troy saw him at school?"

"He went over here after school," Sheilah McCuffy said firmly, "against my express wishes. We still remember what happened to those teenagers in the woods beside your house." She glanced at her husband for corroboration. "But he confessed that he'd been here, because he was just *full* of some nonsense about seeing a parade of fairies."

"Childish claptrap, of course," Sean McCuffy put in staunchly. No superstitious believer he. "God knows what the children thought they saw. But if our Bobby has run off, well, we thought he might have said something to your lass."

Connor bounced promptly to his feet, foolishly abashed because he hadn't even known a young boy was with Troy in those damned woods. Somehow he felt partly responsible for what had happened—whatever it was—and wanted to remove both himself and Troy from the line of fire as quickly as possible. Weren't fathers supposed to know where their youthful daughters were at all times? Why had Troy let him down this way, put him in the neglectful-parent spotlight? "I'll go awaken Troy and ask her," he said roughly, turning.

"It's that Bobby's been gone for more than ten hours now," Sean McCuffy added, shuffling his booted feet. "That simply isn't the way of our boy, sir. He's never done such a thing before."

"We're almost frantic with fear, Mr. Quinlan," the woman said at the same time he said, "Of course." Now she paused. "So we thought we'd check with you and Troy before we went to the authorities."

"No problem," he said over his shoulder, and took the steps to the second floor two at a time. No problem, if you weren't disturbed by vague innuendoes suggesting that your daughter had some mysterious *hold* over a neighbor boy doubtlessly twice her size. Or if the mention of bringing the police in to the matter didn't somehow imply that the Quinlan family would be asked a great many authoritative questions, since they undoubtedly ran a white-slave racket on behalf of gay pirates.

He burst into her room and found Troy sound asleep, the pillow not beneath her pale blonde head but clutched securely in her thin arms. She'd given up sleeping with stuffed toys when she began making friends in the woods. But at night, alone, she had only the old ring Sir Gat gave her for comforting, and a plump pillow was better than nothing.

"Troy, wake up." Connor shook her shoulder and raised his voice. "Troy!"

She lifted a sleepy lid and peered at him. "Dads? What's up?"

"That boy, Bobby McCuffy, seems to have run away from home. His parents are here and they say you were the last one to see him." He paused, trying not to sound like a prosecuting attorney: "Honey, d'you have any idea where he went?"

Her eyes were huge now, especially in the gloom of the darkened bedroom, the only light coming from the hallway. "No, Dads," she said honestly. "He told me he was going straight home from the woods." A thought crossed her mind. "Did he tell them what he saw?"

"You mean the fairies?" he demanded, frowning. "I think we've heard about all of the nonsense we can use, Troy. You're getting old enough to have real friends. I'm not sure all that imagination is good for you." He straightened, running a hand across his forehead with concern. "Well, if Bobby doesn't show up tomorrow, I'll want you to think hard to remember precisely what he said to you. Okay?"

She nodded and Connor turned. Then he turned

back, stooping to kiss her forehead and ruffle her hair. "Go back to sleep, punkin. Don't worry about it."

Wide awake now, Troy watched as her father eased the door shut behind him and then sat up in bed. Troy was angry now. "The little fool!" she exclaimed angrily, slapping one fist into the other open palm. "I'll just bet he went back to my woods by himself. And I warned him *never* to do that!"

There was no answer. It was a quiet, deep night and the skies beyond her single window were jet black, stygian. She stared toward the window, finally sighing and shrugging her shoulders. It wasn't her fault, dammit! She thought for a moment about dressing and going out to her woods, searching for Bobby; but then she reconsidered, for it was clear that the night was absolutely still and Troy knew perfectly well nothing was moving in the woods.

Not any more.

Finally she laid down again, settling back into her pillow and tugging the covers up over her thin legs in a pettish, angry gesture. It really *wasn't* her fault! She'd also warned Bobby about telling his parents about seeing the Dana O'Shea. Now Troy gave the eye of the dark window another angry glance and then closed her eyes, easily dismissing the whole thing from her mind. "He deserves what he gets!" she said aloud, and promptly tumbled childishly back into her innocent dreams.

And (the angel Victorious) gave me one of them, and I read the opening words of the letter, which were, 'The voice of the Irish';

and as I read the beginning of the letter I thought that at the same moment I heard their voice—they were beside the Wood of Voclut, which is near the Western Sea—and this did they cry out as with one mouth: 'We ask thee, boy, come and walk among us once more!'

—*Magnonous Sucatus Patricus*
(St. Patrick, 385-461 A.D.)

thirteen

In the endless eighteen hours since Bobby McCuffy's worried parents appeared at his front door at three o'clock in the night, Connor had found the world beginning to swirl before his eyes like the little black spots he saw, at times, when he straightened up too suddenly. He'd already been tired from a busy day at University College and emotionally on edge from his romantic experiences with Lurene Shanahan, and now there would be no more sleep the rest of Tuesday night. Instead, when the McCuffys returned to the Quinlan house an hour later with Deputy Police Chief Francis Muldowney and several sleepy-eyed policemen, Connor helped them search the woods for the missing boy. That seemed premature, to Connor, because of the way it implied that Bobby might be dead; but he pitched in to help, still strangely troubled by the vague notion that he or his family might somehow be responsible for the lad's disappearance.

It was midway through that stumbling, groping search—three flashlights weren't nearly enough to do the job properly in the thick black night of the woods, and Muldowney instantly struck Connor as an incompetent clown—that he began to separate, in his personal life, the forest from the trees. It dawned on the publisher of Bookquins Newsletter that almost everything had gone awry since he and his family came to County Connaught. It wasn't only the tragedy of Ethelyn's sudden death, on which he had been focused. It was a number of inexplicable terrors, and the impression that life was turning upside down haunted him all day Wednesday.

Originally however, there'd been no time to think it through. When the search for Bobby failed, it was Connor who urged Chief Muldowney to use his phone and contact the authorities in Spiddal, Headford, Oughterhead, and other neighboring communities. They had no word of the boy but promised to begin their own questioning and search. At daybreak, it was Connor who prompted a second journey into the woods, contacting several other neighbors and enlisting them in a more thorough quest. Again, however, they found no evidence that Bobby had ever been there.

Coming back to the Quinlan house, Connor and Muldowney found that Troy and Pat Quinlan were up and around, but neither of them was able to provide a single, workable clue. Not, Connor mused, that the cloth-head, comic-opera cop would know what to do with a clue if he had it.

Finally the McCuffys, exhausted and brooding in their silent anxiety, had headed toward their own home quite some distance down Route T71. Muldowney and his men followed, grudgingly pledging to notify Connor if they received word about the boy. At last the Quinlan family was left alone and Connor's concern for the peculiar things that were happening around him grew stronger. Dad, when everybody else was gone, seemed on the verge of tears and scarcely able to talk about the disappearance. Instead, he fluttered protectively around Troy, patting her shoulder awkwardly and yet, in the glances he gave her, appearing oddly apprehensive. At length the old man excused himself and went slowly to his room, shaking his head, apparently as privately concerned about the missing boy as the McCuffys themselves.

Troy, on the other hand, ate her breakfast as though nothing unusual had transpired. When Connor suggested that she remain home from school, she agreed with a noncommittal air and consumed her eggs with enthusiasm. She asked no questions of her father about the searching of the woods and, when he pointed out that she might show a little concern for her missing playmate, told him flatly that she barely knew Bobby McCuffy and "I didn't like him much anyhow."

In the background, aged Annie, the crone who came to cook and tidy-up, shifted her slight weight brokenly from kitchen to dining-room, occasionally crossing herself with a dagger-like index finger that pricked and prodded her shallow bosom. Trembling involuntarily and whispering ancient imprecations, she seemed to Connor a transplanted Shakespearean witch, dark secrets lurking in the hollows of her eyes. Black and hard as stones, those eyes were heavy with the weight of superstitious terror and, when they met Connor's gaze, the old woman's fright oozed like mucous round the sunken rims. The incongruity, with lithe young Troy eating heartily, furthered the writer's feeling that he had somehow come not to emerald Eire but to an alien land pregnant with imponderable mysteries.

During the afternoon, it rained, one of those abrupt downpours which every Irishman knows will endure only minutes before it is replaced by pale sunshine and multihued rainbows arching above the geometric farmland. Except that this one endured for more than an hour, almost as if God Himself wept for the dreadful things that were happening.

Connor phoned the police department around three in the afternoon, getting Chief Muldowney on the other end only with difficulty and a full explanation of why he'd phoned. "This isn't the Yew-nited States, Mr. Quinlan," Muldowney said in his ear, the acid fairly dripping from his voice. "Things move a wee bit more slowly, ye know."

"I only wanted to know if you had any news," Connor told him patiently, "and what was being done."

"Everything that can be done is bein' done," Muldowney snapped. "Frankly, Mr. Quinlan, we're after figurin' that it's a tempest in a teapot. The lad has probably taken it in his head to go fishin' somewheres—Sligo, perhaps, or the lakeland around Killarney. Or he may turn up in Athlone or Carrick-on-Shannon for the boat show rally. Kids *do* get adventurous ideas in their heads at times."

"Of course," Connor muttered, not believing it for a moment but knowing that he'd get nowhere with this man. He hung up slowly. "Of course," he said again, to no one in particular, staring out the window at the slanting rain.

180

He hadn't done a lick of work by the time they ate dinner and, around six-thirty, Connor telephoned Lurene, mostly to feel that something was being accomplished and partly to tell her what had happened. When he'd explained about Bobby and the search parties, he found himself confiding further in the beautiful blonde. "Things . . . aren't right, Lurene," he said into the mouthpiece. "Indeed, they're very wrong and I'm a fool for not having seen it before."

"I'm not sure I understand," she said. "There's your wife, of course. But you didn't know the McCuffy lad, did you?"

He sighed heavily. "That's only the latest sadness, the most recent puzzle." He paused and spoke the idea that had been lurking beneath the surface even when he dialed her number. "Lovely lady, would you consider coming out here for a few hours? Perhaps you could help me get a little work done on some of my projects, if you'd be so kind? Dad and Troy will be around, so you shouldn't think this is my big seduction scene."

Lurene laughed gaily. "I'd love to come out. I've been thinking about you all day, at university, and I'd enjoy seeing the famous Quinlan estate anyway."

At a few minutes past eight, anxious to see Lurene again but wondering if she was safe coming here after dark, Connor went out back and carefully picked his path across the ground to his garage-study. The rain had left puddles here and there, and it was chilly. Water glittered like fine sprinklings of jewelry on the slabs of stone which seemed to be strewn everywhere in this part of Ireland. *God's rock-garden,* he mused, and instant-

181

ly wondered if he'd chosen the right deity. Long, bleak shadows slid out of the violet mist in anthropomorphic stealth, groping the ancient earth with the fingers of pickpockets. It was growing darker by the moment but Connor paused, before unlocking his study, to stare at the curtain of trees marking the first stage of the deep woods. Was a twelve-year-old boy somehow lost among those silent trees, hungry and hysterical by now, haunted by Druidic or Celtic spirits that waited hungrily for innocence strayed? The big man shuddered and ran a hand through his black mane. There was so much more to Ireland than people thought, back in Indianapolis; so much more than shamrocks and shillalaghs and *When Irish Eyes are Smiling*.

There was the furtive hint everywhere of unseen sprites, discarnate spirits, and beings that knelt on microscopic knees and looked back at you with the eyes of utter strangeness.

Waiting for Lurene, he gave up quickly on doing any work and sat on the edge of his executive chair, drumming his fingers on the desk. It would be nice to turn on the radio, hear some music—something sweetly lyrical and lighthearted, something that spoke of home, and love, and the safety of the hearth. All that he could locate on the radio, he was certain; but suddenly it seemed just another Irish tall tale, a serenely devious coverup for ugliness that lay, like Connaught's poverty, just beneath the surface. And besides, he wanted to be sure to hear Lurene when she arrived and guide her safely to the garage.

It wasn't just Dad, with his damned secret attic and now his unexplained sadness for the missing boy. It wasn't even the way that poor Ethelyn had come here with such hopes for beginning a new life, only to be taken by sudden death.

It was the hideous howling that he, Ethelyn, and Dad had heard, almost as if it predicted—*announced?*—her imminent passing. That was just one of the things that had never been cleared up. Any time he mentioned the shrieking sounds to Dad, the old man simply shrugged and made up another charming explanation. Explanations that had no more to do with truth, Connor was sure, than Troy's playmates.

He stopped drumming his fingertips for a moment and stared outside at the newly ebon night, blinking. *Something* was trying to get through his consciousness, trying to provide a message, a clue. But all he'd thought of was his daughter's imaginary friends and, if he began to question the possibility that they might, somehow, be *real,* he might as well buy a loom and move to the Aran Islands.

Those poor young people who'd been killed by some bearlike creature, shortly after they all arrived in Kylemore. It was no wonder they had dropped right out of the news, their deaths totally unexplained. Francis Muldowney couldn't solve a crime if he saw it with his own ignorant eyes. But there had been *some* menacing animal of some kind in those very woods where they had searched for Bobby McCuffy and, so far as anybody could judge, the damned thing might still be there. Hell, Connor thought with anger and disgust, slapping his typewriter, the creature could have *eaten* Bobby and then Muldowney and his men would simply go on pretending that the boy was somewhere fishing for trout!

When the door to the garage-den opened, Connor fell back in shock against his chair and it shot three feet backward until it slammed against the wall.

He mustered an uneasy laugh and arose. It was Lurene, arm-in-arm with his father.

Now Patrick Quinlan was himself again, affable and clearly delighted to have a beauty on his arm. He handed her over to his son with a show of great regret, sighing. "Faith, I had me own eye on this lass long afore ye ever saw her likes, Connor Quinlan!" he growled in mock displeasure. "But I got t'hand it to ye, boy! Yer taste is impeccable, absolutely impeccable!"

Lurene turned back to him, laughing. "And so is your taste in fathers, Connor."

He grinned at them a little uncertainly. "If you two would like to be alone, I can just go into the house."

"At me age," Dad stated, cocking an eye at them in turn, "mere proximity to a lovely woman like this could put me in m'grave. Yer a fortunate young man."

"You seem to be under some kind of misconception, Dad," Connor said awkwardly, draping an arm round his father's shoulders. "Miss Shanahan is primarily my secretary at University. She's come out here to do some work."

"Work, is it?" Dad chuckled. "I thought ye were more Quinlan than to call lovin' such a thing as 'work!'" He raised his palm to quell an argument. "But have it yore own way, son. Ye shouldn't grieve too long, that's *my* way of thinkin', and a finer lass isn't available this side of the Shannon."

Lurene colored as he squeezed her hand. "How

184

did you get so wise?" she inquired.

"I've lived a long life, me girl," Pat said, turning to leave, "and maybe I haven't learnt everything I should have. But it took only a look at you, when ye came to the front door, t'see the light of love in yore eye." He nodded firmly. "I'll be after leavin' you two by yerselves, then."

She stared at the closed door, then smiled and came into Connor's arms. "He's a wonderful man."

"In his way," Connor said cautiously, kissing her. "But extremely autocratic and nosy when he wishes to be, and always mysterious."

"Mystery beats in the pure heart of Eire, didn't you know that?" she asked, taking her seat. "I'm sure America is a wondrous place, but it's clearly too practical for the likes of your father or me. Too down-to-earth."

"At this moment in my life, my darling secretary," he told her, sitting beside her on the couch and taking her hand in his, "I could use a few entirely pragmatic situations. Obvious ones. I feel like I'm in the middle of a haunting novel by James, except that everyone speaks with this queer, quaint accent!"

"Queer, is it?" She pursed her lips. "And after I came all the way out to Kylemore to tell you that I'd become modern overnight!"

He faced her, intently curious. "What does that mean?"

"It means that we're in the final fifth of the century," she said, looking him in the eye, "and perhaps it's time for me to grow up. Connor, I don't want to wait six months or a year until it's proper to speak of you and me." Suddenly she reached her hands round his head and drew his lips to hers. "I don't want to wait another day."

They clung together, his hands trailing from her throat to her high, heavy breasts, cupping them through her sweater. When he unbuttoned it and felt inside, she let him, and he discovered to his surprise that she wasn't wearing a bra. He spread the sweater wide, cupping one breast gently as his fingers rubbed lightly on the pink-brown nipple. Then he lowered his lips to it, tasting her. Above his head Lurene began to pant. When one hand fumbled at the catches of her skirt, however, she took a deep breath and shoved herself erect on the couch.

"I said I didn't want to wait another day to *talk* about us," she said with her breath catching. Her eyes looked down at his lap, saw the swelling there, and raised quickly to his hungry eyes. "A woman who gets pregnant in Ireland and hasn't a husband to show for it might as well make a sign to carry with her. At that point, my love, it's only a question of how much she charges."

He held her gaze. He reached down again, holding each breast in his hands for only a moment, then kissed her throat above them. Reluctantly, he began to button her sweater himself. "You're a woman who knows her own mind, Lurene Shanahan," he whispered.

"I'm a woman who knows her people, Connor Quinlan. And I don't plan to leave the land I live in. Soon, when we—"

Soft, whimpering sounds. All around them. The effect was, in a way, as sudden and shocking as the screams they had heard before. They seemed to be coming from everywhere and, for a moment, Con-

nor thought it was Troy crying.

"Was th-that a child?" he asked in a low voice.

She shook her head, a swirl of gold. "I don't know," she said helplessly. "But it's gone."

Then the sound came again, from outside the door of the garage-den—just as plaintively sad and heartbroken as the shrieks but somehow more pathetic, more . . . lost.

He hurried to the door, threw it open. Night poured in on them like thick, greasy oil; and, with the blackness, the whimpering once more, but farther away, now, as if leading them. . . .

Leading them toward the woods.

He moved quickly, getting a flashlight from his desk. "It may be the missing child, Lurene. Bobby McCuffy. Sometimes the night plays tricks on your eyes so maybe, somehow, it's carried his voice to us, too." He hesitated, then headed for an unused corner of the old garage. Dad had left a tool cabinet behind and in it, Connor found a shovel. "Perhaps he's caught on something, unable to move and just now regaining consciousness."

"I'll go too." She was on her feet, moving to his side with determination.

"No, sweetheart," he shook his head. "The woods can be dangerous at night. Stay here."

"I insist, Connor," she declared, straightening to her full height. "I'm more familiar with the nature of the woods in Galway than you are. Bobby may need my help as well."

He looked down at her a moment, thinking how everything this lovely young woman did heightened his admiration for her, then shrugged and kissed her forehead above the pert nose. "Have it your way. Let's get going."

187

For a few moments it seemed that the unhappy noises were gone and would not return. Moonlight puddled like a gleaming lake on this side of the wooded area, invitingly; but Connor muttered, "Come into the parlor," and paused.

Then, only yeards from the woods, the sound reached their ears again—eerie, enigmatic, touched by eternal loneliness and regret—definitely from somewhere in the trees. Connor and Lurene exchanged glances. Then, side by side, they took a deep breath and entered the nightmare of absolute night, moving as rapidly as Connor's flashlight beam would permit.

Stillness, Lurene thought, her cheek suddenly brushed by something wet. *It's a new world, a universe of absolute stillness.*

After several more steps forward they were swallowed up by the aged, immense trees looming like Roman columns on every side. In no time there was no trace of moonlight filtering through the leafy canopies far above them and their only guideline was the apparitional beam of the torch in Connor's firm hand. *No time,* he thought, shoving aside branches that seemed adamant about barring their way; *no time is what we have here, or perhaps, all time, the moments and minutes of eternity collected by some giant imp of the primeval forest, so that he can sift through them at his manic leisure, restructuring centuries and reconstructing nations.*

When the whimpering sound came again, each of them jumped, bumping against each other. "To the right," Lurene said in a husky whisper, pointing. "From over there." She shuddered and stayed as near him as she could without either of them tripping. His flashlight beam leaped in the direction she indicated, and together they saw the clear path, the matted grass and weeds underfoot, smelling of old rain and older earthen secrets. Quickly they headed down the path as the sound once more called to them, beckoned to them; *hurry, hurry,* it seemed to say. And, *said the spider to the fly,* Connor thought, his jaw set in grim lines.

"A trap," Lurene said softly, so softly it would never have been heard at the university office. "Could we be walking into some kind of t-trap?"

"Set by whom?" he asked without stopping or slowing his pace. "The primal woods have always been a favorite subject of literary types, you know. The fright they feel is nothing more than their own internal terrors." He laughed humorlessly. "I haven't written my great book yet. So I refuse to be put off by a little darkness."

Lurene didn't answer. But she thought to herself, *I wouldn't call sounds like we're hearing only a "little darkness," or "internal terrors."* She had no idea what they might be, but there was no doubt that they were hearing them—hearing them and being led by them, taken deeper and deeper into the circuitous tangle of midnight woods.

The last sound—gentle, now, almost relieved—came again from the right, summoning Connor and Lurene. The flashlight beam darted toward it and they saw that they were stepping into a clearing, in the center of which rested a quiet, snow-white pool. Moonlight shone again, but hesitantly, as if it feared to be glaring or overly obtrusive at such a time, in such a place.

The sound seemed to have come from a gently rising knoll and, when they approached it, Connor saw that the ground looked freshly turned.

"I think the whimpering came from this mound," he said in a low, nearly conversational tone. He pointed toward it with his shovel. He was striving to sound normal, routine and ordinary, for her benefit. "From *inside* the knoll." He rested the shovel against it and, when he did, his hands were shaking.

Her eyes flickered on his face in fear. "But h-how . . . ?"

"Dammit, I don't know," he answered, close to anger, switching off the flashlight. He shoved it into his jacket pocket, removed the jacket, handed it to Lurene and retrieved the shovel. He looked at her and she saw her fear reflected in his strong, reliable, down-to-earth face. "Sweet Father in Heaven, Lurene, I don't know *anything* that's happening these days!"

He began to dig and she watched his back and shoulder muscles move beneath his shirt. Rivulets of perspiration appeared, as if from nowhere, dark and potent. She noticed that Connor dug carefully, cating aside small shovelsful of dirt like a choosy giant at his meal or like some severe archeologist looking for the traces of a long-dead pharaoh. She entwined her fingers round the top of his jacket in a gesture of helplessness, and waited.

It was still again, totally, but for Connor's gasped inhalations and the slight, susurrant sound made whenever the shovel bit smoothly into the dirt. *The woods,* she thought, shuddering and peering around; *it's holding its breath. Everything in hiding here, unseen and ultimately threatening, is waiting—like so many enchanted loved ones in a Gahan Wilson or Charles Addams cartoon expect-*

ing word from the surgeon but hoping that the news will be bad. . . .

The moon had just come into gloating view like a swollen tennis ball lobbed against the night sky when Connor sprung back, gasping, crying out, "Oh, *no!* Oh, *God,* NO!"

Lurene took three instinctive steps to look down at what he had exposed. "Mother of God," she prayed, her voice half-strangled. Then she sank helplessly to her knees of the opposite side—the farthest side—of the revelation greeting them.

Connor forced himself back to the tattered lip of the grave, holding her hand tight and wondering how he could ever tell Sean McCuffy what had happened to his only son, wondering too why God Himself did not rumble across the heavens in shared despair and, retching, expunge this terrible scene from the face of His raped and sundered planet.

There were a number of small scattered very old bones, enough to have been vital parts of several long-dead human beings. Children, very likely, judging by their size.

But *atop* these slick and shining stumps, similarly scattered, were the more recent remains of young forever-to-be-dead Bobby McCuffy. Now he was a jigsaw puzzle or, perhaps, a toy that had been disassembled with great care. . . .

The head, each small arm, each small hand, each thin leg, and each small foot—the latter still clad in rubber overshoes—had been severed neatly from the torso of the body, and then replaced only a tiny, prudent inch from where they had been joined properly in life. The head still wore its thick glasses. And on Bobby's face, when Connor and

Lurene were irresistibly drawn to see it, was the permanent residue of a dazzled, delighted happy smile....

On Bobby's left cheek, a souvenir for eternity, was the perfect scarlet imprint of an impossibly miniature kiss.

He's gone now, God spare us, and we'll not see him again. He's gone now, and when the black night is falling I'll have no son left in the world.
—John Millington Synge
Riders to the Sea

fourteen

The final, living human being at the site of twelve-year-old Bobby McCuffy's ghastly temporary grave was Bill Fogarty, the aging coroner from Galway. He'd taken a thoughtful stroll away from the knoll once all the preliminary chores were done, and purposely hidden in a clump of bushes till the others left: that pleasant chap Connor Quinlan, who'd returned from America to a terrible thing like this; the lovely blonde university lass, Lurene Shanahan; the horrified policemen; the rickety ambulance and its staring people, taking along not only poor maimed Bobby but the additional unidentified bones from his grave; even Chief Muldowney, who would go the Sean McCuffys with the worst news of their lives. Thankfully, young Connor had volunteered to help Muldowney with his tragic duty. A kinship had been sensed at once between Quinlan and Bill, one that was obviously founded on their unspoken agreement that Francis Muldowney was an ass. It was nice of Connor, Bill Fogarty thought, to accompany the deputy chief; but each of them understood he did it for the McCuffys, not the chief.

There was going to be a burnin' hell of a lot of work to do for awhile, Bill mused now, standing beside the emptied gravesite. He'd required these moments by himself before the examination of the bones began in his laboratory. Not that he was fool enough to expect to find much real peace of mind in a place where such hideous things were happening. But it would be quiet here, he knew; and old Bill hoped that he might get his aging senses going again and somehow feel the nature of evil in these woods. Feel it and, knowing the enemy better, deal with it.

For months now, he and Muldowney had done everything possible to find a clue toward the solving of that animalistic crime which took the lives of two teenagers on the other side of the woods. The autopsy had proved Bill right; Lucy was killed by a toxic substance she had inhaled. Where the boy was concerned, well, it was hard to tell whether the poison or the crushing of virtually every bone took his life. In either case, no one had turned up the slightest evidence of a bearlike monstrosity roaming the woods or, for that matter, any street in County Connaught. It was as if the damnable thing had simply disappeared from the face of the earth.

But that, barring the viability of certain localized myths which tended to turn the coroner's stomach, was patently impossible. With such impressions in mind, he'd attended the burial of Ethelyn Quinlan and was struck by the passing of a customarily healthy woman yet to be thirty-five years old. Afterward, he'd persuaded Muldowney to wire the authorities in the United States for information concerning Connor Quinlan. The possibility that the man had a long psychiatric record and was mad as a hatter—that he had somehow murdered the young people, then his own wife—sounded thrillingly plausible to Muldowney, but never to Bill himself, though the idea to check Connor out was his. He wasn't surprised when an exceptionally complete report came in from an Indianapolis sheriff named Hawkins, showing no record on Connor for anything at all. Indeed, he was well liked by most of those who knew him; the worst thing anyone had to say was that he tended to be a bit of a dreamer.

Now that he had met Quinlan, Bill greatly doubted that Connor was more—or less—than his record indicated. Doubtless Muldowney was thrilled by the prospect of spending several hours with Quinlan, though; heaven only knew what "clues" the chief would try to deduce. The old coroner hoped Muldowney wouldn't slap the cuffs on the poor man if he chanced to cross the road against the traffic.

Where did they turn now? In some respects, this revolting murder was worse than the others. Surely anyone who would dismember a child's body, seemingly wrenching the limbs apart, was too mad, too raving insane, to hide his condition for long?

He made a face; he was glad the first rays of early morning sun were starting to creep around the edges of the clearing. He'd been a fool to stay behind when the murderer might be anywhere.

Consider this woods itself, he told himself cannily, and the countless killers who called it home. He stooped slightly and leaned thoughtfully against the side of the hollowed knoll. It was full of all kinds of life as well as death, yet he could not see a scrap of either. Why, the grass and weeds grew so abundantly here because of the contributory dead who were junked and abandoned in the earth, perpetually fertilizing it with their fur-fringed bodies, multi-eyed heads, and many-legged corpses!

For a lengthy segment of time that passed without witness by the reading of a watch or a clock, the aging coroner simply sat stockstill where he was, reflecting—letting the unconscious antennae of his well-trained doctor's senses reach out, explore, prod, and record the heartbeat and headsounds of the deep woods. Taking the temperature of carnivore, the EEGs of wildness. It seemed to Bill that God must surely have loved the common dead best, for he allowed so many of them. It seemed, as well, on deeper reflection, that the cherishing of life was a luxury of the human animal who could find meaning in *selective* murder, in being *choosy* about the lives he took. Man, the sentimental economist; with a chopping block where his books might have been kept.

A tiny wormlike thing was moving across his foot. He squinted down at it, caught motion from the corner of his eye, saw a spider creep upon his second shoe. Substance, milky and sweet, oozed from the tiny wormlike thing and left microscopic traces which grew slowly, painstakingly. The spider, utterly competitive, began to extrude and entwine a silken rope. Both fascinated and repelled, Bill Fogarty watched them at work and put his money on the spider. *If you sat still long enough,* he reflected, *they came and covered you up. Saved you for a spider's sabbath, a wormy weekend—A surprise for the Little Ones.*

EYES. Unquestionably, from somewhere near the pool, eyes watched the contest between spider and worm. I have become an arena, a sports center, Bill Fogarty realized, shuddering. *But part of me is also the prize.*

Manlike, he used the worm-riding shoe to tramp on the one with the spider, then reversed the procedure. Two tiny specks, one white and one black, fell limply into the grass. *Now what the hell is watching me?*

He stood, unwilling to remain there any longer. It was still too early to die and be covered up. Maybe not terribly early, but too early still. Finally, he had realized what it was he was seeking, what he was trying to remember. Connor and Ethelyn Quinlan and their daughter might be newcomers to Kylemore, one innocent and one newly-dead and one too much a child to harm a worm on her shoe; but the house had been there for years, the nearest structure to the woods, and Patrick Quinlan had been the owner of the house for as long as anyone could remember. It might just pay to exchange a few words with him, and now was an ideal time, since the old man's son would still be with Chief Muldowney.

Bill started back through the woods. It wasn't hard, now that humans had trampled through it in scores, leaving a path as well-marked as a concrete road. He found his car and slipped behind the wheel, yelping in startled fear. He'd left the window open and a bat had squeezed in. For a moment it scared hell out of Bill Fogarty. Then he had the other door open, swinging wide and shooing it away, watching the way it fluttered off, blinking nearsightedly and invoking the cursed name of Dracula. Shaking a little, Bill started the car.

He was slightly surprised to find Pat up and around at such a wee hour of the morning. The elder Quinlan was virtually waiting at the front door, a cup of tea trembling in his veined hands. Bill assumed that Connor must have had Muldowney stop to break the bad news to his father. He was further surprised when old Pat remembered who he was and called him by name.

"The esteemed coroner himself! Come in, William," Pat urged politely. There was a note of heavy sadness in his voice despite the contradictory smile on seeing Fogarty there. He shuffled toward the front room, showing the way. "It's a sad thing, it is, t'see ye for the first time in years at such a toime."

"But typical of my reunions. You knew the McCuffy boy or his family well, Mr. Quinlan?" Bill Fogarty hovered over a slipcovered seat with old, limp flowers staring up at him and eclipsed them with his buttocks. Bill sighed, delighted by how comfortable the chair felt and surprised by how badly he'd needed to get out of the damp. Getting older never failed to provide him with surprises. "I take it you have strong personal feelings about this."

"Didn't know 'em well and I didn't know the lad at all." Pat spoke softly. He appeared agitated now; he needed his morning shave and his eyes were red. The large fingers—index, middle, ring—alternated in nervous rhythm on the sofa where he'd sat. "But it's sorely sad because I have a son meself and can empathize with the pore McCuffys." He broke off drumming to rub his bristly jaw and sigh. "What it says on Swift's grave in Dublin is true, too, of poor Bobby: *'Ubi saeva indignatio ulterius cor lacerare nequit.'*

"My Latin...."

"It means," Pat translated briskly, "'Where savage indignation can no longer tear his heart.' Except in old Johnathan's case the indignation rose from his *own* heart, and not that of some genuine savage."

Bill Fogarty studied the other man from beneath hooded eyes, trying to discover what it was that seemed . . . not *right* . . . about Patrick Aloyius Quinlan. He'd had the impression of something being wrong since he caught a glimpse of Pat at the burial of Ethelyn Quinlan, the daughter-in-law. Now he was sure he was right. But what it might be, Fogarty couldn't quite perceive. Aloud, he asked, "Your son, Connor. I gather you're glad he's returned home?"

Pat beamed. "Delighted beyond description." He smiled warmly, proudly. "For too many years it was always goin' the other way. The Irish leavin' for the States, or Americans comin' to see the old island and then headin' home with the notion they'd seen it all."

"And they hadn't? Even if they stayed a year?"

"Certainly not!" Pat cried. "How can anyone perceive the mystery that is this beloved country unless they learn to *love* her, be *one* with her?" He leaned forward on the couch, index finger lifted in reminder. "D'ye remember, William, what they taught us in childhood? That Eire is no European afterthought, that the spirit of all the clans is buried deep in this precious soil? And do ye recall that *no one has ever known* where the Celtic-speaking people *came from?* That the best anyone knows is that we've been here at *least* since two hundred and fifty years *before Christ?*" He leaned back, content. "Aye, there's the mystery, the rich enigma of it, William Fogarty! And maybe someday, if m'son Connor remains to honor the memory of the long line of Quinlans, *maybe* he'll find just a wee part of the answer to the mystery! Maybe . . . *somehow* . . . he'll *solve* it!"

Bill shifted uncomfortably in his chair. It was only in certain parts of Ulster that speeches like that were made, these days. "In line with the question of mystery, Mr. Quinlan," he began again, "considerin' that two young people were killed on the other side of the woods a few months ago, and the McCuffy boy on this side, last night, what would be *your* concerted viewpoint of what's taking the lives of these youngsters?"

For a moment or two Pat did not reply. He had turned his aging but handsome head in profile, peering beyond the front room, apparently, and down the hallway to the dining room. Bill thought, for a minute, the old man was gazing at the table or chairs; but then he saw that the eyes were raised beyond them, fixed upon the distant window and door which looked out upon the back of the lot, and, beyond it, to the woods itself. Morning sunlight from the high, front room window burned on Pat's cheeks, reddening them as if in embarrassment.

"I want you t'be doin' me a favor, William," he said at last. Looking back at the coroner, his eyes were damp. The sun, Fogarty supposed. "I want you to consider a ridiculous, asinine, completely ludicrous possibility for a few hours. Somethin' ye haven't thought about for decades."

"And what would that be, Mr. Quinlan?"

"I'll say it one time to ye, sir, and no more." Pat took a deep breath. "I want ye to consider that it was perhaps the faeries in the woods who slaughtered those innocent children. I want ye to use your good, well-schooled mentality to consider *all* the better possibilities and then take a long look at the one I just mentioned t'ye." Now his face truly colored. "And if ye ever tell a soul that I suggested this, William Fogarty, I'll damn you as a liar in every pub in County Connaught!"

For some reason the idea did not come as quite such a lightning bolt to the coroner as Pat expected. He took it in quietly, closed his eyes, opened them and blinked. The corners of his mouth did not turn up. "I shall, Mr. Quinlan, I shall consider that possibility." He stood, his legs arthritic again, protesting the sudden motion. "But if it proves to be at the heart of the enigma, sir, then our deputy police chief might just as well be in the hole where we found Bobby McCuffy. And me with him."

Leaving the Quinlan house, backing out of the driveway, coroner Bill Fogarty paused when he was in view of the woods and looked the long distance to it with something like deadening panic in his breast. He wanted badly to bring the killers of these nice young kids to justice and he knew as surely as he sat there, that no one—at least, no one *human*—would ever arrest, charge, and convict the maybe-wee-people of the Quinlan woods.

He threw the old car creakingly into gear, it lurched forward, and he slowly drove back toward Galway, almost annoyed because it was bound to be a beautiful June day. Instead of being able to enjoy it, he had to torture his wits considering the facts that his investigation had disclosed.

For one, the clear fact that he'd last seen Patrick A. Quinlan ten years ago and not a minute later than that, yet the old man hadn't changed an iota. He hadn't aged so much as an hour. Bill would stake everything he'd ever learned in science on that fact: *Pat Quinlan was the same age he'd been ten years ago.*

That, of course, was ridiculous. But a good coroner didn't question it when he ran across cancer cells in the body of an infant. He simply accepted the fact, reported it, and wondered later about the ways of nature.

And what did that old man mean by boasting that, if his son Connor stayed with him on Connemara, he might well solve the mystery of where the Irish people came from? What did that have to do with anything anyway? And from whom could a bluff, ordinary chap like Connor Quinlan acquire a solution of such magnitude? Clearly, old Pat was telling him something—something veiled and, Fogarty suspected, terribly important.

Worst of all, of course, Bill thought as he headed along early-morning St. Vincent Avenue and paused to permit three dappled cows to amble across his path, there was the more immediate mystery of who or what had done such dreadful things to Bobby McCuffy.

Because Bill hadn't mentioned it yet to a single soul, including Chief Muldowney, but the terrible maiming wasn't *all* somebody had done to the poor child.

In addition to being torn apart, little Bobby McCuffy had, as well, been blinded, apparently before he was killed.

Now what in the name of all that was holy *was* it, Fogarty interrogated himself, that Bobby wasn't supposed to have seen?

But winter lingering chills the lap of May.
—Oliver Goldsmith

fifteen

"I'm not asking you, Troy. I am telling you. Do you hear me? Do not go into the woods to play. Not any time, not any more. Not, at least, until I specifically tell you that you may."

Reasonably: "Well, how long will that be?"

"I have no idea. I have no way of knowing when they'll capture the madman who killed Bobby." He paused, standing before her bed, feeling huge and grossly male and hating every word he had to say to the pale, blonde child. "Troy, it may be forever."

"Forever?" She was crushed, heartbroken. More, she was confounded and incredulous. It had never occurred to her that such a diabolical malice existed in the world. You cannot take oxygen away without getting a final protest, nor food and drink. The woods was all these to Troy.

In every human life—age and status have nothing to do with it—there are punishments which cannot be accepted without the suffering of dreadful damage. Most of the harm done adults by other adults stems largely from forgetting that this is true. Fortunately, few people in what passes for a civilized world are ever truly confronted with the dilemma Connor Quinlan handed his daughter; therefore, few of us know just what it is that is, for each of us, utterly indispensable. We may say that it is a mate or child, position perhaps, or income. And when the essential thing is finally taken from us, internal bones begin to break. Precious parts crumble, inside; spirit; the imagination creating personal preference; that nucleus of our individuality which, if it is at last demolished, leaves us mindless zombies or (worse) slaves.

Troy stared up at her beloved Dads without rising from her bed and knew that she hated him most. A deep, wise part of her that would someday be a woman understood that he was doing this fiendish thing for Her Own Good, understood too that people who are not really cruel tend to force such restrictions because there has been inadequate communication. Such fascists of the soul as Connor became have not heard, or believed, the truth of fundamental personal need, simply because they do not share *this* need with us. Because, in short, they can get along without a particular person, without steak, or tobacco, or achievement, or sex, or ice cream, or public acceptance, or booze, or love—or, in Troy's case, her precious woods— they can never feel the identical pain of loss.

Thus do unexpressed words and blunted emotions make monsters of us all. "Then I'll go anyway," Troy said quietly, without a *soupçon* of intended defiance.

Connor had expected her to say that. "If you do, I will take you to a psychiatrist in Dublin who can find out why you stubbornly continue to believe in things that aren't there. And if I have to, Troy, I'll leave you there."

He had never so much wanted to hold her in his arms and tell her everything was fine, or would be; but it wasn't and he didn't know if it ever would be again. So he stood there like a big goddam bully staring at her until he knew that she was beaten, wheeled, ran down the hallway and and down the stairs, found the bottle he'd bought for the occasion in Galway, and got roaring drunk for only the third time in his life.

And a week later, in June—more than two weeks since the dark night when the discarded rubble of human children was unearthed in his family woods—Connor startled himself by asking Lurene Shanahan to marry him.

He was even more surprised when she held his cheeks gently between the palms of her hands and said simply, "I will." Later he would count up the words spoken between them: "Will you marry me?" accounted for four; "I will" totalled two. Six words and the course of his life was altered forever.

It might have been by unspoken agreement that neither he nor Lurene mentioned the propriety of what they were doing. Here in Ireland, unquestionably, Ethelyn had not been anywhere near long enough in her grave for her widower's remarriage. Both he and Lurene knew that she would bear the brunt of any attack that was made, although Connor regarded it as a possibility that he would not be asked to lecture at University again. Yet instead of becoming rebellious or defiant, each of them merely ignored the impact that their news would have on others and began making happy plans.

The wedding would take place in July. It would occur in Dad Quinlan's home, because Connor sensed it was time to make a full commitment, to his father and to Connemara. Afterward, they would take both Dad and little Troy on kind of a family honeymoon jaunt to Croagh Patrick, in nearby County Mayo. They knew how much Dad yearned to go there one more time, to climb the ancient mountain along with fifty thousand other devout Irish Catholics, and honor St. Patrick. In making the climb, Connor and Lurene felt, the four of them would be symbolizing a new family unity, and the family would include Ireland itself.

At first, when Connor told Pat Quinlan their intentions, the old man seemed both shocked and apprehensive. Even fearful, if Connor wasn't being ridiculous. But a few hours later, when Dad came downstairs again after thinking it through, he gave Troy a warm hug and wrung his son's hand as if it was a pump handle. The two men had a strong drink of Irish whisky together and Dad said, with a huge wink at his granddaughter, "This remarriage might just prove to be the salvation of us all!"

Alone in his garage-den, however, Connor behaved like most men. He had painful second thoughts; he wondered if he might be making the mistake of his life. Part of it was that while he honestly believed he loved Lurene Shanahan, he could not be sure that he did. There were sound reasons for feeling that way. Very few of the emotions he'd felt for Ethelyn did he also feel for Lurene. Despite his first wife's clever way with words and the outward independence she'd espoused, Ethelyn had required a steady, protective husband—one who would defend her, not only against all others but against herself, against her own deeply selfish moods. Most of his love had, indeed, sprung from the way Connor needed Ethelyn to defend, almost another child. It was the reason he'd never dared write a book; it was the reason he'd come to County Connaught at all, since that was the only way he could protect Ethelyn from economic insecurity and its accompanying terrors.

But Lurene, in Connor's view, was a woman who required very little protection or, for that matter, help of any kind. Nearly thirty, she'd been on her own since she was nineteen and made a good living at University. A mark of her strength was the incredible fact that she remained a virgin; considering her beauty, Connor would have believed her frigid except for the way she had to fight herself and him every time they were locked in an embrace. While Lurene did not have the brittle, wisecracking manner of modern American women in the bigger cities, she always managed to go her own way and, he was willing to wager, always would.

By the time the evening was over he knew that he did, indeed, love the Irish lass but that it was the best kind of second love: one that arose with fresh feelings and reactions, one that made him feel young and new again too. And he had come to accept his love for her when he realized Lurene had a knack only a few true women of the world had ever possessed, a gift for wanting and needing a man—for doing everything in bed or around the house that he could conceivably desire—but not from any humbling, guilt-generating sense of tradition or duty. She would care for him, he knew, because she *wanted* to, because she *preferred* it to what she had now. In that way it was not a giving, at all, but a sharing—no sacrifice (they both detested the very concept of sacrifice) but a mutual outpouring of desire that defied mathematics and made two people more than that.

Troy, on the other hand, remained a disconcerting problem. Connor had felt the girl would surely adjust, after weeks, to staying out of the woods. God knew there was a large enough front and back yard for her to play in. He'd made it clear to her that friends from school were welcome anytime. Surely, he thought, Troy no long resented being kept from that damnable woods.

But her attitude had unmistakably changed towards him, especially when she learned that Lurene Shanahan was to be her "second mama." Knowing how hard it would be for Troy, Lurene had come to the house many times and paid especial attention to the child. She learned Troy's favorite desserts and snacks and made them for her. She brought gifts from the best stores in Galway. She tried hugging Troy and telling her how pretty she was, and how happy they would all be together.

And yet Troy remained uncommunicative around Lurene and coldly polite to Connor, and that baffled and concerned him. He explained that Lurene would not *replace* Ethelyn, that no one believed for a minute that anybody could fill her shoes. He even tried to explain that just as Troy had chosen her own imaginary playmates, Lurene was choosing her for a daughter.

They might as well have saved their breath. There wasn't one tear shed, nor one tantrum thrown. Troy's reaction was, Connor decided, coldly accepting.

It was almost as if Troy had known it would happen all along.

Alone in her bedroom, Troy was a very different person. She resented the fact that she had finally cried before Dads over the question of going to the woods—bawled her eyes out, like a big crybaby. That would never happen again. Lying on her bed, drying her eyes after an hour of privately renewed sobbing, Troy made her pledge solemnly, to herself: No one would *ever* see her lose control again. If they hurt her like that, all right; just at this moment she could do nothing about it.

But it was such a disappointment. For a while there, after Mommy died, she'd had both Dads and her friends, and Gran-da too. She had been laboriously working out an arrangement, a way to love and enjoy them all—both the real people and those dear friends whom the adults termed "imaginary." Grudgingly, because they had to, her friends from the woods had begun learning how to share Troy with human beings and life had been getting swell again when that old Bobby McCuffy came along and ruined it all. It was no wonder the Dana O'Shea did what they did. The brat had asked for it. She was glad they'd torn him up.

Now, though, she was cut off from all her pleasures and Troy leaned on her doubled-over pillow and swore to the future that *someday* she'd show them if they hurt her, *someday* she'd get even—if that fine day would ever come. *Someday*.

"What about *now*, Troy?"

Looking up with surprise, Troy saw a miraculous procession of half-inch-high humanoid creatures walking across the headboard of her bed. The headboard was only an inch or so thick and the parade looked almost like a tightwire act. The little men seemed so severe and serious yet so comical that Troy giggled out loud. Her friends had come to play with her!

Portunes, she remembered the word from what Kuan told her, months ago. These tiny fellows were *portunes.*

The one in the lead stopped and gave her a merry wave. "Hello! I'm Ruck," he announced with a miniature, beaming grin. "I'm from Great Britain."

She was surprised. "You aren't Irish, like the others?"

"No, Troy. We're *all* on your side now, all the little people everywhere. All over your mortal world, in any case."

She rolled over on her belly and leaned on her elbows to stare at Ruck and the others. "But I thought you couldn't come inside the house," she said slowly. "Except, like Ducie, when you're sort of *asked* in."

"Your concerns have asked us in, Troy Quinlan." He had a voice like an aristocratic mouse blessed with the gift of language.

But it was she who was blessed. She rolled on the bed in delight. "How can I be so lucky, Ruck?" she asked with joy. "Why do I have so many wondrous friends?"

He considered it a moment, then bobbed his head. "It's time you knew the answer to that." He put his fists on his hips. "Because you're *not really* Troy Quinlan at all!"

"I'm not?" The idea confounded her, but pleasantly. Every child likes magic, and disguises. It was how she'd gotten into this to begin with—along with loneliness.

"Actually, child, you are the Queen of the Faeries reborn in human form—Queen Mab!" He paused. "At least, you're *going* to be." Ruck revealed a mouthful of sparkling teeth in such quantity and size that they stretched his cheeks like those of a furry animal. He scratched the tip of one pink, pointed ear. "It's like humans in Tibet, old girl. The priests know the next lama is out there somewhere, but they must go and fetch him, then train him to lead them. Why, when we get through training *you,* there'll be no more Troy at all! Only eternal Mab, our leader returned to us!"

Troy considered that one a moment, vaguely dissatisfied but unable to express it. "How can you *portunes* help me with my problems?"

Ruck grinned. "As you noticed, love, we read minds. Right now you're worried about that human with the yellow hair, Lurene Shanahan. The first thing to do is quite obvious, I think."

"What's that, Ruck?" she asked innocently.

"Why, get rid of her!" The other *portunes* saw his impish grin and burst into a laughter that sounded a little demonic. Several of them did somersaults or cartwheels on the headboard and one tumbled over the side, catching Troy's pillowcase and hanging on for dear life. She let him hop up on a finger, then returned him to the headboard. Ruck waited till he had her full attention. "We'll just *kill* her for you!"

"No." Shakily, Troy sat on the edge of the bed and shook her head firmly. "Honestly, is that *all* you faeries can think of? I don't want anyone else

213

murdered!"

The whole parade of *portunes* looked stunned, puzzled. "Whyever not, for the love of Shob?" demanded Ruck.

"Because death is ugly as sin."

"No, it's not either," the tiny man argued defensively. He looked to his nearest fellow and the other imp shook his head in agreement. "There, see? I'll grant you there's a bloody connection between death and sin, but both of them are entirely natural, child." He inclined his head, conspiratorially, and beamed. "Death is even rather interesting, if you get to watch it happen!"

"Well, I don't *want* to watch it happen!" Troy snapped. "And if I'm truly to be Queen, you gotta do what I say."

The *portune* lieutenant nudged Ruck with a wise expression. "I say, she has something there, old man," he cautioned.

"Quite so!" Ruck cried, making a low bow. "All hail the Queen!"

The string of *portunes* doffed caps containing miniature feathers and bowed to Troy in unison. "Long live the Queen!" they shouted in piercing little voices.

"Now that *that's* over," Ruck said with a sigh, "there are . . . *other* ways."

Troy crossed her legs and listened with her most regal demeanor. "For example, Mr. Ruck?"

He perched on the headboard, a teacher tutoring a royal child. "Well, your majesty, Pan might play his music so that Shanahan never stops dancing. *That's* enjoyable to see. The weight fairly flows from her legs after awhile." He snickered.

"No," Troy replied, shaking her blonde head.

"I have it! A spiral of dust, turning to faery wind and blowing her right into the pool! Old Kelpie, our Scot water demon, would be johnny-on-the-spot. Destroy all the liver and entrails!" Ruck rubbed his hands together with glee.

"I've told you that I don't want her killed," Troy reminded him, but grinned despite herself.

"Bad show, that," Ruck commented wistfully. "She might've been elf-shot with poisoned arrows, a Welsh trick of the 8th Century." Abruptly his marble eyes glittered. "Aha! Let's sic the Poulaphuca on Shanahan!"

Troy gaped in wonder. "What in the world is that?"

"A black dog, more than five foot high at the shoulders and with fangs five inches long." Ruck giggled in anticipation. Then he saw her expression and scrambled to his tiny feet. "I know, m'lady. No murder or eating." He paused reflectively. "But there's something you must realize."

"I mean it, Ruck," she warned him. "Nothing fatal."

Something adamant in her tone of voice must have rubbed little Ruck the wrong way because, in a trice, there was a very different expression on his face, something more mature, definitely less childish. Indeed, Troy edged away from him, realizing with shock that Ruck looked, at that moment, older than time itself. At least, she thought, the age of death. "It isn't only what you prefer, young lady. It is also what's right and good for *all* of us, if the job we do on earth is to be done properly." Then he clapped his small hands and the laughing Ruck was back, bounding boyishly on one foot. "I know! I know what will please everybody! Yes, m'lady, *I know what we're going to do!"*

"What?" she asked anxiously, still shrinking away from him. "What a-are you going to do?"

"I'll offer you a clue, m'lady," Ruck said as he began to fade out of sight. "We're going to do *two* feats of magic for Lurene Shanahan. First something mild the way *you* prefer it—and then what *must* be done in this house. Must, not only to cope with the Shanahan human but with . . . *other forces* working here. And I guarantee you, Mab my Queen, one or the other will send all our enemies packing for good. I double-guarantee it!"

Before Troy could reply, Ruck and his entire procession of *portunes* had vanished.

Something glittered on the headboard of the bed and Troy put out a trembling hand to pick it up.

It was a coin of pure, shining gold.

*She (Queen Mab) is the faeries' midwife, and
    she comes
In shape no bigger than an agate-stone
On the fore-finger of an alderman.
Drawn with a team of little atomies
Athwart men's noses as they lie asleep.*
        —Shakespeare, Romeo and Juliet

sixteen

They intended it to be a small wedding with just the families and a handful of friends in attendance. From the standpoint of Connor himself, there wasn't much reason to get all excited about it nor to spend a great deal of time planning it. "I doubt that the affair will be televised," he told Lurene one evening, kissing her forehead and wondering if he could wait. "And the people there will be our loved ones so we needn't get competitive about it." But she hadn't heard him and her skin tasted salty with perspiration. It dawned on him with some concern that Lurene was perspiring a lot lately, and he wondered if the excitement of the wedding was having an adverse effect on her.

By certain expansive and expensive standards, after all, the ceremony would be simple, brief; largely a matter of formality. As he went around feeling dreadfully neglected, Connor was inclined to think considerably more about their wedding night and, secondarily, the family honeymoon at Croagh Patrick. Even Dad was looking forward to it.

But for any woman of the western world, particularly an Irish colleen who was getting wed for the first and final time in her life, there was nothing more important than the ceremony. Everything had to be perfect, from persuading Father O'Brien to marry them at the house instead of a church to selecting trinkets for the bridesmaids.

These days, when he saw Lurene, she was likely to demand a handful of money for invitations and then breathlessly spin away to make another interminable telephone call. He knew that her father was dead and couldn't give the bride away; but this whole proposition seemed to be getting out of hand. Every time they had a few moments alone, in his university office or at the house in Kylemore, Lurene clutched a list of some kind tightly in her hand and was inclined to check things off at precisely the time he was trying to talk to her. About *important* things. Why, he'd never dreamed Lurene had such a preoccupied side or that she would be expending such energy on their wedding plans that he'd have to fear for her health! She seemed happy, yes, but flushed, frenetic; being alone with her ten minutes tended to give him nerves, or a headache.

Several days before the big event, Lurene had eaten dinner with them, tried once more to make friends with Troy, and then joined Connor in his garage-den. They sat together on the couch and silence settled over them like dust. Lurene looked at him with concern and touched his hand. "Are you well, Con?"

"Oh, you *do* know I'm alive after all," he said acidly, winding his watch. "That's something."

Her lips opened in surprise. "What are y'saying

then?"

He shrugged. "What would it matter? If I tried to explain, you'd just find another list in your purse and start sweating over it."

Lurene smiled with realization. "Ah, I get it! You're feelin' neglected!"

"Well, why wouldn't I?" he demanded, turning to her with asperity. A vein throbbed in one temple. "I'm nothing more than an afterthought around here, a damned *postscript* to your precious ceremony!"

"You're nothing of the sort, Connor Quinlan," she said stoutly, giving him a chaste hug. "It's your wedding as much as it is mine."

For a moment he studied her, sensing hope. "Do you mean it? If so, I do have some ideas I'd like to express. Take the reception after the wedding, for example." Interest turned his face earnest as he began to speak. "It seems to me that there will be people there who like to drink, who even *expect* to drink! Since the reception will be in another part of the house, I don't really believe there's anything ... wrong ... with ..."

His speech slowed to a halt. Lurene, nodding all the while, was dipping a hand into her purse. It produced several sheets of paper, then dipped again.

"... With having an orgy right in front of Father O'Brien," he said acidly, testing to see if she were listening. "It might be contagious. Dad can hump that old lady Annie who cleans for him, and your mother can take on. ..."

He stopped talking. Lurene had located her pen and was clicking it against her front teeth. She made a notation and said, without looking up at

219

him, "Go ahead, darlin', it sounds good to me."

Connor reached out to smash his fist on his desktop. "Damn!" he exploded as papers raised and fluttered like startled birds. "Damn!"

She put back her head and laughed gaily, virtually dissolved in laughter. She was so amused she lifted one hand and struck her thigh with it as the giggles came.

Finally he saw the joke. "You were listening after all," he said in a whisper. "You were teasing me!"

She threw her arms around him and kissed his nose. "I had to," she confessed. "You're becoming such an old bear."

He shook his black head angrily, turned away from her. "It just isn't amusing," he grumbled, "it isn't funny at *all!* A man likes to feel that he's the central thing in a woman's life, that he's more important than anything."

She turned his chin so that he could face her and this time kissed his lips. "You poor Yankee fool," she whispered, reaching down to touch him, "a weddin' like ours is to tell the world that you *are* at the center, to let everyone know how fortunate I am to have won a man like you."

He was only slightly mollified and didn't reply. Lurene took his hands, unprotestingly, in hers and urged his fingers to reach beneath her sweater. His recovery was swift. He found a bra, this time, but groped gently beneath it until he could cup her heavy breasts in his eager hands. His thumbs massaged her unseen nipples and he saw her head tip back in apparent ecstasy, the lips parted.

She held her hands over his, beneath the sweater, so that he could not get away and said quite simply: "Mummy knows what her little boy needs to pacify him. Mummy knows." And again she laughed, shaking with amusement now.

But after he swore his anger and before he could tear his hands away, she leaned the weight of her yielding body on him, tugged down his zipper, and took his treasonous hardness in her fingers. It felt hot, enormous, to each of them. She held the tip against her own clothed lower body with fierce wanting.

"I need you so damn badly," he whispered, burrowing his face in her neck, happily lost in an ocean of silken blonde hair. "So much."

"Me, too," she said softly. "Soon, me love—soon. . . ."

Troy was leaving her bedroom to go downstairs and watch TV—which her grandfather often called Teilifís, pronouncing it "tellafeesh"—when the big, black shadow appeared before her and took her arm.

"Gran-da!" she exclaimed, catching her breath and smiling. "I didn't hear you."

He took her hand in his large one and held on. "I think it's time we were after havin' a little conversation, lass."

The light in the hallway here, a few yards from the stairs leading to the attic, was burning low and his face was bathed in shadow. "What about?" she inquired.

"Important things, Troy," he replied, turning and pulling her along. "*Terrible* important things."

Her heart caught in her thin chest. "Are we going to your attic?"

Gran-da didn't answer. Instead, he opened the

door to his bedroom and gave her a light whack on the bottom to urge her inside. Troy hadn't been here, either, not because she wasn't allowed in Gran-da's room but because she wasn't at all curious about him. He was a nice, funny, crinkly person to have around but he had never been especially important to her. Certainly he'd been no threat to her friendships, the way Dads had proved to be.

Now he indicated an uncomfortable-looking straight-backed chair with a fading antimacassar and lean pillow and, confused by his new hardness of manner, she quickly took her seat. Rather demurely, she folded her hands in her lap and waited, expressionless.

"This begins," the grandfather said from a chair of his own, "as a sort of history lesson, lass. Ye needn't take notes but I warn ye: there'll be a test afterwards."

Troy swallowed hard. What had she done to make him angry?

"Our country of Ireland is a marvelous place to be," he said, his voice dry and purposive, "from the beauty of Shannon, the longest river in Eire, to Lough Ree. Here in Connemara, the mountains seem made of blue stone and bog streams flow in every color from translucent browns to pale tans. What ye want, ye can find here. For the gamblin' sort, there're over nine hundred bettin' shops to place a wager with Turf Accountants, legal and proper-like. Because we're honest folk; we pay cash when we settle a deal. And if ye like sport, why, ninety thousand people fill Croke Park at Dublin for All-Ireland football and hurling."

Troy raised her hand, using the child's right to

interrupt. "What's hurling?"

He paused. "There are fifteen men to a side who play on a pitch—a field—one hundred yards long and one hundred and eighty yards wide. The lads bang away at a leather ball with bats called hurleys." He gave her a wise, hard look. "And only *three* substitutions are permitted, exclusively t'haul away the injured. Now, where was I? We Irish provide leadership for the world and not alone in authorin'; for yore so-called 'American' presidents include Chester Alan Arthur, Andrew Jackson, John Fitzgerald Kennedy, and Ronald Reagan. Ireland is so pretty she's smog-free and the temperature don't fall below forty. Ye can hear excitin' tales of gore and rich stories of our fabled past from wild West Cork to clever Killarney and the Ring of Kerry. But sometimes, me lass, I think it may be the way James Joyce himself had it: 'O Ireland my first and only love, Where Christ and Caesar are hand in glove!' Peace and goodness on one hand, evil and ugliness on the other." Suddenly he leaned forward in his chair to touch her hand. "Which is it with ye, girl: Christ and beauty, or Caesar and the corruption of the grave?"

"I d-don't understand, Gran-da," Troy cried, pulling away from his touch.

He leaned back, thoughtfully, and pursed his lips. "I'm sure now, Troy Quinlan, that all them grand, gory stories I mentioned ye've been hearin' in yore woods. The game's up, colleen. I know now your playmates aren't creatures of the imagination. I know for a fact they are *real*."

She didn't answer him for a minute. It was close in the old man's bedroom, somehow sweltering. Here, Troy felt echoes of Indiana's summer heat.

223

She inserted an index finger at the neck of her pullover and swallowed. Behind Gran-da the one window in the room was tightly shut. Through it, at a distance, she could see the tops of trees swaying in the woods. "I never told anybody they were imaginary."

"What? Speak up, child!"

She looked him in the eye. "Gran-da, I always *said* they were real. It was all you adults who thought I was makin' things up."

"Then ye must look in yore own heart for what those friends of yours have done, Troy." He cleared his throat. "The redhaired woman, Ducie, was a banshee. A creature who came to steal your very own mother's life away. You saw her first, washin' something in the water, didn't you?"

"Yes, but how did you know?"

"I'm Irish, darlin'," he told her reasonably. "It's what we Irish have always believed in. Creatures like banshees—and others, some far worse. D'ye realize Ducie *murdered* Ethelyn Quinlan?"

This was nothing new to Troy. She had wept over it, considered it frequently over the months. She wished Ducie hadn't done it, but that was what banshees did; she had done it, and now it was finished. "Yes, I know that, Gran-da," she answered the old man, sounding completely cold and uncaring. "But I didn't *ask* her to do it."

Patrick Quinlan drew in a sharp breath, thinking that this girl-child was more like the Quinlans he'd known—more like himself—than his own son. He studied her keenly. "There's more'n one way t'ask spirits to do things, and ye should know that. The strength of an idea is absolute. Havin' the idea of dislike or hatred toward your parents was like

224

invitin' the faery kingdom to have power again. I'm thinkin' the responsibility of that lies with you."

"One thing is stronger than an idea though, Ducie said." Troy remembered. "Belief is."

"And I fear ye believed your mother was between you and your father. Ye wanted him all to yourself." The lovely image of Lurene Shanahan was in his mind. Perhaps he could never save her from the forces of his own attic but he could try to save her from this small female child. "Then there was your real, human friend, Bobby McCuffy."

Her attitude was abruptly airy, detached. "Well, I didn't have anything t'do with what happened to that little brat, either. Not that I care about the damn ole sneak." She added, firmly and defiantly, "I warned him, you know!"

Despite himself, Pat was shocked. "Ye must break with them once and for good, Troy," he said, trying to keep the whining plea out of his deep voice. "Honestly, lass, ye must. They could hurt you. Child, they could destroy all of us!"

"No," she disagreed, getting up from the chair and moving lazily to the door. She hesitated, her brows arched. "Not *us*, Gran-da. Not *all* of us."

Before he could stop her, she was off down the corridor and dashing down the steps. In a moment the front door slammed.

He got unsteadily to his feet, crossed the room, and squinted into a mirror. It was all so unnatural. It did not surprise him that, while he looked tired, he continued to give an impression of late youth. It was the face of a man in his fifties, but one with a sallow, unhealthy complexion. Ah, Lord, he realized it would not be long until he was again powerless to stop the relentless Quinlan forces. Not long at all. And not that he would; for every man, so long as he likes the flavor of life at all, grasps the sustaining straws advanced to him. *Bitter is the wind tonight,* he recited softly to himself, remembering the anonymous Irish message; *It tosses the ocean's white hair....*

Downstairs, feeling he had done all he could, the old man poured himself some ever-ready hot tea and sank down over the cup at his kitchen table. Annie would be along soon to fix supper. He wondered idly how it was that Annie, whom he could still picture as a much younger woman, never mentioned his own protracted youth. What could she possibly think about him when she was alone on her farm, counting her widow's beads and muttering outdated prayers to her Lord? What explanation for Pat A. Quinlan had formed in her crone's mentality; or was she, unlike him, so old and beyond common help that she no longer bothered to explain anything?

Outside—at times, when he looked, he could catch glimpses of her pale yellow hair blowing in the early-summer breeze—Troy was jumping rope. She was good at it, he knew. He'd seen her before, cat-nimble as she twirled the cord, swinging it easily beneath her bounding feet. It was Lurene whom Troy meant, Pat thought sadly, when she alluded to "not *all* of us"; that was clear. He had no idea why she'd turned against her Dads but she intended to mar his fresh happiness, wreck his new life. She meant to do something, through the horrid cooperation of her damned playmates, to that pretty, sweet Lurene Shanahan. And he was helpless to stop her.

Troy's lilting voice carried to the old man as she began to chant:

"'*Are you a witch,
Are you a faery?
Or are you the wife
Of Mi-cha-el Cleary?*'"

He blanched as she sang it again. Over and over, droningly, perhaps even pointedly.

After the second verse, Gran-da turned away to put his hands over his ears. It was an old nursery rhyme from his childhood and he hadn't heard it since then. Troy had been here only a short time, still, despite the things that had occurred, she could never have heard the rhyme. Never.

But of course, she *had* learned it. From her companions in the woods.

Pat put the tea cup down because it was starting to slosh over the edges, staining the fine cuffs of the smoking jacket Connor and poor dead Ethelyn had presented him.

Ah God, don't let it be that Troy knows this story, he prayed. He'd remembered the story, a true one, behind the seemingly innocuous jumping-rhyme, recalled that it dealt with a variation of one of the most frightening myths of all: the story of the diabolical creature called a changeling.

Know you what it is to be child? . . . It is to have a spirit yet streaming from the waters of baptism; it is to believe in love, to believe in loveliness, to believe in belief; it is to be so little that the elves can reach to whisper in your ear; it is to turn pumpkins into coaches, and mice into horses, lowness into loftiness,

and nothing into everything, for each child has its fairy godmother in its soul.
—Shelley, by Francis Thompson

seventeen

On the morning of the wedding, Dad surprised Connor by asking him to join him for a drink at his favorite pub. A toast to the bridegroom, a man-to-man thing, Connor imagined, grinning affably and agreeing to go. Perhaps Dad had lost sight of the fact he'd been married before. While Connor certainly hoped to renovate and refurbish the mysteries of marital union, they weren't exactly new to him. But what harm could a wee one with his father do?

They drove west, toward rugged seacoast, and he found the area at once wildly beautiful and shockingly desolate. There were random farms that sprung before the eyes like fairy villages but so distant from others that it was hard to believe their occupants traveled only by bicycle or horse-drawn cart.

There was a sharp breeze this morning that bit at the neck and made Connor roll the Mercedes' window up. Dad assured him, with the rapport some old men had for the weather, that a rare heavy rainfall was coming. Already the lakes they passed were stirring restlessly, changing colors as they roiled; it would have been easy to believe it was autumn instead of early June. It was in this region that settlers were chased from the fertile heartland of Ireland in the 17th and 18th centuries, obliged to roll away huge boulders in order to create the struggling fields in which they planted potatoes and prayers.

Though the road signs here were largely printed in Gaelic, Dad knew the way well and unerringly led them to their destination. Connor parked in a lot that seemed to have had the stones removed only yesterday and followed Pat Quinlan into Kelly's Pub.

There were more people than Connor expected at ten-twenty in the morning. A number of the patrons were old fellows like Dad who sat around tables with such stoic seriousness on their faces they might have been attending a board meeting. More, however, were plain-talking big men from the Aran Islands, wearing hand-woven white sweaters and the moccasin-style, homemade shoes for which they were known. They crouched over the long bar as if they were defending it, muttering in monosyllables. One or two tourists had also discovered the pub and, dressed in sports jackets and brightly-colored shirts or blouses, stood out like sore thumbs.

Dad squeezed between two islanders and plunked a banknote down on the bar. A tall, leather-faced man of fifty approached, giving the old man a silent smile. "Two pints," Dad ordered, lifting his index and middle fingers. "Me son and meself have a slight thirst." A pair of immense mugs appeared as if from nowhere.

Connor followed his father to a table, took his

seat in a hard wooden chair, and looked around. Kelly's Pub was the size of a small neighborhood bar in middle-western American but better lit, less guilty of that distinctive cloak-and-dagger clandestine-meeting ambience with which Connor was familiar. There was little advertising posted around and no telephone or game machines. The place had a family feeling; at the back, adjacent to an area of larger tables ready for evening meals, a father and his small fair-haired son played darts. To Connor's delight, he spied a great black shillalegh mounted ominously on the wall above the bar. Anybody daring to start a brawl would surely have Mr. Kelly himself to deal with.

The stout proved to be strong, warm, and frothy on his lips and quickly took away the lakeland chill. "I'm glad you brought me here, Dad," he said softly.

"I'm glad too," Pat said simply and placed his big hand over Connor's. "It's me hope that the events of the day will set ye on a new course, Con. That ye'll be done with the troubles of late."

"I'm sure I will be. Lurene makes me very happy, Dad." He shrugged. "Besides, none of what's happened is your fault. Somehow I've seen you take everything on your own shoulders. But it isn't your doing."

The old man's dark eyes shifted slightly away from his son. "Not all of it, leastways," he said with a sigh. He removed his hand and took his mug of stout to his lips for a hearty draught. "Not all of it."

Connor laughed, a trifle awkwardly. "Now, what does that mean?"

Pat looked away, stared out the window at

thunderclouds beginning to take shape in the low skies. "Soon enough, son, ye'll find out precisely what it means. Very soon now." He looked back at Connor and it was one of those remarkable mood changes of the man, the expression now a challenging one. "Tell me, Con. D'ye know the story of the changeling?"

"I believe I do," Connor said slowly, nodding. "You explained it to me years ago. As I recall, the faeries sometimes have need of a genuine human child. Not for anything hideous like sacrifice, I guess, but for reasons we mortals cannot perceive. At these times of need, if they see a human infant left alone even for a moment, they take it."

Dad also nodded, "And bein' principled people in their strange way, they don't steal it but make a swap. A change. In the place of the human infant, the wee folk leave a baby of their own imaginative concoction. Now, at a glance, it may appear fine and normal. But even so, the creature is unreal. At best, Connor, it is bound t'have some kind of be-zarr eccentricities. Attributes which mark it as . . . *unhuman*."

Connor twisted uncomfortably and put his stout back on the table. "You have a point to all this, don't you, Dad? What is it you're trying to say?"

"I'm sayin', flat-out, that you and Lurene must never have a child of your own." The old man swallowed hard. "I—have sound reason t'believe it will be . . . *exchanged*."

"Dad, that's ridiculous!"

Pat bristled. "It is, is it? Then explain to me what happened to your first wife, Ethelyn? Go on, tell me what took her life! Ye heard the hideous screams yourself, Connor lad—ye cannot have forgot them.

232

It was a *banshee* who murdered the poor girl, nothing less. A banshee!"

"I can't believe you're saying this to me in all seriousness," Connor said, frowning. "You're a well-read man, despite that quaint brogue you effect. An intelligent man. I didn't really believe it when that coroner, Fogarty, told me you'd said some such thing to him. I thought he was lying, or that he misunderstood."

"Connor, damn it, *listen* to me!" He grabbed his son's arm, squeezed it tightly, as he leaned across the table. "I can *prove* it—prove that they've *already gotten into our home!* Not just when Ethelyn was killed, but *yesterday!*"

With that, Dad spread his other palm beneath Connor's nose. Three silver coins, undated but obviously reaching back to antiquity, sparkled in his hand.

"Where in the world did you get these, Dad?" Connor took one between his fingers, curious despite himself. "They look ancient. Priceless!"

Pat closed his eyes. "In Cornwall, son, the pixies often leave silver coins as a reward for tidyin' the house for a special occasion. I've done that, y'see, worked very hard with Miz Annie to get everythin' nice for the weddin'." He opened his eyes, staring. "Con, these coins were left on the cabinet by the sink in the kitchen. T'reward me."

"That's nonsense. I don't know where you got those, but this is idiotic."

"Even more, son, I'm sure it's a warning of what's to happen after yore marriage. Ah, they're great for notifyin' folk—informin' us of their intent. It's one of their ways, maybe the way they brag, tellin' us that we can't possibly stop them.

233

Because we believe in *other* things, and that makes us helpless. But I'm *on* to them, don't ye see? Connor, I *know* why they're here and what's brought them."

"Why?" he asked bluntly, withdrawing his arm. "What *has* brought them?"

Dad blinked and looked away. There was nothing he could say that wouldn't involve Troy, and there was already a sizeable gulf between her and her father.

"We have to get back," Connor said, standing. "I enjoyed the drink."

Pat Quinlan stayed where he was another moment, watching his modern, half-American son wend his way through Kelly's patrons to the front door. Then he sighed heavily and arose.

He left the three priceless coins on the table.

The majority of the guests at the wedding were colleagues of both sexes of Connor and Lurene from University College. The likeable department head who had originally persuaded Connor to lecture agreed now to act as his best man. Again, as it had in the past, it occurred to Connor how solitary writing-types could sometimes be. Lurene's mother, Mrs. Belle Shanahan, was present—a handsome middle-aged woman bravely blinking back tears and dressed, Connor was sure, in her only fine dress. Lurene's matron of honor was an old friend who'd moved to Limerick after her own marriage, a petite auburn haired woman named Mary Clancy.

There were also people there who had known Patrick Quinlan for years, but not as many of them as Connor had anticipated. Oddly, only a few of them were Dad's age—all appearing vastly older—and at least half the old man's guests were people in their thirties and forties. Dr. Bill Fogarty, the coroner, and deputy Chief Francis Muldowney had been invited by Connor as well. He genuinely liked Bill, his wry humor and honest, industrious ways; he considered Muldowney's obvious suspiciousness comical. Two little girls whom Troy knew slightly from school were also present with their parents. And looking wrung-out and perpetually perplexed, yet dressed in their best, were Sean and Sheilah McCuffy, poor Bobby's grieving parents.

Troy herself looked so much more like a teenager than she had when they moved to County Connaught that sentimental Connor found tears in his eyes just looking at her. Troy wore an elaborate and absurdly expensive imported gown Lurene had insisted upon buying for her. And this afternoon, at least, Troy seemed to her father more her old, sweet self—not exactly blossoming with happiness over the occasion, but at least polite and acquiescent. There was something else in her expression, too, Connor thought. Something of curiosity, or even anticipation. . . .

The Quinlan house itself looked lovely, Connor observed, uncomfortable in a dark blue suit he'd brought to Kylemore from Indianapolis. *(Odd,* he caught himself, *that he now thought of it that way—as Indianapolis, not home. Perhaps it was as an Indiana composer named Maryesther once wrote and home, truly, was where the heart was. In his case, he had finally to confess that it was wherever Troy, Lurene, and Dad were.)* The old man had indeed "Tidied up," as he put it. Together, Dad and Troy had gathered greens and field

235

flowers to twine in a beautfiul trellis arch beneath which Connor and Lurene would stand. Although the weather outside was threatening—it seemed the sky must burst with rain at any second—nature had permitted all the guests to arrive dry. Everything, really, was perfect.

Then why, he wondered as he approached the trellis at the appointed hour, *did he have the impression that it wasn't fine at all? Was it the way Dad sat on the precipitate edge of his folding chair in the front row, nervously tapping his foot? Or was it Troy, still looking vividly expectant, filled with childish mischief?*

At precisely three P.M., Father Jason O'Brien appeared at his post. The trellis arch had been mounted in the space between the front and dining rooms and the priest faced out into the former, the faintest of tight smiles budging his stern lips. He was resplendent in white surplice and a white silk stole, the very picture of authority required, here in Connemara, for such a significant step. From behind Father O'Brien, in the dining room, old Annie took her cue and pushed the button on Connor's tape recorder, just the way he'd instructed her, and music poured sweetly into the house.

Movement behind Connor. He knew that he did not dare turn to see who it was, but he knew anyway. His beautiful, virginal bride, his beloved Lurene Shanahan, gracefully proceeding down the aisle made by the parted rows of folding chairs. Wasn't this when he was to have his real attack of nerves, of second thoughts? Well, he'd have to let the tradition down. Connor smiled openly, from ear to ear. There wasn't a doubt left in his mind or heart. He wanted this woman for his wife.

There had been no one to give the bride away and, mostly as her escort, Pat Quinlan arose to lock her arm in his and lead her the rest of the way. "Ye look beautiful," he said under his breath, but received no reply. She looked straight ahead, her gaze soberly, steadily fixed on Connor. From around them came gasps of pleasure at her loveliness. Because she was a woman who'd never married, Lurene was permitted to wear white and every male heart in the room took an extra beat as she passed. Surreptitiously, Dad gave her arm a squeeze of encouragement. Again, no response. Beneath the long white sleeve her arm felt cold, icy cold. *Nerves,* the old man told himself as he deposited the bride beside his only son and released her, *it must be nerves. But why is it, then, I have what the young 'uns call 'bad vibes?' Why is it that everything I'm after seein' looks . . . obscene?*

Pat took his chair on the edge of the front row again and patted Troy's knee. Another surprise. Her leg was sweaty; so, he saw when he stared at the child's face, was her forehead. And she did not so much as turn her head to glance at him. Instead, her gaze was intently focussed on Lurene; and Pat, like Connor, sensed the anticipation welling up in young Troy. What was happening? Had some creature of the woods cast a hypnotic spell on everyone present?

He realized he hadn't heard the opening lines of Father O'Brien's services and tried to concentrate. ". . In the sight of God . . ." Was it? Pat wondered helplessly; was it really in the sight of God? His eyes swept from Lurene to Connor, to Father O'Brien, to the surrounding scene. Certainly the

237

bride and groom were handsome, especially the way they stood beneath the trellis arch he and Troy made. The flowers. . . .

The flowers!

Those near his son Connor were fresh and pretty, springlike in their bloom. The ones closest to the bride *were dying even as he stared. Fading; falling apart. Petals began to rain softly down on her shoulders, unnoticed. And now the morbid sickness was spreading; even the ones above Connor's head were wilting, beginning to tatter and fall.*

He'd expected something terrible and he was prepared.

Before anyone could stop him, to the utter shock and horror of the wedding crowd, Dad Quinlan vaulted into the aisle and grabbed Lurene from behind, around the neck, instantly dragging her away from Connor and the priest into a corner of the room. She struggled with surprising strength, arms flailing, although no sound came from her lips. For a moment it seemed she might tear away, freed of this crazy old man, *but then he brought the butcher knife from his trouser waist and, as women shrieked in terror, lifted it high above Lurene's head.*

"*Tell* me, damn you!" he shouted in her ear. "*Tell me where she is!*"

The bride, half-choked, merely struggled more energetically until he pricked the side of her throat with the sharp point of the knife.

Connor, who'd been frozen in shock, began moving forward, uncertain what he should do but convinced that his father had gone horribly mad and that his wife-to-be was in mortal danger. Deep in the front room crowd, Francis Muldowney had produced a revolver and was shoving through other people in his manic effort to reach Dad and Lurene.

"I warn you," the old man howled in her ear, "this knife is treated with the proper herbs and ointments. *Where is the lass?*"

"At the pond," came the gurgling answer, the face purpling from the arm round the neck.

"Is she *well?* shouted Dad, seeing Connor and Muldowney yards away and getting closer. He twisted the bride so she faced the police deputy's pointing weapon. *"Is she unharmed?"*

"Yes, yes, damn you!"

"Then *this* should bring her to us!" Dad Quinlan's arm reached high into the air, paused to gather strength, then came hurtling down. The butcher knife plunged deep into Lurene's stomach, just below the breasts.

Connor, almost paralyzed by the worst sight of his life, managed to stagger forward. His own arm was raised belatedly in a pathetic, passionate protest. Because of his motion, he'd stepped directly in front of Muldowney, spoiling his aim.

Then as each man watched—at the instant the knifeblade reached the hilt—a fiendish hissing sound issued from the punctured body, like the air from a balloon. Simultaneously, thunder cracked in the heavens above the house and, from the awful gash in Lurene's abdomen, a greenish stream of reeking smoke began to curl into the air. Her face contorted in a grimace, not of pain but a mixture of amazement, disappointment, and maniacal fury. Her features immediately began to run, as if some vicious poison had been passed across them—the nose made a popping noise and disappeared—the eyes sank into flaccid skin, like two globules of putty, and the chin dipped lower, and lower, becoming a grotesque melting goatee that dripped and trickled all the way between her breasts.

There was a stench that gagged, that nauseated; and then, the bride was gone. Vanished. Gone, as if she had never existed in fact; which in fact, was the truth. Lurene's prized wedding gown tumbled limply to the blue carpeted floor in a heap and the last thing left was a corkscrew of red smoke drifting to the ceiling.

"Look!" cried Troy from her seat, her body turned to the front part of the house, pointing with excitement.

Lurching through the door into the living room, drenched in water and as naked as the day she was born, came the real Lurene Shanahan. "Connor . . ." she called weakly. He tore across the room and caught her in his arms as she collapsed.

Yet each man kills the things he loves . . .
  —*Oscar Fingal O'Flahertie Wills Wilde*

eighteen

"It happened in real life, in 1894," said Dad slowly, recalling the details, "that an Irish gent named Michael Cleary shoved his wife into a stove, and turned it on. Simply stated, he roasted the woman till she was well-done."

They were gathered before a roaring fire in the old man's seldom-entered library: Patrick Quinlan, Connor Quinlan, Lurene Shanahan, coroner Bill Fogarty, and perspiring, frustrated deputy police chief Francis Muldowney. He had accepted the hot tea only when old Bill insisted and because, for the life of him, he couldn't decide whether to arrest Pat Quinlan or not.

"He did it to her, children," continued Dad, folding his hands comfortably across his stomach and leaning back in his chair with a grateful sigh, "because he knew she wasn't really his wife. Why, his wife's own family *helped* him, for the simple reason that they agreed with Mike Cleary: the woman cookin' his meals and sharin' his bed was a changeling."

Connor lit his fifth cigarette of the hour and tossed the match in the fire. "What happened

241

next?"

"Well, it took days to do the job proper, just the way ole Michael felt was necessary. Until the woman's—or the changeling's—legs and abdomen were burned clean away. He was arrested, of course—even the Irish authorities have t'make a pretext of bein' logical and modern—and put in prison. Yet Mike went on swearin' to his death that he killed a changeling given him by the faeries in exchange for his real wife. When twenty years of hard labor were in the past, Cleary claimed, 'It couldn't have been my wife. She was two inches shorter than the changeling!' The inter'sting thing is, Michael Cleary was buried in a decent Catholic cemetery after receivin' the proper last rites. In death, it seems, certain authorities couldn't deny him the truth he had comin'."

Connor shook his head, staring at hands which felt might go on shaking the rest of his life. Lurene, who was wearing his bathrobe and still trying to get warm, touched his arm sympathetically. He saw how pale she looked and hugged her. "God, Dad, what if you'd been wrong?"

"I *was* wrong, when we were at Kelly's," Pat replied candidly. "Dead wrong. I thought Troy's jumpin' rhyme meant they was gonna wait till you had a child of your own, then make the swap. But today, seein' how Troy looked forward all at once to your weddin', I remember the whole Mike Cleary story. How it was a variation on the old changeling legend." He chuckled a little and turned his head. "To answer your question, son, I s'pect Chief Muldowney would see to it I did twenty years, if I'd been in error."

Muldowney's stubborn gaze met his and the

policeman's face crimsoned. "I still think it's some kind of trick. Mebbe a deceit t'undermine law and order in County Galway, but a trick all the same." He slammed down his tea cup and pointed a finger at Pat. "Don't think ye're safe yet, old man. I'll be after checkin' the statute books."

Fogarty glanced over at him. "That right, Francis? How long have they had pictures now?"

Angered, the burly chief rose and the aging coroner followed him. Muldowney swore at the thudding rainfall, turned up his collar, and made a clumsy run toward his official car.

But Bill Fogarty paused beside Dad Quinlan for a private conversation. "Why it is, sir, that I have the distinct notion you've had everything but the details worked out for many months now? That you've always had a pretty good idea that certain supernatural creatures killed all those kids in the woods?"

"Probably because ye're one damned smart Irishman, Billy," Pat answered with a twinkle in his eye. His heroic, decisive action of the afternoon seemed to have taken away another collection of years, like a sauna bath of time soaking away the months and minutes. "'Course, I can't be sayin' for *sure*."

Fogarty's tired, faded blue eyes stared deep into those of the other man. "I'm remembering that you told me about the way we Irish have roots lost in the bowels of time. And how you thought young Connor may be learning the truth before long." He stopped, scratching his cheek thoughtfully. "I tried to conceive of the only man who'd be able to teach your son such fantastic facts and the one man I could imagine—is you."

243

"That's purely flatterin', Bill," Dad said smoothly. "Thank ye."

The coroner's gaze swept to the dining room, where incredible things had occurred that afternoon. "This won't be the end of it, will it, Mr. Quinlan? That's all I want to know right now. I ask you this because I don't want to get into my bed for a good night's sleep and be awakened once more by a horror story bleated into my ear by that fool Muldowney." He put his hand on Pat's shoulder. "There's more comin', isn't there?"

Pat sighed and slowly raised the fingers and cast the hand aside. "Let an old man be a hero for a day, eh, Billy? One last day?"

But when coroner Fogarty was almost to his car, Dad Quinlan's bass voice boomed after him and what he said made him colder than the drenching rain: "Bill? Unplug your phone awhile. Or just don't answer it."

He rejoined his son and the woman who was nearly his daughter-in-law, warming his heavy hands in the blaze from the fireplace. A single look told him how done-in they were, especially the colleen. He looked away from her, troubled, privately trying to think of alternatives.

When he took his seat, it was clear that both the younger people understood at last that they were under seige from the little people of the woods. Without the pressuring stare of Muldowney, Lurene told in her own words how she had been lured to the forest pool by a strangely compelling, intuitive feeling that Troy was in danger. There, she had felt a rustling activity at her feet, as if the grass and weeds were coming to menacing life. She had tried to run but instead found herself

244

"mentally suspended, in a sort of floating, emerald-green cloud. It was foetus-like," she went on, her voice trembling, "almost like I was waiting to be born."

"That wasn't new life you were expectin', child," Dad said firmly. "It was death. At the moment that monstrous changeling and Con exchanged vows, you'd have ceased to exist."

Connor hadn't said a word since his father returned from seeing Fogarty and Muldowney off. He felt rather as though he was being submerged, even drowning, in a past not of his own making. *Déjà vu* was part of it; he could remember sitting in this enormous armchair as a boy, listening to his father tell stories, and smart enough—practical enough—to put little or no stock in what he heard. Now he was forced to admit that he'd been wrong and he felt the tug of generations, the tenacious pull of ancient Ireland and a universe of bizarre mythology which he could no longer ignore.

He turned his head wearily to peer out the window. It was past ten o'clock now and the storm outside thrust itself against the old stone house in torrential battering-ram fury. How odd it was, these sudden, heavy rainfalls when Ireland scarcely ever suffered them. It was as if nature itself was divided, torn between its creatures of the cities and its tiny creatures of the forest. Sulking, angry, it chose to beat upon them both and inject its own bleakly savage mood into the eternal debate. He caught Lurene's eyes gazing at the way the water on the panes seemed to swim frantically in another grotesque parody of life. When she shivered with cold, Connor stood, his mind made up.

"We must talk with Troy," he said, surprised by the way the very thoughts he'd tried to banish insinuated themselves in the forefront of his mind. "I'd say it's pretty clear that she's at the root of all this murderous nonsense, however she's managed to enlist their cooperation."

Dad raised his wide palm and shook his head. "You have it wrong, boy. The wee folk came after Troy, *chose* her, enlisted her unwilling cooperation by confusing the fact of what they've planned to do."

"Nevertheless, Dad, she must be stopped once and for all from going near that woods again."

The old man shrugged, scarlet flames reflected from the fireplace against his deep cheek bones. "I've tried talkin' with her, Connor, and failed. Besides, you've seen the way they can come *inside* now. It no longer matters if she speaks to 'em in the woods or here." He took a sip of his tea and found it cold, making a face as he put the cup down. "But I have a good feelin' about things now."

"Why in the world would you feel that way after today?" Lurene asked, shuddering.

"Simple." He smiled at the younger people. "She's seen that they lied to her again. They promised only to chase ye away and they tried to steal and t'kill ye instead. Troy has learned, the hard way, that the creatures of belief, just like human beings, can't always be trusted. And certainly haven't earned her *believin'* in them."

"I have to get some rest," Lurene said abruptly, feeling her long blonde hair and discovering that it was still damp. She looked up at Connor. "Please, hon, let me sleep in your bed tonight. It was meant to have been our honeymoon evening." She looked at the old man, appealing to him. "We won't dishonor your house, Mr. Quinlan, I promise. But I c-can't go home in this weather and I won't feel safe sleepin' alone in this house, not after this afternoon."

Connor, too, looked at Dad for his permission.

"I trust ye, Lurene Shanahan," he said lightly, getting to his feet and beaming at her. His eyes gleamed in the light from the fire. He seemed at once ancient and wise. "But I think it's safe enough here tonight. Little Troy won't be cooperatin' with the cray-tures of the woods again for quite awhile, y'can wager a pretty banknote on that one! My guess is, the child's been sound asleep for hours now."

"I hope you're right, Dad," Connor said with concern, putting his arms around Lurene and leading her toward the stairs. "I hope and pray that you're right about Troy. I love her so!"

Troy wasn't asleep at all, and hadn't been. She was sitting at a small child's desk for which she was getting leggy, her face an expressionless mask but her oddly colorless eyes darting everywhere.

She did not know where to turn. Her friends had betrayed her, lied to her about their intentions. Her family knew all her most cherished secrets now and that took the fun out of it anyway. Even more than when Ethelyn had died, Troy felt alone. Truly alone.

But even now she thought her independent thoughts, placing blame where she felt it should be. And even now the rising, throbbing heave of conflicting emotions in her mind were beginning to communicate on a beckoning tide of their own.

None of it was really Lurene's fault, she knew that now. It wasn't fair to blame her for falling in love with Dads, because he was handsome, nice, a fun kind of person who needed love and sponged it up without half trying. Dammit, it was *his* fault everything had gone wrong!

Troy hit the desk with her small fist, tears in her eyes as she figured it all out. Dads simply wasn't *worth* loving anymore, not by anybody. First he turned aside from Mommy to put his dumb work first. Then he put the *new* lady, Lurene, ahead of Troy herself, always lookin' out for his own needs, no matter who it hurt. And then Dads had just stood still while Gran-da grabbed the changeling and *watched* while he killed it.

That made Gran-da partly responsible too, clearly it did. If he'd kept his big nose out of everything from the very beginning, everything might still be fine now. But no, *he* had to show her and everyone how smart he was about the faeries in the woods—when he didn't really understand them, or know them at all. Not the way *she* did!

Slowly, as her pain at losing her friends in the woods grew, as she realized they'd all spoiled her chance to become Mab, Queen of the Faeries, Troy's hatred mounted—a fierce, overt, uncontrolled hatred common to children. And any parent who has heard a child say "I hate you" and doesn't believe that the child means it, at least for that particular moment in time, is foolish and vulnerable. Troy Quinlan knew perfectly well, just then, how she *detested* Dads and *loathed* Gran-da.

Tendrils of potent searching reached out, swept beyond the house, questing, seeking a meeting, unconsciously, with forces capable of matching such black, bleak, guilt-free, absolute hatred. There was nothing apologetic about the emotion, nothing halfhearted and nothing that remembered the good times they'd given her. Only detestation and loathing, unsullied and as pure as only thoughts of evil can be in their lack of complexity. The feelings probed the edges of the woods, entered them, delved deep inside—searching, questing, craving a contact that was hideously capable of doing something about the way Troy Quinlan felt. . . .

Where does electricity come from? What is it? Doesn't it come as a product of belief from the electomagnetic mind of man?

Who created the atomic bomb, the hydrogen bomb, nuclear power? Wasn't it man who envisioned these things, fully believed in their potential—man who had the mad temerity to cross the unmarked, tremulous bridge between reality and the fearful universe of possibility?

Things, born of atoms disassembled and rearranged; of particles, neutrons, and quarks agitated and vivified and redistributed, given uncanny life by the only power of eternity entrusted to man: The power of *belief*. A belief generated by wild need and fervent, unmodified desire. . . .

It came to the shallow pool in the deep woods from the Irish Sea, transported by no means understandable or even humanly conceivable, summoned principally by a child's desire and belief. It turned, and tumbled, and rolled there, well beneath the shining surface, unseen by human eyes—a blessing for them.

Water was its preferred, natural habitat, although it was not truly fish-like except in the flat, dull, staring orbs set virtually on the opposite sides of its grotesque head. There, deep in water, it had some of the attributes of an octopus because of its liquid grace and its implacably calm acceptance of the customary tides.

It had a knack for living like a swollen, imperturbable blob of jelly in friendly depths where its mindless blood-lust and blindly murderous appetites were calmed by the swirling, acquiescent waters.

But here, in the pool deep in the woods, the *Nuckelavee* was quite uncomfortable. Discontented, for which read: Hideously angry. The water wasn't deep, it did not sting with the taste of salt, there were no darting schools of flashing fish with which to slake its casual appetite.

Slowly, its fury a banked bomb of madness anxious to explode, it turned over on its obese form and half-rolled, half-drifted, to the bank with no sound at all. It had heard the call, and it was responding.

Erect now, on its legless great bulb of a body, it allowed air to rush into its porcine mouth and, as it did so, the body began to swell. A stink arose round the *Nuckelavee* until it formed something palpable, like cloud-cover. It was almost lost itself in the poisonous, filthy mists of its own foul smell.

And as the air continued to enter it, the swelling continued, the obscene body expanded. Had human eyes been so unfortunate as to penetrate the offal-covering they would have discerned a creature nearly thirty-five feet in height.

Flattening grass and flowers, it began to move.

It had it bearings now, it read the message deep in its lunatic brain clearly, and it turned to the path leading out of the woods. *Rolling.* Rolling laboriously but unstoppably through the immense trees it bumped and sometimes tore up by the roots, heading undeviatingly toward the old two-story house of Patrick and Connor Quinlan.

> *An' the Gobble-uns'll git you*
> *Ef you don't watch out.*
> *—Little Orphan Annie,*
> *by James Whitcomb Riley*

PART THREE

Is there Life Before Death?
—Graffiti on an Irish wall

nineteen

Patrick Quinlan sat ramrod straight on the hard chair in his solitary bedroom for a very long time, reading and reflecting. He'd done little to renovate or modernize the room since his son had gone to America, a long while ago, and the place might have appeared to be a monk's cell to another adult who experienced its undecorative, Spartan aura. It wasn't even comfortable; Pat slept with a board under the mattress and had for years.

He didn't look at his clock to check the time; it might have been two o'clock in the morning, or three. Despite the bizarre events of the day, all the others in the old house must have been sound asleep because it was still as death now. And how still was that, Pat wondered, giving a sardonic chuckle. He resumed his reading of the Bible, concentrating. He read the holy verses a great deal of the time lately, because of his precious beliefs.

Unfortunately, those beliefs had little to do with the Roman Catholic faith in which he and his son Connor had been reared, many years apart. In a way, they weren't Pat's beliefs but unyielding restrictions imposed upon him. Soon, they would also be imposed on Connor.

Having finished what he chose to read, he went back to reread other portions of the Book, both the Old and New Testaments. He tried to commit the sacred passages to memory, but the weather outside distracted him. It was still raining, enough that his arthritis was again flaring up in his neck and limbs. At last he arose with some pain and difficulty, sighing and stretching. He slipped the volume in a pocket of his smoking jacket, which he wore, rather incongruously, over a Connemara sweater, and slowly crossed the room to a mirror hanging above a chest of drawers.

He stared at himself for a considerable length of time, touching his forehead, his cheeks, the still-taut flesh at the corners of his mouth. This was done not with masculine vanity but with a soft, fleeting flash of the old wonder. He'd come to the mirror hoping that merely seeing his familiar reflection, observing his youthfully spurious self, would make him more sanguine about the ponderous, revelatory hours which lay ahead. The way he looked was the obvious reward for the faith foisted on him; years ago, it had given him cheer, and resolve.

This time it didn't work because he kept meeting his own gaze in the mirror, and there was no way to avoid seeing the penetrating wealth of guilt residing in those clear eyes. Pat knew the timing was off, that everything might fail now. But he had adored having a granddaughter like Troy, who was like him in so many ways, and he was growing fond despite himself of Connor's second wife-to-be. Inwardly, it was obvious, he was softening, letting himself and the others down. But he couldn't help it, not even if he jeopardized the decades that he—and those of the attic—had invested.

Of course, it was speculation, whether he'd ruined things or not. Something else wasn't. At the instant he told Connor the entire astonishing story, everything would definitely change around him forever, just as it had changed for him the moment *he* was told. Dammit, there was no way in the world he could be wrong about that. Connor might well hate him. The lad was a sturdy, reliable man with a mind of his own and an active conscience. He would have strong feelings about this, resentment that the awful old burdens were now to be piled on his own shoulders, and Patrick Quinlan didn't blame him. Not now, as he planned for the confrontation, nor, the old man was sure, when it actually happened.

He took several aching, plodding steps to his nightstand and picked up the miniature of Margaret, his late wife, framed in antique silver and beginning to fade badly now. Yet there she was, forever suspended at the ideal age of twenty-nine. Lurene Shanahan's age, today. Despite the way the colors were slowly softening, Margaret was still alive there, beneath his big-knuckled fingers, her beauty and vitality of spirit somehow unblemished after all these years. Sadly, with remembered tears in his eyes, he studied her well-loved features and thought for the thousandth time how damnably sad it all was. Never in his life had he wanted another woman, not before or after death took her. Yet he, her lover, was partly responsible for the way she'd left him at such a youthful age. He shook his head, trembling. A man did not dare die with such things on his conscience, not ever. Somehow he had to go on keeping himself alive and away from judgment, whatever the cost. Anything, rather than face the ultimate consequences of his actions.

It wasn't God, or Jesus, whom he feared to confront when he died, however. It was Margaret. It was impossible to face the hurt that would be there in her eyes.

Carefully, Pat kissed the painted lips and replaced the picture on his nightstand. He crossed himself, rather wishing he'd never removed the crucifix from his room. He'd done it himself, on his own, because he wasn't in favor of such sacrilege even if he was one of the offending parties. Faith, he was so *tuirseach*—so exhausted—and yet he intended, this very night, to make it again impossible to lie down and rest. Whatever the exact nature of Connor's reaction to the news, he knew he himself was doomed to sleeplessness, and to walking the aged corridors of his house like a restless spirit.

Now he looked at the clock on the other wall and decided it was time. He couldn't really afford to wait much longer, not with Bill Fogarty on the job, already half convinced of the need of a search warrant. Once that clown Muldowney got his mitts on one and began poking through things, discovering the secrets of the attic, it would be too late to give Connor a careful, thorough explanation. And the lad was owed that much, certainly, even if it would really work more effectively if Connor was farther along in years. Because of Troy's unplanned-for psychic attunement with the folk of the forest, and because of his own hesitation to seize the opportunity when it arose, Pat would simply have to screw up his courage and tell Connor now.

Right now.

He shut his door behind him and, without switching on a light, began walking stealthily down the dark hallway. After all these years he knew every inch, every step, and didn't require light. But despite himself, Pat shivered, almost willing to believe that *they* were lurking here, watching his every movement, urging him on. He stopped before Troy's door to make sure she was asleep. Regular as clockwork, her breathing whispered out to him, and he went on, stopping at last before Connor's door.

Lurene—Lurene was sleeping here too. Pat withdrew his knuckled hand, changing his mind about knocking. If the door were locked, he didn't dare rap and risk awakening the young woman. She was the last—the *very last*—person in the world whom he wanted to have hear his legend, the Quinlan legend. So perhaps this was a sign that he should, after all, wait—until the turn of the century, perhaps, when Connor's loins had cooled and he was deeply puzzled by the mysterious way his old da stuck around at such an advanced age. Then, twenty years from now, Connor would have a little age on his *own* shoulders. The filthy, groping creatures of the grave would be breathing down *his* neck, then, and the lad would be happy to learn the Quinlan fairy tale. Why, he'd be relieved, *anxious* to take the place of Patrick Aloyious Quinlan and assume the burdens of eternity.

When he could distinguish Lurene's breathing from Connor's and was sure she was there, he turned his back on the door, shakily anxious about

259

his next move, and peered through the swallowing shadows in the direction of his granddaughter's bedroom. Ah, how unfortunate it was that the sweet lass's inadvertent interference had brought it all to the fore this way, forced him to play his cards.

Or was it truly unfortunate? Troy had certainly saved her own life because of making friends with the wee folk. And despite his own self-interest, Pat was glad of that. But he wondered if the faeries themselves knew what they'd done. In their desire to use Troy as their own queen, had they also fathomed the incredible mystery of *human* ways— *Quinlan* ways? Besides, there could be no guarantee that they were done with little Troy, simply because the adults knew her secret. So long as she believed in them, she could keep them alive. Was it at all possible that, even without the girl's knowledge, they were still protecting her—or worse, that they were taking steps against him?

For a moment it was all simply too much for an old man to handle. Images came into his mind of the period in his life when he was like everybody else, neatly stacking reality in one corner and unreality in the other, certain they'd never mix, sure they had nothing in common. It had been a younger, gentler Ireland then, as Pat Quinlan had been himself, a time when there were still beginnings, middles, and ends.

Tell him, voices seemed to cry in his mind, *tell Connor now! You must take the risk!*

He spun in a circle and impulsively reached out to try the knob. Gently, he pushed against the door with his shoulder.

It was unlocked; it opened without a sound. He

was in the room.

The *Nuckelavee* had burst away from the trees and was drawing nearer now, approaching the large stone house at the edge of the woods as water dripped off its obese, circular shape. It knew that it was hidden from sight, both by the riveting rainfall and its own stench-filled cloud, but it didn't care at all. Whether people were around to see it or not could not have mattered less. If anyone was there, it would simply roll over the being, absorbing it and feeding its evil perpetual hunger.

At Connor Quinlan's garage-den the *Nuckelavee* paused for a moment, getting its bearings. No, this wasn't the source of the call; the call came from the larger place, the house. If flowed forward, wet green grass adhering to its body and then consumed, vanishing inside it along with enormous handfuls of insect life. Its cavernous digestive system purred, but only for a moment. It required much larger prey than bugs.

Of the *Nuckelavee's* present thirty-five feet in circumference, nearly twenty feet consisted of the fantastically ugly head which slipped and lolled stupidly from side to side as it proceeded. The incredible, spineless skull gave the thing a deformed and lunatic demeanor, caused the creature to seem to have no mind and no purpose.

But that was a lie, part of the ruse, the deceit, perverse nature had given it. The *Nuckelavee's* mind might have been devoid of knowledge of what it actually *was,* but it knew perfectly well what it could *do*—what it was *meant* to do. The mind itself was also spongelike, in many respects, a servant-brain of sorts which came running when it was called. Once there, however, it did what it *could* do, and details were of no importance to the creature.

And its central purpose, as it rolled dripping wet to the front of the stone house and, ghostlike, became a drifting cloud of stink tumbling smoothly to the front door—as it propelled itself forward on gangling arms that reached the ground and added obscene *scooting* to its rolling gait—its larger purpose was the total annihilation of life.

In her own bedroom on the second floor, Troy turned restlessly in her sleep, curling the pillow tighter against her slender, fetally-curved form. She was having a nightmare and it was about something huge, round, staggeringly ugly, trying to get into her house in Indianapolis. Mommy—Ethelyn—struck at it with a broom and Dads, her beloved Dads, was himself again, protecting Troy with his own sturdy body and daring the thing to come near him.

It was only—mostly—a dream and she was unaware of the *Nuckelavee* she'd summoned herself, subconsciously, unaware of the hideous danger to people she loved, and fully unaware of the fact that Ruck and several other *portunes* were on the headboard of her bed, doing a jubilant dance as their future queen slept on.

Some say no evil thing that walks by night,
In fog or fire, by lake or moorish fen,
Blue meagre hag, or stubborn unlaid ghost,
That breaks his magic chains at curfew time,
No goblin, or swart faery of the mine,

Hath hurtful power o'er true virginity . . .
Comes the blind Fury with th' abhorred shears
And slits the thin-spun life. . . .
Hence, loathed Melancholy,
Of Cerebus and blackest Midnight born.
                                        —*John Milton*

twenty

It was graveyard-dark in Connor's bedroom, but for the small rectangle of window high and cell-like above the bed, and Dad stopped inside the door, squinting in the gloom. Finally, lightning flashed against the night—midnight old man with a raincoat revealing a dazzling secret—and momentarily illumined the people in the bed.

Dad caught a glimpse of the naked Lurene Shanahan, milk white lying on her back, her beautiful upthrust breasts like vanilla sundaes topped with cherries, her golden hair fanned out over Connor's hirsute barrel chest, a triangular patch of nearly colorless pubic hair, and one sweetly curved leg raised in nonchalance. Glad when the lightning faded, Dad went to them and shook his son's arm. When there was no response, he shook it again. Harder.

Connor awoke startled, a little afraid, and tried to sit up. But the old man had a palm flat on his chest. "Dad! What's up? Why—?"

"It's truth time, son." It was a whisper but it projected an odd combination of relief and weariness. Or perhaps the combination wasn't really so odd. "Time to satisfy your curiosity, once and for all."

Again, an illuminating flash and distant rumble. Connor blinked and seemed to understand. He paused only long enough to raise Lurene's arm and place it carefully across her own side. Softly, he kissed her neck below the ear. "I'll just get my robe and slippers," he whispered.

Pat Quinlan waited in the hallway, the door discreetly pulled to after him, clicking his teeth with his tongue, impatient for it to be done. Over. When Connor came out, closing the door tightly, he gave his father an ashamed look and a turn of the head.

"This was to have been the night, Father," he said, scratching his ear. "I just couldn't wait any longer."

For an instant Pat didn't know what he was talking about. He'd heard clearly the word "Father" and wondered how long it had been since Connor called him that. When he understood that the lad was talking about making love to his woman, he made a disdainful sound in his nose and clapped Connor on the shoulder. "You young people honestly believe that goin' against the sexual rules is the most sinful thing ye can do. Or that it is what will offend your parents the most. Ah, boy, I wish that were the only bad thing, I really do!" He sighed and pointed ahead, down the corridor to the steps. They led up to the attic and Connor could not even see the door in the dim light. "Sex is a wee thing over the course of life, boy." His jaw was set in grim lines. "I'll be showing ye *real* sin."

Connor gave him a somewhat relieved smile and

fell into step with his father. "It's hard to believe you're finally letting me in on your secret. Are you sure you want to?"

"I'm positive that I do *not* want to. But there are few options left t'me. Connor, ye must be ready t'take me place. But before you can do that, ye must learn how to prepare me. What to *do* with your da, when it comes down to that."

"I've no idea what you're talking about," the younger man replied, shaking his head. "But I'm eager to find out."

"One thing about secrets, lad," Pat warned him as they passed like two spirits down the carpeted corridor. His hand was affectionate on Connor's shoulder. "Once they're out in the open, ye can never put them back. *Never.*"

Downstairs, there was a secret that had been let out and there wasn't an ounce of affection in its heart or soul. In order to accommodate the nine-foot ceilings, just barely, the ghastly caller shrank and paused inside the front door. It sensed, above it, the motion of two men moving down a hallway and its prudent mechanism hesitated to feel for danger. It felt other lives as well in this strange four-walled container. One of them, it knew, was the source of the messages it was receiving, but now, peculiarly, they were somewhat vague. Then Troy Quinlan's nightmare reasserted itself in her young mind and, below her, the *Nuckelavee* was satisfied. Unhurriedly, a blasé and confident stalker of life to devour, it began rolling forward. Ahead of it a few yards was a staircase to negotiate. That required further prudent attention.

But that was all right. It had ample time. And it

knew that the human creatures upstairs had no chance at all to hurt or slow it down. Really, there was no rush whatsoever.

They climbed the steps together for the first time in their lives, father and son, and then the old man was getting his keys out of his pocket and unlocking the door. Connor was surprised when his heartbeat accelerated and kept beating faster with anticipation. There was, quite literally, a lifetime of wonderment, of curiosity and expectation, built up in him by now. Finally Dad threw the door open.

A gust of surreal heat came blasting out the door at the younger man, strong and surprising enough to make him take a step backward. Along with it came the remembered, seemingly unchanged smell of remarkable mustiness. He was about to step forward and enter, when Pat touched his chest with a finger and caused him to wait.

"Son, this is not what I'd call an optimum time for what you're about to see and hear. Someday in the future, when you're older, it would have been a lot easier for me and doubtless for you. But as I told ye, there's no choice. You must be told, immediately, and what you learn in this attic is for *your ears alone*. It is a *male Quinlan knowledge* and not for anyone else. Ever." He paused, his face shadowed slightly on the stoop outside the attic, his expression earnest and peculiarly ageless. "I realize ye will find it hard to keep your word, even if ye give it to me, but this is the *solitary catch:* Connor, ye must pledge—*now*—to be still about this. T'keep it between the two of us, regardless of how awful it may appear. If ye loves your da, lad, pledge that now."

Connor frowned. It had always annoyed him, being asked to give his word blindly. Yet this was his own father asking, a man he once feared, a man he had come, in his middle years, to love and respect. The man who had saved his Lurene's life, perhaps her very soul. He nodded briskly. "Understood. You have my word."

Pat waved an arm and Connor stepped by him, into the attic.

The stench of mustiness, of immense and somehow heady age, was overwhelming when the door closed behind him. At first he felt his stomach turn, uncomfortably informed of the olfactory disturbance by his twitching nostrils. But he learned quickly that it wasn't as bad, as offensive, as it was simply unrelenting. He began to peer more attentively at the great, long attic room which, for so many years, had plagued and mystified him.

It looked close to a hundred feet in length; it ran the full depth of the old Quinlan house and the high ceiling was buttressed by sturdy, aging oak rafters. Everything was clean; there wasn't a trace of a spider's handiwork. At the nearest side wall were machine-like objects, cabinets, and a chair. His eyes were drawn by gigantic space heaters at each end of the room, pumping out blasts of heat. Connor frowned again; what was the need of heaters in June, in a country that never became very cold? The intestine-like coils of the heaters glowed pinkly and he decided it must be more than one hundred degrees Fahrenheit in the attic. Perspiration beaded his forehead and seeped from the crown of his dark head to ooze soggily into the fine hair at his temples. He wished he'd had time to dress in more than a bathrobe; then he would have had a handkerchief to mop his brow.

Directly in front of him, a screen obscured his view. "There," he said quietly to his father. "What's behind that?"

Let the revelation begin, old Pat thought, lifting and folding the screen, getting it out of the way.

Beginning some twelve feet inside the attic entrance was an elongated, tunneled contraption which seemed to stretch the interminable length of the room. Heart pumping, Connor took a few tentative steps forward. He felt hesitant—fearful—of actually drawing abreast of the tunnel. From before it, he saw that it was walled by compartment partitions of the kind used in many offices. They were approximately five feet wide and somewhere between six and seven feet in height.

Puzzled, Connor raised his eyes. Although open at the top, there was a formidable, endless string of oddly-shaped emerald tubes suspended above the individual tunnel "rooms." Each set of tubing apparently divided the contraption further into dozens of smaller, man-sized booths—perhaps hundreds, Connor couldn't readily tell. The emerald tubes *glowed,* intermittently, like so many strangely bright insects who'd hopped atop the partitions to bask in an alien sun.

And from just beneath each glimmering green tube, corresponding precisely with each sporadic, silent glow, arose an almost invisible puff of pure white smoke. It was almost as though myriad mad elves were in there, getting high on Colombian pot, Connor thought wildly. . . .

No! he realized; *it was more as if the tunneled booths were . . . breathing.*

What the hell was going on here? He swallowed hard, got his nerve up, and began walking along the side of the tunnel. It was impossible to see what was inside any of the partitions. Peering closer, Connor observed that each seamless partition bore either three or four letters. *Initials,* he saw; *they're initials.* And following each set of initials, a number.

Remembering what he'd seen from the corner of his eye, he turned and identified a number of heavy steel filing cabinets set against the wall. Connor looked back at the tunneled partitions, back to the cabinets, again to the booths. The last initial on each of them was *Q.* It was the same with the drawers of the filing cabinets.

When he spoke, his voice sounded loud in this place and that was unthinkable—like shouting in a funeral parlor, or a cemetery. "The cabinets," he began. "They provide full data—complete explanations—for what the initials and numbers suggest?" He paused. "For what the partitions . . . *contain?*"

Dad nodded but his smile was tight. "Yes. A brief, factual history for each." He yanked open a cabinet door at random, lifted a neat manila folder into view and glanced at it. "Quinlan, Francis Cavanagh. Birthdate, November 7, 1801. Occupation, cobbler. Wife, Siobhan Mary." He glanced up from beneath his brows. "There's a good deal of data. The word, ah, '*biography*' comes to mind as an accurate term."

Slowly, an agonizing chill began at the base of Connor's skull and trickled like ice water all the way down his back. His lips formed the word when he repeated it but no sound came with it: "Biography?"

Pat Quinlan walked toward an object, partly concealing it with his sturdy old body. At a glance, it looked almost like a television set with the screen removed. It might also have been some kind of exotic computer. But it wasn't. There were vivid electronic dials and rubberized knobs, several rows of plush crimson buttons. The old man hit a switch at the side, swiveled a knob, turned a dial.

"*Watch,*" he commanded Connor.

It was a simple word but the ponderous inflection in his father's voice made Connor freeze, staring helplessly at the remarkable length of bizarre tunneling.

That was when the dozens of partitions of the tunneled contraption raised a steaming black cloud of musty, repugnant smoke that made Connor instinctively back off, lightheaded.

When he saw what there was to see and reached out behind him, groping shakily for the chair, tumbling back into it without removing his astonished gaze from the scene, his mind almost blacked out. His mouth was open in amazement. His eyes protruded from their sockets in plainly stupefied disbelief.

Each of the booths was occupied. Seemingly suspended in midair or possibly fastened neatly by its back to a segmented half-wall hung a cadaverously thin, yellowish, mouldering and deteriorating human body. There were dazzling dozens of age-tarnished dead—well-kept, perfectly mummified old men set in a precise line beneath the intermittently-glowing green tubes, reaching all the way to the distant far wall. It was a clothing-store rack with the suits filled—filled with dead men.

Connor struggled to his feet, an arm wildly thrashing out; he was unable to find his own voice.

He didn't have to. "Go *close*, son," the father urged him casually, offhandedly. "Peer straight into their faces."

Connor blinked, as if the old man had suggested he fly out the window. Except that there was no window. He felt faint now, literally inclined to drop to his own face in this nightmare ward; but he nodded like a good, obedient son and willed his feet to move.

Staggering, Connor reached the closest, facing mummy; and the closer he got, the more it reeked of age—of a death too far-gone to be saddening, or memorialized—and chemicals.

It dangled there before him like a pinned moth, its dark business suit voluminous on its shrunken old form. The face was parchment-like, brown and gray and yellow, beginning to crumble. What hair remained on the head was left there at random, short shocks of off-white growths aimlessly springing from the crown, or a spot on the forehead, and *there,* at the temple.

"That's the most recent fellow, son," said Dad, chatty behind Connor, in much the same affable tone of voice he'd used to discuss Kelly's Pub. "Everything is in neat chronological order, of course. From the newest one, on back."

On *back?* On back to *what,* to *where?* Connor blinked into the mummy's face, beginning to be fascinated despite his horror. *What* was in chronological sequence? And who the hell *were* these aged dead men? Worse, what were they *doing here,* for the love of God and human decency—in the

Quinlan attic? Could this mean his father was a grave robber or that he performed experiments? What *process* had he used to mummify them; *how had he done* this ghastly thing—and why?

Connor swallowed his fear, putting his face within inches of that first old man in the line . . .

And, shrieking hysterically, vaulted back a full yard, reaching blindly out for his father's arm in order to keep from falling—fainting—on this awful attic floor.

Because the mummy at the head of death's procession had lifted a veined and dessicated hand, opened its rheumy eyes, and winked at Connor!

St Francis and St. Benedict, Bless this house from wicked wight, From the nightmare and the Goblin That is hight Good Fellow Robin. Keep it from all evil spiretes, Faeries, Wezles, Bats and Ferrytes, From Curfew Time to the next Prime.

—William Cartwright

twenty-one

"Sit down a moment, son," Pat Quinlan urged him, then handed him a glass with some water in it. He squeezed Connor's shoulder comfortingly. "Ye've had a bit more of a shock than I expected. I s'pose yer old man is immune to it all, by now, and forgot a bit of the initial shock."

"Dad . . . ?"

"Sh-h, just ye rest a moment, all right?" Pat fussed with the younger man, smoothing his dark hair, adjusting the collar of his bathrobe. He grinned a little. "But ye have no reason, Connor me lad, to fear that poor old fellow." He chuckled. "After all, he's *yer own gran-da!*"

Connor's gaze shot to the "corpse" heading the line—"The most recent fellow"—and he saw that while the head and body were again perfectly quiescent, the eyes remained open. Watchful; staring; intelligent—and *friendly*.

Feeling that he might well be going mad, Connor got to his feet again and started moving down the line of now-revealed partitions. After the second one in line, he found that he was half-dancing, half-jogging sideways along the tunnel, peering first into one booth and then another, and another, and another.

Each time he looked inside, there was *movement*—faint, scarcely discernible, perhaps only a twitch of the awful cracked lips or a waggle of a corrugated index finger—that told Connor Quinlan these grotesque mummies were . . . *alive*.

Ah, but this was no life with which he was familiar. His creative mind groped for explanations, for parallels. Perhaps they were related to the slumberous, immobilized existence of certain slugs, but certainly not to any human beings. This was a feeble, tenuous life so incredibly fragile that the ancient beings were obliged to be supported from their spines, sustained by—by *what?* He looked closely at the emerald tubing above them, remembering the white puffs of smoke which, he calculated, had to be laborious, turgid human breath.

His head whirling with wonderment, Connor raced one-third the length of the tunnel again, verifying the other things he'd seen. The clothes worn by these poor creatures—all of them, he saw, seemed to be men—were different, significantly, in both style and condition the farther back he moved in the procession. Gradually, yards away from the front of the room, perhaps halfway down the nightmarish line, suits gave way to simpler garb. Tattered, homemade shirts. Rough-hewn trousers. Eventually tunics with short skirts, even robes. Yet regardless of how far back he moved—*was it a journey into the past?*—there were the telltale signs of human life; each unbelievably old man was breathing: shallowly, piteously, just enough to maintain this mockery of human existence. Alive, yes; but in a fantastic museum of such immense and unthinkable age that Connor could not imagine what the answers might be, could not even assimilate all that he saw.

"Dad." He stopped before his father, breathing hard, his eyes wild. "Dad, who *are* all these men?"

"I told ye that the first one is your gran-da, me own father." Patrick Aloyious Quinlan remained calm. "This is your *family,* son. These men are your heritage—your *living ancestors.*"

"That's impossible," Connor said flatly.

"Ye didn't recognize your gran-da from his pictures?" Pat's eyes flickered to the second decrepit figure. "That's *his* da, your great-grandfather. Behind him, why, it's your great-*great*-grandfather." He laughed a little. "Let's see, Con. If we count back *nine* men, for example—" he did so, ticking them off with a brush of his fingertips on each old hand—"Why, this fine Irishman is yer great-great-great-great-great-great-great-*great*-grandfather!"

"How many," Connor gulped, "how many a-are there?"

Dad shrugged. "I don't rightly know. I'd have to check the files to be certain. The human body isn't customarily very thick, y'know, at the chest or waist. It doesn't actually take a great deal of room." He lifted a finger to make a point. "I *did* make some calculations a few weeks ago. I can be tellin' ye that there's still room in this attic for another eighteen generations of Quinlans!"

"How old?" Connor whispered. "How old *are* they?"

"Now, ye'll be thinkin' your own da isn't as bright as he should be, but I don't have the answer

277

to that either." He paused, clearly trying mightily to keep this fantastic topic as free of tension, of dispute, as humanly possible. "As I told ye, lad, it's easy t'take all this for granted after years of carin' for yer family. The details, well, they lose some of their importance."

"But—*how?*" Connor blurted out, gesturing at the racks of Quinlan ancestors. "*Why?*"

"Sit down here, me boy, right at the console." Dad's voice was steady and firm, somehow calming. His smile remained affectionate and gentle as he helped Connor take his seat. "Are ye after rememberin' your Bible? Just a bit, perhaps?" He paused. "Can ye recall *Genesis?*"

". . . Some of it . . ."

"It contains some marvelous passages, Con. Such as, 'And all the days that Adam lived were nine hundred and thirty years; and he died.' Others like 'And Methusaleh lived a hundred and eighty and seven years, and begat Lamech: And Methusaleh lived after he begat Lamech seven hundred eighty and two years, and begat sons and daughters: And all the days of Methusaleh were nine hundred sixty and nine years; and he died.'"

When Connor shook his head it was nearly with anger; but the nucleus of it remained disbelief. "Dad, that was . . . *legend, allegory!* Or an error; perhaps they calculated years differently back then."

"No, that isn't true." Dad was finely paternal, certain. "No error is made in the Book. It's all precisely stated. Now, will ye consider this: 'There were giants in the earth in those days . . . mighty men were of old, men of renown.' It seems some translations of the ancient holy writings were in error. 'Giants' don't mean men of exceptional *bulk*, son. It means the *special* men. Men with gigantic powers."

"Your point, Dad?" The temperature seemed to be rising now. The hair on Connor's forehead adhered to it like a witch's kiss. "What's your point to this?"

"Simple, lad. *We* are those men, Connor. Your da, and *all our fathers*—and *you,* Connor Quinlan. You; me; my da there, his father behind him; his father's father; and so on back to antiquity. *All* male Quinlans, lad, go back to that Biblical race of gigantic intellects." He pointed at them. "Because we continued to live."

"Let me think a moment." Connor held his forehead, steadying himself, forcing his brain to begin pumping facts. He had to hold to them for all his might, grasp the reality which made his world go round. At last he looked up at Pat. "There is a serious flaw in what you're saying, Dad. *Noah.*" He held his father's gaze. "When the flood came, according to the Bible, everything was destroyed, except Noah's family and—and the animals which the Lord made him take."

"Not quite, me lad, if ye learn t'read the Good Book attentively." Pat's eyes twinkled with a glimmer of his old charm. "Genesis says, as well, 7:23: 'And every living substance was destroyed which was upon the face of the ground . . . and Noah only remained alive, and *they that were with him in the* ark.' Remember now?"

"Well, what are you saying? That we weren't left on the ground? That our family was—was on the mountains or flapping around in the sky?"

Dad chuckled softly. "Not at all. It's quite simple, Con. We were on the ark with Noah. Recall, God told Noah t'take two of *each kind.* 'Of every living thing of all flesh, two of every sort shalt thou bring into the ark, to keep them alive with thee...' And *ours,* young Mister Quinlan, was a very different 'living thing' than the regular folks of Noah. *We* were of the mighty men who always lived, four, five, eight, nine hundred years, and Noah knew that to be true. Thus, *our kind* was saved. D'ye see? And the point is," the easy, amiable manner fell away from him, replaced with the most inflexible, dogmatic expression Connor had ever seen on old Pat's face, "it has been our *duty,* ever since, to *stay alive.* Until the Lord asks us to take a walk with Him, like Enoch. It is our *divine commandment* to remain alive, until our proper time has come. Connor, lad, it is *our personal covenant with God!*"

Did he mistake it, or did Connor, he wondered, hear a tiny smattering of applause from halfway down the strange corridor of corruption behind him? He stared weakly into his father's sparkling blue eyes. "All right, even with these men you keep here, there isn't enough for all the generations since Noah."

"Aw, ye always was a bright lad!" Dad beamed. "The ancestors of the Quinlans are not alone here but in Europe, and Asia—everywhere." He leaned forward, conspiratorially. "Ye want to know how it's done?" He saw Connor give him a helpless nod. "Well, there are several kinds of life around a man and for each there is a different kind of death. Connie, have ye ever been so wrapped up in life— so *involved* with those around ye—that ye felt a *part* of *everythin'?* Of *all* life?"

He nodded tentatively. "I guess I have," he admitted.

"The end of the 'I' is a visionary experience, boy, even for a single moment. Most of the time, however, you are you, and nobody else, only because your own multiple senses *reason* for your aloneness. But Connor, son, what of a beehive?" He was flushed with enthusiasm now. "Nowhere and nothin' is more sane, more organized and ordered than a beehive. But y'know, if the queen bee dies, the others—the bee 'cells'—become gibberin' idiots. Bereft of direction and doomed to die, because they're set *free* . . . turned into isolated individuals. No longer a cohesive collective organ operatin' for the good of all."

Cohesive collective organ: Was that Pat Quinlan speaking? "What are you telling me, Dad?" Connor asked as the words were absorbed and the stunning idea arose. "That my individuality is . . . imaginary, a form of madness? That we Quinlans are created like bees in a beehive?"

"I told ye, son, we're a separate race." He nodded with certainty. "Only the males, however, and only partly imagined, for we have been diluted by interbreeding with ordinary folks for centuries. But so long as we *all* survive, the youngest, newest Quinlan cannot die and, literally we *all* survive. When it is our time—and mine is comin', I fear—we only fall back into the semi-sleeping stage ye see before ye. Our brains are fully intact, but at half-speed."

"No, I can't buy any of this!" Connor was on his feet again, striding nervously toward his dessicated gran-da and back again. "What if a male Quinlan *prefers* to be an ordinary man? What if he goes his own way?"

"There have been those, from time to time," said Dad, nodding, "who, like the queen, withdraw from the hive. For awhile there is chaos. You had a younger brother, y'know, and he was one of those who wished to leave. The lad died, of course. Y'see, like bacteria, there's no death from old age for Quinlan males so long as no virus appears. When it is unimpeded, as scientists know, bacteria is immortal. So are we." Now he looked hard at his living son and his expression was powerful, tempered by the steel of ages, the steel of a man's total, absolute belief. "Ye cannot ever become that murderin' virus, Connor. Ye must understand that as ye promised ye would." Finally he shrugged lightly, and grinned. "Why would a healthy fellow like ye choose to die anyway?"

"I don't know," Connor said with a sigh, striding once more beside the tunnel of time. When he saw that his ancestors followed his movements with sunken, half-sentient eyes, he shuddered. Yet what Dad said was true. He had no brief to make for the grave. "How did it all begin?"

"Well, I might say it's God's way. Indeed, it surely was." Now Dad loosened his smoking jacket, opened it. His expression became that of the reflective pedant. "But I've had consider'ble time t'think it through. In evolution, there once was dead, inorganic matter but one fine day, bacterial life appeared. The stage of immortality, son. It's an odd fact that most folks don't realize somethin' astonishing: Once, *nothing* was under a mandatory death sentence; once, dying wasn't an absolute necessity at all; once, that which lived *went on livin'*, sometimes forever. D'ye know how science, to this day, finds *living organisms* in stone, millions of years old?"

"But we're talking about *people,* Dad," Connor put in with some asperity. "Mortal, living human beings."

"Con, what I'm tellin' ye was that mandatory dyin' didn't come along until *after the Flood!* It was a part of God's punishment for man, payment for his dreadful sins. I've even discovered that Biblical fellows didn't merely 'begat' their children, Connor Quinlan—they *duplicated* themselves in a natural cloning process." He smiled as his son's lips again parted in consternation. "Now, we Quinlans didn't do that like the others. We simply escaped the Flood, with Noah, and went on livin'—till the virus happened to us."

"What virus? What went wrong?" Connor demanded.

"Ah, now ye're startin' to b'lieve your da! Because we constantly married women from the generations coming along after the Flood, we Quinlan males were weakened. Some of the young ones didn't take proper care of their fathers. The Bible," old Pat grew meditative, "meant for the sins or burdens continuing through their reproduced sons. But as we began marryin' ordinary womenfolk, we inadvertently caused . . . occasions of death. There became one way—*one way only,* son—t'make sure our immortality was guaranteed. One of the survivin' Quinlans learned that way and he . . . struck a bargain."

"How? How was the guarantee made?" A part of Connor felt that his father was mad, merely senile and insane; but each moment his rational mind sought that explanation, a glance at the unbroken

283

procession of scantly-living forbears whose toothless lips and beclouded eyes observed him, he knew he was hearing the truth. "How did we continue our immortality?"

Pat approached him then, deliberately, resting his strong hands on his son's broad shoulders. His expression was at once sad and cautious, the look of a man who wept for the Christians but feared the lions might escape. "This is the hardest part for me to explain to ye, Con. Ordinary people—people who are other than Quinlans, I mean—must sometimes die. Younger folk must perish for us, in order to keep the whole line of our ancestry alive. Die a wee bit sooner, perhaps, than they otherwise would."

Connor threw off the placating hand, snarling, "Are you telling me that other people must give up their lives for us—" he gestured to the enclosures—"to keep *them* extant?"

"Some must die, yes." He said it apologetically, meekly. "Folks who are yet on the happy side of middle age, most of them women, and children." Knowing the shocked look he would see in his son's eyes, Dad looked away, peering at the tunnel and the living history it contained. "The release of other life energies—their electrical or magnetic forces—gives Quinlans a new lease on life."

"*That* kind of pathetically creepy, grasping sort of life?" Connor pointed.

"Yes, all our fathers and grandfathers. But *me,* Connor, as well. And you." He let it sink in. "Yes, *you,* my son. Because ye happen to be the next in line after me. If ye do not take care of your da when the time comes, lad, it won't be just him and all the others who perish. It will be ye, as well, at an earlier age than ye can imagine."

The profile of his father was mere inches from his own now, that face so much like a smudged or aged mirror image of his own face. "Lurene, you're saying. And Troy, too, if it comes to that." Suddenly the thought occurred to him. "Ethelyn! Did you—?"

"That was the banshee's work, Con," the old man said sadly. "But had she not been taken, I believe she'd have been next. The next one to go." He paused. "I have done everything in m'power to keep them from Troy. When Lurene came along, soon to be a part of the clan, I rejoiced. I'll admit that. Better her, I felt, than me granddaughter."

Connor shouted into the aging face. "Are you saying I'm expected to—to *murder* my own wife or child? *Are* you, Dad? Kill them so this decrepit parade of immortals can continue its charade?"

Pat Quinlan moved with remarkable speed. Incredibly, his sturdy arm shot out, cutting musty air as he slapped Connor's face, stinging it, sending the younger man a step back, blinking. "Don't ye *ever* make such an accusation to yer father again! No Quinlan ever stole a human life and ye must remember that!" He was shaking, a little, with indignation. He took a deep, slow breath. "It is the . . . the *dark folk* who take care of the killin'. Not Quinlans."

Connor was puzzled. "You mean, Troy's playmates?" he asked, touching his smarting cheek.

"No, Con, I mean another kind of . . . creature." Pat shook his head. "The *Old Ones,* they're called. Have been called for an eternity. Closer to ghouls or to imps than Troy's friends." He tugged his lower lip thoughtfully, his overall expression reflecting distaste. "There's a mighty big difference between the two. The Old Ones exist *in* the earth, son, beneath the ground. I suspect it's from our proximity t'them that Troy happened to be contacted by her own wee folk."

Connor read his face. "And?"

"And I suspect that there exists a terrible and eternal conflict between the spirits of light—such as the bee-zarr friends of our sweet Troy—and the dark forces beneath the earth."

"You call the banshee who killed my wife a 'spirit of *light?*'" Connor demanded aghast.

"The works of the Old Ones are vastly worse, son. It is one thing to lose your temporary existence. It is quite another to lose your immortal soul."

"The rest of it, Dad," Connor prodded.

He sighed again. "I have had time to think it all through and I suspect they *both* wish t'take us people over—and the earth itself—when we humans are through at last. Isn't it obligin' the way we do their work for them—the way we kill ourselves off, year in and year out?"

The younger man lifted his palms. "Let me see if I've managed to get this fantastic story straight," he said, his brows turned down in thought. "We Quinlan males do not have to—to take life ourselves. Conveniently, it is done for us by the Old Ones. The question is obvious: *Why?* Why would they cooperate with us, if they wish to seize the planet for themselves?"

For a full tick of the clock there was no reply. At last Pat answered him in carefully screened tones. "They want us to defeat the faeries once and for all, and then take the earth over from us. That's the distinction, I think."

"No. No, that isn't it." Connor caught his father's arm. "That bargain you mentioned. What was the nature of it?"

"Ah, that was made two thousand years ago, when Christ Himself walked the earth." The old man seemed ready to shrug it off.

"Go on," Connor urged him.

"Well, it wasn't . . . *just* Jesus . . . who was present then." He was clearly anxious to change the subject. "I'm told there were . . . *others*."

"The name, Dad," Connor persisted in a hoarse whisper. "What's the name of the person or entity with whom the bargain was struck?"

Slow, creeping, pale horror crossed Pat Quinlan's face. "We never mention that name, lad. Not that—hideous name. *Not ever.* For when it was last known, last mentioned, the pact was officially forged."

Understanding what his father said, Connor sank again into the chair, looking with consternation up at the man who had fathered him. "It's exceedingly hard to accept all this, you know. But it is harder still to accept the concept that my own father's fathers made compacts with the Devil."

"Come on, lad! Nothin' is ever quite as it seems. Don't ye know that's the beginning of wisdom?" Pat rushed to stand before him, boldly and unabashedly staring down into his face. "We were all goin' to Croagh Patrick t'climb the mountain in honor of St. Patrick, till the changeling ruined everything. Remember? Fifty thousand of the devoted climbin' a rocky path until daybreak, watchin' the sun rise over Clew Bay and seein' all them sweet islands come into focus—from the hills of Achill to the north and west and the Atlantic Ocean itself. But Connor, good old St. Patrick *himself* had another side—a *hidden* side!" He snatched his son's hand, held it tightly. "Why, Patrick was charged with killing his own *sister,* by runnin' back and forth over her in his chariot! He cursed hills and lakes, rivers with the little fish in 'em, causin' fishermen t'starve to death! Why once, they say, old Patrick made an entire road sink until it closed over a whole train of chariots filled with people! Just because they wouldn't stop t'let him pass!"

"Didn't he do good works, too?" Connor peered up at the old man, knowing he begged not for St. Patrick but for his own father.

"Surely he did, lad! He drove the serpents from Ireland, it's said. He slew the Monster of the Lake—evil Pisthta-More. He did miraculous things, and he founded many good Catholic churches!" Pat was perspiring freely now, bent low to persuade his son to follow in an entire history of footprints. "The point is, boy, none of us has a perfect record, *none.* We're all fallible, left in this vale of richly available sin t'do the best we can—or drown in it. And if it's God's sweet will that Quinlans are to live forever, ye have no right t'question *how* it's done!"

For a moment Connor couldn't answer. When he did, his voice was his own again, steady and resonant. Firm. "I have every right, Father, because I think that I may well prove to be that virus you were talking about. The one which takes the life of your immortal bacterium, which disrupts that precious beehive you described." Gathering defiance, he stood and faced Pat. "I'm not about to let either Lurene or Troy be sacrificed for such ancient claptrap, old man. Nor anybody else." He swallowed. "Somehow I still can't believe you'd even ask such acquiescence of me."

"Well, *believe* it, Connor, or be damned to ye!" Patrick Quinlan stood tall and powerful before the younger man, his expression fierce now with a weary youth he would cling to somehow until his death—or that of anyone else. "Believe it because I have told ye, as me lifelong duty. Believe it because I have learned the hard way about life and the numerous tricks she conceals in her skirts." Abruptly his hard hands clutched Connor's resistant shoulders and held on, almost shaking them. "Darlin' boy, *look* at yer old da! I'm not seventy years old, Connor. *Hear me out and believe me.* Con, lad, your father has spent *more than one-hundred-and-thirty-one years* on this planet!"

Again stunned, Connor glanced from his father to the shocking procession of ancients—forever's frightening parade; pale sticks of frozen time—and heard them rattle their booths and their bones in applause for what Pat Quinlan had told him.

But each and every one of them stopped—staring, along with Connor and Pat *when the door to the attic burst off its hinges, and it was there.*

> *Proof enough for those they have happened to, proof that there is a memory of Nature that reveals events and symbols of distant centuries. Mystics of many countries and many centuries have spoken of this memory.*
>   —*William Butler Yeats*

twenty-two

In her room, lovely Lurene Shanahan awakened to find her lover, her almost-husband, gone from the bed. In an instant her bosom and the private place between her legs tingled with their own memory of Connor's presence, there. She felt warm all over, satisfied and yet newly needing, and peered into the shadows of the room from a seated position. Where had he gone?

She waited several moments for him to return and heard the forbidding creaks and undescribed silences of the old house breathing from the walls, from the hallway. When it seemed that he would not come back to her that night, Lurene decided that he must have gone out to his garage-den to work, and smiled. She would never be a woman who stood between her man and his honest work. Regretfully, she pulled the covers up over her abdomen and breasts, up to the chin, and curled up in a little ball, ready to seek sleep again.

Lurene shivered. She wondered if she'd ever forget the horror of what had been done to her, that day, of awakening naked and drenched in the woods. But when she recalled and considered the tenderness as well as the fulfilling passion Connor had brought and unleashed in her, she smiled like a wise little girl and closed her eyes.

What's that? Lurene sat upright, startled and afraid. She heard it then, outside the room, beyond the closed door. It was a *weighted, slithering, lumbering sound,* like that of a slimy bowling ball being laboriously rolled down the dark corridor. Shocked into wakefulness, she stared at the crack between the door and the doorframe, saw its massive, round and rotund shape ooze by.

When it was gone, she crossed herself and began to pray.

Troy Quinlan didn't hear a thing as it approached. She was lost in a nightmare of her own, one that seemed to be growing more and more threatening. For the first time she felt that she herself might be in danger from the terrible things in the eye of her unconscious mind. Whimpering, she turned over in bed, exposing her small bare feet.

And the message came to her, in the midst of her ghastly dream, that they were *all* threatened by her association with the wee folk of the woods. All of them, indeed, were meant to die terrible, agonizing deaths. Still sleeping, she murmured, *no, no,* in a tiny child's voice even as her own mind told her, in ponderous certainty, *yes, yes—all of you. All of you must die.*

The *Nuckelavee* half-rolled, half-lurched into the attic room on its globular form and thin, absurd arms, and stopped to survey the scene. It saw the living men across the way, and knew that they were its target—Connor and Patrick Quinlan. Its porcine nose sniffed the musty air for danger; its wall-eyed gaze swept the tunnel partitions and they made it pause, considering the alien life lined before it. Its great, bulbous body shifted frantically for a moment, anxiously determining its next step.

Then, adapted to the high-raftered and lengthy attic room, the *Nuckelavee* began swelling up. It fattened, it grew, it blew itself up to a full ten feet in height, the towering summit of it matched by its gross, astonishing bulk. The stench-filled cloud it carried with it for camouflage, gaseous and sickeningly foul, was instantly dispersed by the high temperature of the attic, and the other beings in the room saw the thing clear—gasping.

The implausible, repulsive head, still comprising more than half its prodigious enormity, lolled in displeasure and bitter puzzlement. *Who were these others?* Neckless and maniacally resentful, furious with an anger that was its own avaricious motivation, the preposterous head perched atop a nakedly hairless torso and gaped from one to another of the Quinlan family.

Connor, fallen back against the steel cabinets by the wall, felt his pulse double in erratic search of escape. He saw the piscean eyes of dull loathing, of killing, programmed purpose in the spineless caricature of a head, its limp and dangling arms, its incomprehensible body-bulk. Connor realized quickly that its weapons were the dizzying odor of its death-decaying breath and the ovoid, murderous weight of its steamroller carcass.

But what appalled him that moment—sickened Connor, made him wish more than before to turn and run—were the *raw wounds* that yawned and

293

seeped pus everywhere on its body—yellow-green veins clotted with something like bug-like, black cockroach blood—in a mass of repugnant sores. There was very little actual skin left on the *Nuckelavee;* but where skin was intact, it was ashen white and revoltingly naked, with a bristle of coarse pig-hair. The loosely-hanging child's arms, Connor saw, it used as a balancing factor when it moved forward. . . .

Even as it did now, toward Patrick Quinlan!

The old man hurled his terrified hands up, before his face, as he saw the unspeakable monster picking up amazing speed, rushing toward him now like a runaway locomotive. Pat stumbled helplessly away, right into the wide space between the wall and the endless tunnel of partitioned Quinlan ancestors. He strove to run from the oncoming creature, perhaps put the tunnel between them.

But he caught his foot at the last moment on the Bible that had fallen from his smoking jacket pocket, and tripped, falling even as the *Nuckelavee* moved unstoppably forward.

Connor's lips parted to shriek his horror as the monstrous entity thundering with all its fierce, compressed weight crushed the prone body of Patrick Aloysius Quinlan.

Then the steamrolling creature squeaked to a stop, wheeling to face Connor himself.

Spread some eleven or twelve feet across the protuberant width of the Nuckelavee's legless midsection was the nauseatingly staining remnant—a blurred, scarlet smear against the devouring and consuming mouths of the million gaping wounds—of Connor's beloved Dad.

Even as the younger man stared in horror, he saw the fragments of his father's body sucked into the countless wound-mouths and heard the sounds of digestion.

Panting with fright, at once terrified and grief-stricken, Connor came to life. Turning swiftly, he looked at the door across the room and tried to gauge his chances of making it to the opening. On the one hand he remembered vividly the incredible speed of the monster as it had crossed the attic width in a second, and he knew there would not be time. If it snatched even his foot, it would *absorb* him, suck him into its plentiful apertures. On the other hand, however, he was a man. He could not stand there in simple, mindless, trapped-beast *waiting*—could not merely allow himself to be smeared to nothingness and then eaten by a legendary Irish beast.

He looked bravely back at the *Nuckelavee,* seeing the disgusting way a million things that might have been tongues extruded from the obscene holes to lick the fat carcass clean.

Fascinated and gripped by loathing, he did not see the *other* figure as it moved to fill the torn doorframe.

Instead, in a mortal mind already wracked by more consummate terror than a living man had ever experienced before, Connor saw . . . the *others,* watched the old men of the tunnel come to life.

A male Quinlan had died. Died before their staring eyes. Barely sensate, their aged minds were at once alerted and infuriated by the great loss, their frail and hungry bodies energized and newly vitalized by the gift of life force. And as Connor stared in wonder *the column of emaciated*

295

mummies who were his ancestors began disentangling themselves in one collective move from the hooks which had supported them for centuries.

While Connor Quinlan's eyes widened in further shock and utter bewilderment, *dozens upon dozens of antediluvian patriarchs—wrinkled, withered, some skeletal and little more than loosely-connected bones clothed in the wretched rags of bygone generations, the cloth voluminous on their shrunken limbs—moved deliberately toward him. Shuffling and tottering on legs that had not been used for perhaps three or four hundred years, keening and chattering among themselves in tremulous high voices, they moved to form a circle around Connor Quinlan ... the only surviving male Quinlan heir.*

Meanwhile, the *Nuckelavee* was confused, bewildered. Did one remain, or *many?* Were they all his enemies—the reason he had been summoned— or just the strong human being at their center? In its microscopic brain, there was no room for fear and so there had never been a need for courage. Nothing had stood successfully before it in the past; nothing had ever stood in its dull-witted presence which seemed simultaneously alive and dead.

In a way, at that second, it was a momentary stalemate between the creature of faerydom and the ancient men of Quinlan. They met on common ground. The monster had never actually "lived," except for the vivifying belief given it by the minds of the superstitious and the very young. The old men were no longer entirely alive, but for the belief in a tradition that, like the *Nuckelavee* itself, found its distant source in antiquity.

Troy Quinlan skittered from the smashed door across the attic floor, running toward her father, the man whom she had hated and who, because of that, had brought this nightmare tableau to a culmination. She did not remember, then, how she had despised him; she did not think at all of Troy Quinlan. She simply hurled herself into his startled arms—how could he protect her *here!*—and hugged him in love and terror. "Dads, oh, *Dads!*" she cried, kissing him. "My Dads!"

"My kitten," he said softly into her ear, hoarse and petrified with fear for them. "My own dear pumpkin-princess!"

Incredibly, the ranks of antiquated men closed and started forward. Sweet Lord, Connor marveled, *they're attacking!*

Then the *Nuckelavee* recovered its aplomb, faced with something it had seen before. Recognizing the bold and outrageously brave march toward it for what it was, the bulbous beast exhaled its puissant and obscene breath. A thunderhead mist of acrid foulness poured from its uncountable mouth-pores like the blaze of a flamethrower. Crying out, Connor dove for the protection of the sturdy tunnel, Troy clinging to him. They ducked behind it as the walls themselves began cracking and the emerald tube lights above the partitions blinked on and off like the blinded eyes of a sinuous centipede. The fallout of the dreadful stench was almost palpable; poisonous. It caught at Connor's and Troy's nostrils and seemed to rend them as their tears streaked down their cheeks. Doubled over, they hid in one another as the war began.

And one by one, the valiant old Men of Quinlan

began collapsing, withering before a diabolical blast they could not confront. As each of the aged beings died, an assortment of bony rags tossed to the floor, he crumbled—crumbled into small, heaping mounds of calcium dust until the customary odor of the endless attic was cursed with the cloying memory of long belated death.

Connor winked back the tears and peered above the ruined tunnel. The ovoid beast with the tumorous, lolling head was still there, rolling back and forth on the ashes that were all that remained of an entire familial history. It was rabid about its work, livid at being defied; it ground the Quinlan remnants into the floor and issued a queer growling whine that might have been the triumphal song of the *Nuckelavee*. Connor saw how it was occupied and stood on shaky legs, Troy held tightly against him as he braced himself for the dash to the door.

"Oh, Dads, I love you so!" Troy whispered in his ear. She had seen what her thoughtless beliefs, her misplaced hatred had done. Even now, she gaped at the immense and vindictive form. "I don't wanna believe in such horrid things as that. I don't! I just believe in *you,* Dads! It's *you* I believe and love!"

Two piggy eyes looked back at them, stunned and shocked. There was, as well, an expression of resentment, as if the *Nuckelavee* felt aggrieved, even hurt. It spun on its round rear and clammy arms; the large-knuckled miniature hands raised before its voluminous abdomen in disbelief; it made a sighing sound that Connor thought he would never forget—and then it was *gone*.

Vanished. As if it had never existed at all.

In a moment he put Troy down, but she insisted

upon holding his hand. Together, father and daughter peered down at the secret place of old Patrick Quinlan—or what was left of it.

Suddenly the partitions of the ruined tunnel looked like so many stalls in a men's room, and Connor laughed in relief.

Troy heard him and looked up at her father with a smile. "C'mon, Dads," she urged him, tugging his hand. "Let's go tell my new mother all about it."

I am certain that (visions) draw upon associations which are beyond the reach of the individual 'subconscious.'
—*William Butler Yeats*

epilogue

Eight years later...
It took time. She had been in hospital awhile, first in Galway and then under the care of a skilled psychiatrist in Dublin. No ordinary man would have been adequate to the task of caring for Troy, because it wasn't a question of convincing her that she'd only had imaginary visions, unreal "playmates." It was a matter of helping her to accept the idea that reality took many forms but that, in the last analysis, a person has to decide for herself which ones would receive her endorsement, her faith.

Blessedly, many of the problems of the young, physically as well as mentally, prove to be impermanent. The kind of loving care and understanding she received from Lurene and Connor Quinlan didn't hurt a bit.

Now Troy Quinlan was almost twenty years old, a statuesque blonde who attended University College in Galway. On weekends, she often telephoned her father and her stepmother, speaking happily and confidently of the future. Because she was an affectionate child but a child of the age, she did not speak of the young man from Kilkenny with whom she was living.

Recently, pretty Troy was sitting in a chair in her apartment, knees up to her chin, feeling grumpy. "I wish I had something really good to read."

"What about Tolkien?" inquired her roommate, picking up a paperback book and tossing it to her. "I really groove on his stuff."

Troy grinned at him, impressed by his American slang. "No, honey, I don't think so." She peered at the cover and threw the book back. "I'm not into fantasy much." For a moment she studied her hands and added tonelessly, "I guess I don't have the imagination to believe in things like that."

Meanwhile in the new house they'd built in Connemara, Connor and Lurene were also living a peaceful, loving life. Connor was happier than he had ever been in his life. With Lurene's support and encouragement, he had written a book at last. Oh, no one knew yet whether the regular American publishers would take it or he'd have to settle for his own handiwork. But he'd conquered his block and put his thoughts on paper. Besides, Troy was healthy and happy and Lurene Shanahan Quinlan was the perfect wife he'd yearned for all his life.

Best of all, in some respects, there was the seven-year-old product of their marriage, a lad named Patrick Aloysius Quinlan II.

Little Pat had few playmates in the vicinity. He lay with his back against a huge oak tree in the front yard, alternately yawning and sighing. His mind was unoccupied by any thoughts except a tiny, nagging resentment for the absolute joy his father and mother shared between themselves; and so he merely stared into space....

Until, miraculously, the space was filled.

"Hi!" came the high, piping voice, apparently from nowhere at all. Handsome little Pat II peered round and round, and finally looked down at the ground. His eyes opened wide and a delighted smile played upon his youthful lips.

"My name is Ruck! May I be your playmate? We'll have lots of exciting times together!"

Yeats knew something that Paracelsus and Bruno glimpsed only in flashes: that the efficiency of magic is basically a matter of inner pressure ... He mastered the first principle of magic: focusing his dream world and holding it clearly in his mind's eye as he transferred it to paper ... Yeats recognized the connection between magic and Magic: that is, between moods of deep and intense delight and the ability to summon 'paranormal' powers.

—Colin Wilson
Mysteries

QUEEN OF HELL
By J.N. Williamson

PRICE: $2.50 LB995
CATEGORY: Occult

A DARK LEGEND
BECOMES A HIDEOUS REALITY!

Three desirable young women, Diana, Soni, and Marcia, enroll in a special course for liberated women at the University of California. Only after the blood, the bizarre sexual encounters, and the mindless horror of random murders, does anyone realize that one of the young women has become: QUEEN OF HELL!